TWO MINUTE WARNING

James Gurtner

Battle Press
Satellite Beach, Florida

TWO MINUTE WARNING

Copyright © 2022 by James Gurtner.

Battle Press books may be ordered through booksellers
or by contacting:

Battle Press
1-919-218-4039
steve@battlepress.media
www.battlepress.media

ISBN: 979-8-9854-2997-8 (softcover)
ISBN: 979-8-9854-2998-5 (eBook)

First Edition

Contents

The Players

Primary Characters:

Jason McVay	Private Investigator, Owner of McVay & Associates
Laura Sparks	CIA Senior Agent; Jason's friend and lover
Samantha Talley	"Sam" Jason's protege investigator
Emily Cast	FBI Agent working with Jason's team
Diane Stockwell	Kidnapped wife of John Stockwell
Owen Whittaker	Rogue FBI Agent working with Russians
Sergei Dimitrov	Leader of Russian Espionage Team

Secondary Characters:

Tara Wayne	Director of Security for Dynamadics Corporation
John Stockwell	Director of R&D, Dynamadics; Husband of kidnapped Diane
Madison Winslow	"Maddy" Jason's Secretary
D'Arby Grande	FBI Agent assigned to Agent Whittaker
Jaydan Sanders	CIA Agent, Interrogations Specialist
Sandy McVay	CIA Senior Agent; Jason's sister

Incidental Characters:

Baylin Sanders	R&D Director, NASA; CIA Senior Agent
Tucker Henry	CEO of Dynamadics
Jennifer Deveroux	Receptionist, Dynamadics
Officer Thomas	Security Officer, Dynamadics
Robert Dumont	Security Chief, Briar Patch Estates
Kaitlyn McBride	CIA Director
Ken Upton	FBI Director
Sheriff Brown	Orange County Sheriff; good friend of Director McBride

Michael McBride	Kaitlyn's brother; sold P.I. Practice to Jason
Richard Winslow	Maddy's brother. Orlando Real Estate Agent
Demonia Nogudum	aka Scarface. Sexually assaulted Samantha Talley
Shorty the Redneck	Drunk at O'Doul's Pub; acquaintance of Scarface
Al Wainwright	Bartender at O'Doul's Pub
Vladimir Kaslov	aka Nikita Vaslov. High Echelon Russian Agent
Kathy	Waitress at Brunch 'N Lunch
James	Maitre'D at Starlight Terrace
Sally	Housebot (domestic robot) for Sandy
Andre Asimov	Leader of the Russian crew; only one fluent in English
Pavlov Kruska	Medically trained member of the Russian crew
President Sarov	Current head of the Russian Government
Emily (the younger)	Abducted girl rescued by Sam, Emily

Acknowledgements

My son, MIchael

For being there every step of the way; offering insightful suggestions and helping to smooth out the rough patches along the way. Your special contribution is much appreciated.

Susan Scott, Susan Kneeland

Who I fondly think of as The Susan Twins.
Thanks to you both for taking the time to read
Two Minute Warning as a work-in-progress.
Your suggestions were much appreciated;
your encouragement invaluable.

Preface

The story introduces Jason McVay, a 44-year-old Private Investigator who has a small, but very successful practice. His secretary/receptionist, Madison (Maddy) Winslow and apprentice investigator, Samantha (Sam) Talley are his only employees. The narrative is set in the mid twenty-first century.

Jason has been in private practice for just over four years. The practice is located in Orlando, Florida where he set up his own private investigation agency after working four years at the renowned Michael McBride Investigation Agency in Boston. He has one sister, Sandy McVay, currently a senior agent in the CIA.

Jason has a unique ability: he knows what is going to happen two minutes into the future. He acquired this ability in Afghanistan after the MRAP vehicle he was in was destroyed by an IED. The son of his secretary (Maddy) was killed in the same incident; he was the sole survivor. Jason was honorably discharged after 2 months of hospital convalescence. This new ability manifested a week after his discharge while he was staying with his sister, Sandy. At first, he was very disoriented and extremely anxious. Sandy introduced him to her best friend, Laura Sparks. Laura was gifted with a powerful extra-sensory perception ability and reassured Jason he would be all right. She convinced him to keep his "gift" quiet beyond his sister and herself. She taught him how to use his mind to control this ability - allowing him to function normally. He quickly learned there were limitations with his "future vision." Most significantly, he could only "see" what involved him personally and only within his immediate physical environment.

In other words, he could only *react to* what was coming to him personally; for instance: he could turn to the left instead of a now "foreseen" right to be spared what would have been an otherwise unavoidable pitfall.

He couldn't go to the racetrack and foresee which horse would win - his gift was exclusive to his immediate and personal future. He would *not* see the car speeding down the street in front of him about to hit the person crossing that street - unless the person was *him*.

Jason is hired by Tara Wayne, an executive of Dynamadics Corporation, a large Aerospace company headquartered in Orlando, to find another executive, John Stockwell's missing wife, Diane.

That is the starting point of a much more significant issue involving cloaking (stealth) technology developed by Dynamadics for the U.S. Government and coveted by the Russians.

During the course of the investigation, Jason is in constant peril from the Russians while simultaneously dealing with the CIA and FBI, as often as not, on an adversarial basis. And there is a mole within the local FBI field office to be ferreted out.

The story unfolds with a background of evolving character relationships. As one might expect, Jason's "future-casting" ability is a significant feature, and a source of comic relief in addition to its more serious aspect.

There are several plot twists in the second half of the story that will make sense to the reader by the conclusion of the story. I like to think of them as my little "aha" moments. And a couple of surprises no one could have seen coming...

** ** **

Chapter One
Betrayal

The warm, muggy night air was a rude slap in the face as she shut the sliding glass door behind her, strolled over to a pool side table and sat down in a nicely padded deck chair. Setting her Margarita down, she surveyed the expansive yard, its lush tropical foliage manicured to perfection. Having made the transition from the comfortable cool of the air-conditioned interior to the tropical warmth typical of a June evening in Orlando, she reflected on how nice it was to live in Briar Patch Estates. One of the more exclusive communities in the greater Orlando area, its 20 homes were inhabited by the elite of the local high-tech research industry. To live in the "Patch" spoke volumes about one's status. As she sipped her Margarita, she thought about the events that had brought her here tonight; the party for the retiring Comptroller had become exceedingly boring. From her grab bag of excuses, she selected the "unbearable migraine headache" option and excused herself.

Diane Stockwell was a beautiful woman by any measure. Now 35, she still had the looks and figure of the cover model she was 15 years ago. Tall, lithe, perfect facial structure...she had all the requisite qualities the agencies sought. She had been relatively content - if unfulfilled - in her modeling career. Then she met John. Average looking but possessed of a most interesting personality. Charming with a good sense of humor. Not to mention he was an up-and-coming executive with Dynamadics, a rapidly growing defense contractor with very close ties to the University of Central Florida and its well-respected Science Research Park.

He pursued her relentlessly. Eventually, she gave in, agreeing to marry him...a very generous prenuptial sealing the deal. Diane told herself she would grow to love him over time. Unfortunately, his increasingly negative attitude toward her quickly took that possibility off the table. So, she accepted the role of the loyal trophy wife, but not without resentment.

John Stockwell believed his wife to be - *at best* - of average intelligence. Diane gave him no reason to believe otherwise. Unbeknownst to him, actually anyone outside her family, she was far smarter than she let on. To her lasting regret she had chosen a career path based on her beauty rather than her brain. Diane had a Mensa-level I.Q. and an intense interest in all things scientific. She enjoyed eavesdropping at the various company social gatherings, picking up little tidbits of information. Moreover, her considerable computer skills allowed her to access his computer; passwords and file encryption notwithstanding. For her, the hacking provided an entertaining distraction from an otherwise mundane life.

Diane knew all there was to know about *Project Expose'*, Dynamadics' code name for the de-cloaking software they had developed to counter the recent Russian theft of the advanced cloaking technology NASA, the Space Force, and the Air Force used for their craft. This new software would effectively neutralize the Russian's ability to use the stolen technology. She was also aware Dynamadics worried about the ongoing Russian attempts to obtain the *Project Expose'* files.

Diane was looking for an opportunity to exit the marriage while taking advantage of the infidelity clause in the prenuptial agreement. To this end, she had hacked her husband's phone to monitor his conversations. Surprisingly, there was no evidence of anything untoward. But two days ago, he had begun communicating in what she quickly recognized as "coded" phrases with a man - *a man with a Russian accent.* After reviewing their conversations, she concluded that her husband was about to turn over the *Project Expose'* files to the Russians for twenty-five million dollars! Her husband had many character flaws, but *traitor* had never entered her mind. Disappointment didn't begin to describe how she felt.

Then this morning, she intercepted a call he received while driving to work. The call lasted precisely three and a half minutes, just under the time necessary to trace the caller. After analyzing the conversation, she deduced that he was going to leave a flash drive containing the Project Expose' files for retrieval while they were having brunch at the River's Edge Country Club with neighbors Ed and JoAnn, a Sunday morning tradition.

Having been raised in a military family - her Dad was a newly retired Air Force Brigadier General - she had been imbued with a strong sense of patriotism. She knew what she had to do. Tomorrow she would pay a visit to the Orlando FBI Office. She finished her Margarita, got up and headed back to the house and its promise of cool comfort. If she was going to be miserable, might as well have the creature comforts.

Just as she shut the sliding door behind her, she saw a figure emerge from the shadow of the front entrance hall.

"What the hell are you doing here?" ...was all she was able to say before seeing a brilliant field of stars that quickly faded to black nothingness.

** ** **

At precisely 11:15 PM, John Stockwell exited his BMW, now parked adjacent to Diane's Lexus. As he entered the house, he voice-commanded the Home Control System to close the garage door, followed by "Enable entry," to momentarily turn off this door's alarm. He was surprised when the Security System's Robotic manager responded, "Cannot comply. Security System has been disabled."

Now alarmed, Stockwell took a step into the Great Room. Glancing around furtively, he shouted, "Diane! Diane! Where are you?"

The System Manager immediately intoned, "Mrs. Stockwell is not on the premises."

"Well, *where* is she? *Where did she* go?" He asked anxiously.

"I do not know," responded the Manager. "The security alarm and camera functions were disabled at 9:10 PM."

"*Who* disabled the security system?" asked Stockwell, already knowing the answer.

"You did, Sir," the Manager responded. "Using your personal keypad code." The keypad code system was designed as a backup in the event of a voice control malfunction.

The highly stressed Stockwell directed the Manager, "Call 911, request a police response then get Tara Wayne on my cellphone!"

"Processing," acknowledged the Manager.

As Stockwell nervously paced back and forth in the Great Room, his thoughts running amok through a series of bad scenarios, he finally heard his alert tone announce a call. It was his associate and fellow executive Tara Wayne.

"What's up John? Forget something at the party?"

"I need you to get over here as soon as possible!" Exclaimed the thoroughly distraught, extremely agitated Stockwell. "Diane's not here!"

"What do you mean, *not here?*" queried a now alarmed Wayne.

"NOT HERE!! *Gone. Vanished into thin air.* Something bad has happened. I'm sure of it! Please, Tara, *please...just get over here...I need you right now!!*"

"Okay I'm on the way," replied Wayne anxiously.

** ** **

Wayne had the autopilot park the Lincoln next to the Orange County Sheriff's cruiser currently occupying the left side of the driveway. She exited the vehicle, walking briskly to the front door which she noted was wide open, the soft amber light of the front entry hall spilling out into the moonless night. The usual 15-minute trip had taken 25 - a consequence of the autopilot's programming to strictly observe speed limits. She would have driven, but for an abundance of caution about the alcohol imbibed earlier at the comptroller's retirement party.

Tara Wayne was the Vice President of Corporate Security, the executive title indicative of just how seriously Dynamadics viewed this function. As such, she reported directly to Tucker Henry, the CEO. This unusual autonomy conferred her with an outsized influence, which, to her credit, she wielded with subtle discretion.

She stood 5'9" and at 140 lbs. was on the "husky" side. But not fat. The woman was fastidious when it came to fitness. Blonde with deep set brown eyes and rather pronounced Anglo-Saxon features, she was an attractive lady. Not beautiful. Many thought of her as a "handsome" woman.

Wayne nodded at the departing Deputy as he brushed past her on the way out.

"Would you shut the door behind you, Deputy?" requested Stockwell.

"Certainly, Mr. Stockwell," he replied. "We'll contact you as soon as we have something."

"Thanks," said Stockwell as the Deputy closed the door behind him.

Wayne and Stockwell engaged in a brief hug. Wayne took a step back, glancing around the room, looking for nothing in particular.

"So, John...tell me all you know...in detail...chapter and verse."

"Okay," he answered tentatively. Stockwell reprised her with the greatest detail he could muster given his current emotional state. When he finished, Wayne stopped recording on her iPhone.

She told Stockwell, "All right, John. You're understandably upset. We'll get this handled. I know someone that can help us. Right now, I want you to pack some things for a short stay in a Bungalow at the UCF Research Park campus. I'm going to secure the house and have one of my people stay here. Out of an abundance of caution, another one will be assigned to you twenty-four seven for at least a few days. I'll get Tucker up to speed first thing tomorrow. Try to relax...I know, easy for me to say - but *try!* You will be in the loop all the way. We're gonna find Diane...I promise."

"Okay Tara," he acknowledged. "I know I can count on you."

As Stockwell went up the stairs, Wayne opened *Contacts* on her phone, scrolled to the desired number and clicked. After 4 rings, her call was answered.

"Hello, Jason, really sorry to bother you so late...I have a situation that needs immediate attention. On the surface, it appears to be a missing person case...but there are serious underlying security issues involved."

"Yes...*Great.*" Let me give you the address...I'll be here when you arrive." She clicked off.

** ** **

The melodious door chime announced the detective's arrival. Wayne terminated her call, briskly walking to the front door. Opening the door, she caught a subtle scent of bayberry. Tara recalled having asked him what after-shave lotion he used, then was taken aback when he said he never used any. Imagine, having a *natural* scent like that. Most unusual. *Most pleasant.*

"Hello, Jason," she warmly greeted. "Please come in. Thanks for the prompt response."

"No problem, Tara. That's the advantage of you having us on retainer. Plus, I owe you, anyway. So... bring me up to speed."

"Well," she answered. "The short version is she vanished without a trace. The responding deputy couldn't find any evidence of a break-in or foul play, so technically it's a routine missing person case."

"Obviously, you're not buying that - or I wouldn't be here."

"An astute observation, Jason," joked a sarcastic Wayne, eliciting a smile from the detective. "My instinct tells me something nefarious is afoot. Her husband is the lead on *Project Expose'*, a highly classified project for the military. I haven't the clearance to say more...I'm sure Tucker will enlighten you tomorrow."

"Is Mr. Stockwell here?" Inquired McVay.

"No, actually you just missed him...I arranged for him to stay in campus housing at the UCF Research Park along with one of my staff."

"You *are* taking this seriously. First question out of the gate, what's the status of their marriage, or do you even know?" Asked McVay.

"To the best of my knowledge, their doing OK. That said, he really doesn't talk much about his home life. So, I guess it's kind of a "grain of salt" thing."

"What about the security system? Anything there?"

Wayne shook her head. "I reviewed the Home System Manager log. The security system - all sensors and cameras - went off-line at 9:10 PM. And - *get this* - it was *Stockwell's* keypad code. Of course, he denies he entered it. I checked both exterior keypads and - you guessed it - no prints. Wiped clean. But here's the kicker. They *both* had their own codes. Sort of a His and Her deal...you know, like the towel thing." She chuckled at her little aside, Jason politely acknowledging with a nod and smile.

"But" interjected McVay, "it doesn't matter. What possible reason would she have to shut down the system...unless she was having a tryst," answering his own question.

"True," responded Wayne, "but I don't think so. Too obvious. Too easily discovered. No, whoever entered that code has got Diane...and I don't think it's sexually motivated. Which brings me back to the security issue, *Project Expose'*. No, this is more than a missing person case. *Much more.*"

"Sounds like a case for the FBI. When it goes beyond missing person status, they're sure to get involved. Again, why me? I don't have their investigative resources."

"You're right, Jason. Two reasons. First, you're one of the best private investigators in the country. And while you don't have their resources, you're also not wearing their bureaucratic handcuffs. Second, I believe there is a mole in the FBI Orlando office...I'm not prepared to elaborate just yet. So, are you in?"

"All in," he confirmed.

"Great!" said Wayne. "Tomorrow we'll meet with Tucker and devise a strategy."

The pair conducted a thorough sweep of the home and grounds. Just as they finished, the first surveillance team arrived. Wayne gave them instructions, then bid goodnight to McVay as they got in their respective vehicles for the trip home.

** ** **

Jason entered the vehicle, sat back, and fastened his shoulder restraint before instructing the autopilot to take him home. He settled in for the 20-minute trip to his apartment in downtown Orlando. A spacious 2-bedroom unit overlooking Lake Eola, it was pricey, but he felt he got his money's worth of satisfaction and enjoyment out of the place. He was lucky to have it. Fortuitously, his secretary, Madison Winslow had a brother who happened to own a real estate firm specializing in downtown properties. Jason preferred the urban lifestyle, albeit traffic was a hassle. Florida's highway and hi-speed rail system was on the cutting edge. Unfortunately, the same couldn't be said for the inner urban areas. Nearing the midpoint of the 21st century, he expected more...

Fortunately, his commute to work was...well, it *wasn't.* Maddy's brother - Richard - had found the perfect location for his office at the same time he had secured Jason's apartment. It was a great 3 room office suite on the sixth floor of the ten story *Lake Eola Professional*

Tower building directly across from his place on the other side of the lake! The *Tower* was mostly occupied by attorneys, accountants, and assorted "consultants." Oh, and the Orlando branch office of the FBI took up more than half of the ground floor.

He gazed out at the approaching lights of downtown Orlando as the car glided along a mostly empty I-4. A beautiful, albeit muggy evening in Central Florida. His mind wandered back to the wonderful time he had with Laura in Savannah Heights. That was two weeks ago, and he couldn't keep her from dominating his thoughts, even now recalling in exquisite detail that magical week.

** ** **

Chapter Two
Jason's Story

*T*wo *weeks earlier...*

The knock on his bedroom door gave Jason a bit of a start. He had been awake about five minutes debating whether or not to go for a morning run when his sister made it an easy decision.

"Come in, Sandy," He invited.

The door opened to reveal a smiling Sandy...*way* too perky for this early on a Saturday morning.

"Listen, I'm gonna pick up Laura at the Lexus dealer...she's having some routine maintenance done and then we'll be coming back here for breakfast. I'll be gone a couple of hours if you want to squeeze in a run."

"Sounds great," responded Jason. "I should have a pretty good appetite worked up by the time you're back."

Jason was delighted at the prospect of seeing his friend again. He hadn't seen Laura Sparks for what seemed forever. He owed her a lot - she played a big part in his becoming the person he now was.

"See ya in a little while," he heard his sister say as she went down the stairs.

Jason climbed out of bed and headed into the shower. After toweling off, he decided to shave (*Laura's coming, he thought*). He looked in the mirror and was satisfied with the guy looking back at him. 44 years old and holding up pretty well. At 6'2" he could get away with the 200 lbs. he carried, though, to be sure, he'd rather be closer to 185. Nature had been kind so far; still a full head of light brown hair and hazel eyes, with just a hint of age wrinkles creeping into the corners. He had the high cheekbones and aquiline nose common to his Scottish ancestry.

He donned his jogging shorts, snagged a clean t-shirt, slipped into his Nikes, and stepped out onto the balcony off his bedroom. He looked out on the sun-splashed day and the beckoning trail that ran along the Choctaw River bordering his sister's property.

After 30 minutes and nearly 3 miles, Jason slowed to a walk as he entered the winding driveway leading to his sister's home. She had bought the house 12 years ago, just before Jason was discharged from active duty. Sandy had wanted to live in a more rural environment and had lucked into this beautiful riverfront house on the outskirts of Savannah Heights, Va. At 3000 sq.ft. the four-bedroom chalet style home was a perfect fit for her. Built into the hillside adjacent to the river, it featured a master bedroom and two large guest bedrooms on the second floor, each accessing the large balcony running the entire length of the front elevation. The first floor featured a large great room that melded nicely into the open kitchen/dining room. In the rear a fourth bedroom sat next to a large den/media room. The house had all the bells and whistles and even included the latest version of Robotics, Inc. Housebot, a nice bonus. Jason especially liked the unique stone fireplace he felt added a real "country" flavor.

Having hardly broken a sweat, he opted to just change into a fresh tee, after which he went downstairs and out to the patio, plopping onto a chaise lounge to await the arrival of Sandy and Laura. Sally (the Housebot) suddenly appeared and inquired if he needed anything.

"Yes...a cup of coffee would be great Sally," he said. "Oh, and some music... light jazz would be nice."

"Certainly, Jason I'll be back in a moment," Sally said in the cockney accent Sandy had playfully programmed for the robot in a moment of whimsy. True to her - *its* - word, the Housebot quickly returned with a steaming mug of freshly brewed coffee.

** ** **

Jason sipped his coffee, his thoughts returning to the first time he had met Laura Sparks 12 years ago. He had been staying with his sister after 3 weeks at Walter Reed Hospital where he had been treated for life-threatening wounds sustained during the MRAP incident in Afghanistan. His team had been returning from routine reconnaissance when they struck a very old IED left over from the conflict in the early part of the century. He was the only survivor.

He recalled how happy he had been to finish his convalescence at Sandy's home in Virginia. And extremely grateful. Truth be told, he had expected no less - the siblings had been close all their lives. He would, of course, done exactly the same were the shoe on the other foot. Still, she hadn't been in her new home 3 weeks, hardly long enough to "settle in". Sandy had taken 2 weeks leave from her CIA job. Not a convenient time for the newly minted Senior Agent. How lucky he was to have someone so close with just the right experience to understand his plight. Herself a Marine Corps veteran with 2 tours in Afghanistan, who better to understand his feelings and help him get his "head straight."

The first couple of days at his sister's house had been quiet and uneventful. The morning of the third day changed his life forever. He awoke with the mother of all headaches - it took all his will power to not scream out from the excruciating pain in his head. Then the pain left as quickly as it came. But his *mind*...something had happened to his mind. He was sitting on the edge of the bed looking around the room when, all of a sudden, he *saw himself* - as if he were watching a movie - get up and walk to the balcony; turn, walk to the other side of the room, open the door, then step out. Just as he stepped out, the "movie in his mind" showed him approach the head of the stairs, then step on an empty tennis racquet cover. As he lost his balance, he screamed Sandy's name, tumbling head over heels down the length of the stairs, ending up in a twisted heap at the bottom.

Returning to real time - he got up, walked to the balcony, turned; walked to the door, stepped out and approached the head of the stairs...*but this time he glanced down and saw the tennis cover.* He stopped abruptly, thereby avoiding the fall he had just foreseen.

Now thoroughly shaken, Jason sat down at the top of the stairs, yelling for Sandy. Sweating profusely, he held his head in both hands. Sandy, who had been outside on the patio when she heard his panicked scream, barged in the front door, and tore up the stairs, two at a time. When she reached him and saw that he was un-harmed, she walked him back to his bedroom. He sat on the edge of the bed with his sister sitting down next to him. After a few moments, he gathered himself and related in exacting detail what had just happened to him.

"I'm going crazy...right?!" Exclaimed Jason. "What the hell is happening to me?!"

"I don't know how that happened," answered Sandy, "But *You're Not Going Crazy.* I know someone who can help us figure this out. Why don't you get dressed? I'll see you at the breakfast nook."

Jason nodded absently. Sandy got up, and seeing he was calming down, left the room. On the way out, she picked up the empty tennis racquet cover, chastising herself for leaving it there in the first place. When she got downstairs, she snatched her phone from the bar and told Siri to *"call Laura Sparks."*

Laura Sparks was Sandy's best friend. She thought of her more as a sister. They had met six years earlier when Sandy, a CIA Field Agent, was teamed with Laura, then an FBI Agent, for a dangerous covert mission in Afghanistan with two specially trained SEALs. Long story short - they were successful. Laura had saved Sandy's life, though to hear Laura tell it, it was the other way around. Regardless, they quickly bonded and had been together ever since. Laura left the FBI to become a CIA Agent...still teamed with Sandy.

The thing Sandy especially liked about her friend was her quirky personality. That, and her ever cheerful nature. And Laura had *extraordinary* ESP. It was almost like she was from another planet. She had downplayed this ability to all but Sandy, who had loyally kept her friend's secret. Now she needed Laura to help her brother - and her - understand what was happening.

Laura picked up on the first ring. "Hello, girlfriend. What's up so early on a Saturday morning?" She listened intently as Sandy related her brother's strange experience. When Sandy finished, Laura said, "Hang tight, I'm on the way...see ya in about a half hour."

Jason and Sandy were sitting at the breakfast bar discussing the recent event when they heard the crunch of tires on the gravel drive-way announce her friend's arrival.

"That's got to be Laura," said Sandy as she got up and went to the door.

Sandy opened the door, hugging her friend hello. She walked her over to Jason, who had already risen from his seat at the bar.

"Laura, this is my brother, Jason. Jason, this is my friend, Laura Sparks."

Jason shook hands with Laura and greeted her with "I am so very pleased to meet you - to finally meet you - Sandy has told me so much about you."

"And likewise, Jason," responded Laura. Glancing at Sandy, Laura continued, "I trust it was all good, though your sister is known to embellish now and then." Sandy smirked at this last remark.

Jason was quite taken with this attractive...no, beautiful creature standing before him. She was casually dressed in jeans and a pale beige chiffon blouse. No makeup. No matter. She didn't need any. Close to six feet, he guessed. Luxuriant dark brown hair, worn shoulder length. Blue eyes. Almost violet. Wow. But he turned his mind away from this pleasant distraction. *A much more serious topic is at hand.*

While Jason was appraising Laura's looks, she in turn was impressed with this excellent specimen of masculinity. Not surprising, however...good looks often run in the family. That aside, she took an instant liking to this man. There was definitely something special about him.

"I've got some things to take care of, so I'll leave you two to get acquainted," said Sandy, discreetly excusing herself.

"Coffee?" asked Laura as she walked over to the carafe at the end of the bar.

"Yes, thanks," replied Jason.

"How do you take it?"

"Cream, 2 sugars, please."

"As do I," Laura said. "*I just knew we were going to hit it off.*" They both laughed.

After fixing their coffees, Laura put the two oversized mugs on a tray. "Let's go outside and sit on the patio," suggested Laura. Jason opened the sliding glass door for Laura, and they took seats at a table halfway to the pool.

After a few minutes of small talk...the unusually warm weather, the D.C. traffic, etc... Laura said, "So, tell me what happened, Jason... please be as detailed and precise as possible."

As requested, Jason rendered a very nuanced telling of the sequence of events, including his intense emotional response and concern for his state-of-mind...indeed, his very sanity.

Laura reached across the table and took Jason's hand, enfolding it within both of hers. He felt a calm slowly settle over him...his racing mind slowed.

"I'm going to come over to you...you'll have to trust me on this...and we're going to make a connection that will allow me to help you. Are you OK with that?"

"Sure, Laura. Whatever you need to do, I'm ready."

Laura stepped around the table and stood next to Jason, who remained seated. She brought her forehead down, gently touching it to his forehead while simultaneously holding the sides of his head and slowly increasing pressure on his temples with her two forefingers.

Jason felt the strangest sensation course through his body as his mind went blank. Then he saw "stars" like he'd just taken a blow to the head, but without the pain. What he experienced next, he would never forget. For just an instant he *felt her mind - her thoughts - the very core of her being -* intertwined with his own. A vision he would never forget...for the briefest of moments; scenes of stars, planets...the kind of things one might see in a science fiction movie, ending with strangely dressed people strolling around futuristic buildings. Laura suddenly removed her forehead from his and let go her grip. She returned to her chair, both sitting in silence for what seemed a very long minute.

Finally, Jason exclaimed, "What *Just Happened??*"

Reaching for his hand, Laura said, *"I understand.* I know what's happened to you. You've received a *gift."*

"A gift! A gift? What are you talking about?" Asked the perplexed Jason.

"When you were injured in the IED incident, your brain chemistry was altered. Your non-physical mind was simultaneously changed. The process took a few weeks before manifesting, which turned out to be a good thing."

"And *how* do you know this?" Inquired an incredulous Jason.

"I don't know exactly," she truthfully responded, "but my people - er, *my family* - has had ESP abilities for generations. The range and scope vary greatly. Some of us perceive things beyond the physical world. Others, like myself, perceive people's intentions, good or bad. My greatest gift is the ability to meld my mind with another - if willing - to discover extra-sensory capabilities. You have a very rare ability - the gift of *personal* foresight."

"What does that mean? How do I turn it on...or off? Do I alter the future, maybe cause bad outcomes for others? I'm *very worried...actually scared to death!*"

Once more, Laura reached across the table to take his hand. As before, her touch had a subtle calming effect on him.

"Here's what I know," she began. "This new ability is unique to *you.* It's more a *personal* thing. You won't be able to "see" your future, much less anyone else's. Think of your new ability as a paranormal defensive tool. Sort of a *guardian angel* if you will. You don't turn this thing on or off. Your "foresight" activates in the presence of *any danger to you.* Remember the empty racquet cover you would have slipped on...with catastrophic results, as you saw?!"

"Yes...and I instinctively stepped out of the way, saving myself."

"And what happened in the next moment?" Prompted Laura.

"My future sight went away..."

"Exactly!" Exclaimed Laura. "You don't have to worry...you're not changing the future; you can't go the racetrack and make a ton of money. This ability is specific to you within your immediate environment...and it automatically activates 2 minutes before a threat occurs."

"Your Right!" Enthused Jason. "It is a *gift.* But...*how do you know all this?*"

"Honestly, I don't know....*I just don't,*" she answered. "Anyway, are you going to look this gift horse in the mouth? Really? Seriously?"

They both laughed, all the residual tension melting away. They heard the door open. Sandy stood there glancing tentatively in their direction.

"Everything OK? Making any progress?" She asked with just a hint of anxiety.

"Yes, Yes," said Laura with a broad smile. "Come...join us!" waving her friend over to the table. Without getting into too much detail on the process, Laura related what had happened to Jason and her conclusions.

"One thing...," stated Laura. "We need to keep this between the three of us."

"Of course," said Sandy as Jason nodded in agreement.

One week later...

Jason hugged Sandy tightly, feeling a bittersweet combination of love and sadness.

"Well, Sis," he began, tears welling up, "thanks for everything, mostly giving me my life back. God, I'm gonna miss you!"

Overcome with emotion, Sandy silently looked at her brother as she also teared up. Finally, she spoke.

"I love you, Jason. I'll always have your six. *Simper Fi!*" referencing their common Marine Corps heritage. "You have the address I gave you...right?"

"I do...and please tell Director McBride how grateful I am."

He was referring to Sandy's supervisor, CIA Director Kaitlyn McBride's job referral. Her brother, also a Marine vet, operated a small, but prestigious private investigation agency in Boston. He was looking to hire an assistant investigator, preferably one with little or no experience. Someone without "baggage" ...someone he could mold from scratch. McBride immediately thought of Jason, feeling he would be the perfect fit. So, the arrangements were made and he would soon be on his way to interview (just a formality, the job was already his).

"Speaking of grateful," he continued, "tell Laura I am forever in her debt. I'm gonna miss her...more than you know."

"Oh, *but I do know,* brother," she countered. "You do realize that Boston is a mere 2-hour plane ride from Savannah Heights...right?"

"Right...of course," he said, brightening as she pointed out the obvious. "Be well Sandy. I'll be in touch."

Jason put his luggage in the trunk of his sister's car, got in, and with a final wave goodbye backed down the driveway. That was the last time he had seen either of them...until now.

** ** **

The next four years were what Jason came to regard as the pivotal point of his life. Michael McBride had molded him into a topflight investigator. He would be forever grateful to Mike - and Kaitlyn for getting them together in the first place. But Michael sensed Jason needed to be his own man. He knew Jason would eventually come to resent always being in the shadow of his mentor.

Then, out of nowhere, an opportunity arose. Michael had been in Orlando, staying with an old flame, now just a really good friend, Tara Wayne, who mentioned in passing, that her brother was looking to retire and sell his very successful private investigation practice. Michael instantly thought of Jason...talk about your perfect fit...one thing led to another, with win-wins all over the place. Michael provided financing for his protege; Tara's brother walked away happy, and Jason had his very own practice...with a considerable leg up on the competition!

Oh, another bonus! Michael's very experienced secretary of twenty years, Madeline, was leaving for Orlando to be with her ailing mother. And she would need a job. 'Viola'! Jason quickly offered her a position as his secretary, with a nice raise in the bargain. She immediately accepted. He trusted her completely and she was quite fond of the up-and-coming detective.

** ** **

"Talk about detailed memories...," Jason said aloud, his mind abruptly returning to the present. Sally the Housebot suddenly appeared. "What did you need, Love?" she asked in her amusing cockney accent.

"Nothing, Sally. I was just thinking out loud."

"Well, all right then," she said. "If your Lordship needs anything, just holler."

"Sure Sally," replied Jason, amused yet again with Sandy's quirky Housebot.

He heard the car pull into the driveway, setting his heart racing in anticipation of seeing Laura again. Jason got up, quickly striding back into the house just as the front door opened, Laura coming into view. They both stopped dead in their tracks, but only for the briefest of moments. They wasted no time coming together for a tight, seriously affectionate hug.

"Laura, you look wonderful!" gushed Jason. "I'm so happy to see you again!"

In his mind, he heard Laura say, *"I've missed you so, you're often in my thoughts."*

Looking at Laura quizzically, he said, "I feel the same way...wait, what did you just..."

She put her finger on his lips to silence him, then drew him in close for a welcoming kiss. He noticed Sandy standing in the doorway, arms folded, a bemused expression on her face. Jason straightened up, let go of Laura, looking at Sandy with a sheepish smile.

He said, "Hi Sis! ...we were just saying hello."

** ** **

So began Jason and Laura's "magical week." It was as if they had been separated only a matter of days...they were more than lovers, true soulmates sharing a unique bond. In the intervening years, neither had met anyone that remotely sparked a romantic interest. Now, they made a pact to see each other as often as possible...even given the devotion each had for their chosen career paths. The feelings they had for each other remained as strong, nay stronger, then their first encounter twelve years ago.

** ** **

The autopilot parked the car in the designated space, abruptly bringing Jason's mind back to the present. He walked the short distance to the elevator and punched in the code for his fourth-floor apartment. Tomorrow he would begin the Diane Stockwell investigation, about which he already had a bad feeling.

** ** **

Chapter Three
Dodging A Bullet

Good morning, Sir. How may I help you?" Asked the perky young women sitting at the receptionist desk. Very attractive. Very professional. Her tone was friendly, albeit business-like.

Jason smiled; dropping his gaze from the beautiful young lady to the nameplate on her desk replied, "And Good Morning to you, Ms. ...*Deveroux.* I'm here to see Miss Wayne."

"...And do you have an appointment, Mr. ...?" her voice trailing off as she looked at the computer monitor sitting on her desk.

"McVay, Jason McVay," he replied. "I don't have an appointment, but if you would be kind enough..."

"Certainly, Mr. McVay," said the receptionist, this time with a notably *less business-like* smile, "one moment please." She tapped her computer keypad, announcing, "Miss Wayne, there's a Mr. McVay here to see you. Yes ma'am, I'll tell him." Glancing up at Jason, she allowed that Miss Wayne would be down shortly. He took a seat across from the receptionist to await Tara's arrival. He noticed *Miss Perky's* occasional furtive glances in his direction.

The elevator door opened, Tara stepped out, quickly walking over as Jason stood to greet her. Releasing Jason after a brief hug, she turned toward the receptionist.

"Jennifer, hold all my calls. Oh, and do the same for Mr. Henry."

"Yes, Ma'am," acknowledged the young receptionist with a smile, stealing a glance at Jason.

As they walked to the elevator, Tara confided to Jason: "Jennifer finds you most intriguing. Rarely have I seen her break professional demeanor."

After they entered the elevator, he replied, "Way too young for me...but she won't have any trouble in the dating department, I can tell you that."

"Which reminds me, the last time I spoke to Michael (McBride), he said you were pretty serious with a *Lana...*"

"*Laura,*" he corrected. "Laura Sparks. She's my sister's best friend and work mate. And we've already passed the "pretty serious" stage. Beyond that, long-distance romance is a bitch."

"Yeah, I know from personal experience," said Tara.

The elevator arrived on the fourth floor. Jason followed Tara to the end of the hall where they entered the Executive Suite Reception Office. The handsome middle-aged woman sitting at the desk glanced up, then stood and said, "Go right in Miss Wayne, Mr. Henry is waiting for you."

"Thank you, Erin," Tara responded, as she walked into the CEO's office with Jason in tow.

Tucker Henry stood up, walked around his desk and strode directly over to Jason, who extended his hand. Tucker reached out, grasping Jason's hand firmly with both his hands.

The CEO of Dynamadics Corporation was a husky, athletic looking individual. Jason judged him to be about six feet, just a couple inches shorter than himself and about the same weight. Certainly, in great shape for a 60-year-old man. Thinning grey hair and a nicely sculpted mustache accented a weathered, but nonetheless handsome face.

"Welcome, Jason," he said with a broad smile. "Tara has been singing your praises all morning."

Glancing over at Tara, Jason said, "Easy for her to say, tougher for me to live up to."

All three laughed as Tucker returned to his desk. After he sat down, he indicated two plush chairs facing his desk at either end.

"Please...have a seat, make yourselves comfortable. Coffee is on the way...if you would like anything else, please..."

"No... thank you," interrupted Jason. "Just coffee would be great."

"So... nasty business from what Tara has told me. John Stockwell is a well-respected associate here at Dynamadics and plays an important role as Executive Chief of Research. I don't know his wife, Diane all that well. Of course, I've seen her at numerous social functions, but while always pleasant, she's on the quiet side...keeps a low profile."

Just then, there was a light knock on the door, with Tucker inviting entry. A young lady, probably a college intern, came in carrying a tray with three large mugs and a good-sized carafe of coffee, along with the requisite creamer and sugar. She set the tray on the table between their chairs and asked the CEO if there would be anything else.

"We're good, Teresa, thank you," Tucker said with a warm smile. As the young intern turned and left, he remarked, "Teresa is interning from UCF. She's a graduate student working on a Master's Degree in Chemical Engineering. Brilliant girl. We are paying her tuition and she has accepted a position with Dynamadics' research department upon finishing her degree."

"Very impressive," Observed Jason, thinking *...and that's how you make a company successful.* "Is there anything else," he continued, "you can think of concerning Diane?"

"There *is* one thing," said Tucker. "All of John's peers regard her as being a "trophy wife" and a pretty dumb one at that. I know better. She is extremely smart. A member of Mensa. I know this because I have a cousin, also a Mensa member, who recognized her at a company function and pointed out that fact to me. For whatever reason, she keeps it to herself. Obviously, her own husband is unaware, so I wasn't going to bring the subject up."

"Interesting," observed Jason. "I wonder why she would keep such an impressive distinction to herself?"

"She was - *is* - a pretty reserved person. Perhaps she simply doesn't want the notoriety and inevitable attention," interjected Tara. "Beyond her disappearance, there is a much more nefarious side to this, Jason. Actually, the reason we need your expertise. Tucker, if you would..."

"Yes, of course," began the CEO. "Tara told me about your investigative background with the McBride Agency. I am also aware that Michael McBride's sister, Kaitlyn, is head of the CIA. You have the requisite experience as well as the security clearances necessary for this type of sensitive investigation."

"To get to the point...Dynamadics has developed cloaking technology in collaboration with NASA scientists that is years - if not decades - ahead of the rest of the world. The Russians managed to steal a significant amount of that technology. Fortunately, they lack a key piece of the formula. To be on the safe side, the Military contracted us to develop software which enables us to remotely deactivate the cloaking ability we had developed, essentially rendering the technology they appropriated useless. The Russian espionage apparatus is making a "full court press" to obtain this new deactivation software at any cost."

"So... where do I fit in?" Asked Jason.

"You have a key role," the CEO continued. "Tara believes...as do I, that we have a mole within the company and there is a good chance he *or* she is conspiring with someone in the Orlando FBI Office."

Tara, weighing in, added, "We believe you can ferret out the bad players, using your missing person investigation as cover."

"*Not* to diminish the importance of Diane Stockwell's having gone missing. To the contrary, Tara believes her disappearance is inextricably bound to the espionage case," said Tucker.

"That's right!" exclaimed Tara. "She's almost certainly been kidnapped...and it's all tied up with *Project Expose'*. Her husband is, after all, the executive head of research."

"For starters," requested the detective, "I'll need dossiers for both Stockwells and whatever you can provide regarding any suspicious associates of Dynamadics. And... I agree with you both - the missing person investigation is absolutely the perfect cover."

Tucker opened a side drawer of his desk, retrieved a medium-sized briefcase, and slid it across the desktop, where it came to rest in front of Jason.

"I think you'll find most of what you requested in the briefcase," announced the CEO.

He stood, walking around to the front to shake hands with the already standing Jason.

"It's been a pleasure, Sir," said Jason, "I can see why Dynamadics is such a successful company."

"Flattery will get you everywhere young man," Joked the affable CEO. "And please...call me *Tucker.*"

Tara and Jason laughed at his humorous remark. As they turned to leave, Tucker put a hand on each of their shoulders as he walked them to the outer Reception Office.

Before turning for his office, he said, "Anything...*Anything* you need, don't hesitate to call me directly. And Tara...be sure to give him the "nickel tour."

"Thanks, Tucker," said Tara, followed by Jason's "Goodbye Mr. ...er, *Tucker.* I'll be in touch."

As they walked to the elevator, Jason remarked, "Most definitely *one of the good guys.*"

In the elevator, Jason suggested they go over to the Stockwell residence and do a detailed walk-thru in daylight, Tara readily agreeing. The elevator door opened to the ground floor, and they walked past the Receptionist Desk where *Miss Perky* looked up, giving him an especially warm smile while pointedly making eye contact.

"Jennifer for sure finds you interesting," teased Tara.

Jason looked at Tara with *faux* petulance. "Stop it!" He said gruffly. They both chuckled.

They walked to the Security Station by the front entrance. Jason was about to place his briefcase on the scanning conveyor when Tara, looking at the Security Associate said, "That won't be necessary Officer Thomas."

He quickly responded, "Yes, Ma'am," and the pair continued to the entrance door. Then Jason felt a chill descend over his body. He knew what was coming as he went into "out-of-body" mode. The *movie in his mind* showed him walking out just behind and to the right of Tara. He heard a loud crack, instantly followed by the back of her skull coming off, landing on his chest. He felt the projectile continue on its path through his left lung, exiting his body and striking a large planter by the door. Two people, a young man and woman who were headed for the entrance suddenly dove to the ground. As he and the mortally wounded Tara fell to the pavement, he heard panicked screaming with Security Officer Thomas tearing out the entrance, gun drawn; quickly scanning the entire area.

Real time returned. This time, when the entrance door slid open, he roughly shoved Tara to the ground, landing on top of her, just as a loud crack shattered the peaceful environment. He grabbed the confused woman, pulling her with him to cover behind the large planter.

He yelled for the Guard to get back inside and secure the door. He was about to tell the young couple lying on the pavement to crawl toward him, when they arrived at his side, having made a crouching run for it.

After a few minutes, they heard the distant wail of sirens. Jason stood up, then helped Tara to her feet.

He said, "Okay you two. The threat is gone. You can go inside now." They got up and ran to the front entrance where Thomas escorted them inside.

"What The Hell Just Happened?!" Said a visibly shaken Tara.

"Someone just tried to take you...*us*...out!" Replied an excited Jason.

He helped her over to the entrance, the security man letting them in. The first of an arriving gaggle of law enforcement vehicles pulled up to the entrance. A deputy sergeant came in and Jason waved him over. He quickly told the deputy what had happened and the direction from which the shot originated. The deputy ran out, got in his vehicle and along with several more cruisers, headed in the direction Jason had told him.

The elevator door opened, and a very tense Tucker Henry hurried over to them. A multitude of Dynamadics security staff began descending on the main lobby, just as a cadre of three ambulances arrived. After assuring the medical personnel they were OK, they briefed Tucker about the incident. The CEO then gathered the department heads together to begin the process of neutralizing the chaotic environment and resuming normal operations.

Jason noticed four deputies, clipboards in hand, walking toward Tara, himself, and the young couple that had been approaching the entrance when the gunfire erupted...no doubt to begin the documentation process.

Tara and Jason finished their respective interviews about the same time. The interviewing deputies got up, thanked them, and abruptly left, presumably to complete the witness statements.

Turning to Jason, Tara said, "Thanks for saving my life! *But how on Earth did you know that was coming??*"

"A stroke of luck," he lied. "I saw a glint of light and guessed...*correctly*...it came from a rifle barrel. My military training told me to "*duck,*" so I did, grabbing you on the way down. That's all there was to it."

"Again, my heartfelt Thanks...and I guess, a shout-out to the *Corps* as well. Listen, I think I should stay here...get with Tucker to review our security strategy in light of current events. Plus, five will get you ten that the FBI shows up today."

"Agreed," replied the detective. "I'm gonna call Sam -Samantha Tally, my associate investigator and have her meet me at the Stockwell residence."

As Tara headed for the elevator, Jason took out his iPhone and called his office.

Now the young detective had a very real sense of what he was up against.

** ** **

Sam picked up on the first ring. "*Sam?*" said Jason. "Where's Maddy?"

"She's not in yet...she had a dental appointment," explained Sam.

"Oh, right," he replied. "It's you I want to talk to anyway."

Samantha Talley was Jason's first *true* hire. Technically, Madison Winslow was first, but he had worked with her almost 4 years at the McBride Agency in Boston. Sam, he had known many years; her older brother, Randy, was one of his best friends...they had enlisted in the Corps together. He had gone on to Officer Candidate School. Last he knew, Randy was in line for promotion to Brigadier General. Good for him. They had managed to stay in touch all these years, so Jason had watched his kid sister grow up. After a 3-year stint in the Marine Corps, she bounced around, from fitness trainer at a gym to becoming a fitness training consultant specializing in large private investigation agencies

.

She was a big girl, but *a very fit* big girl. At six feet and a well-muscled 150 lbs., she could physically hold her own with any man. And a martial arts expert in the bargain. She wore her auburn hair short. Attractive in an off-beat sort of way, she possessed deep green eyes offset by a slightly crooked nose, the end product of numerous breaks and resets. She had a great personality; a playful prankster tending toward hyperactivity; just now, at 29, learning how to relax. From a professional standpoint, her ability to implement a concerted focus at a moment's notice was a particularly useful quality.

Best of all, she - like Jason before her - was essentially a blank canvas. No bad habits to unlearn. He could mold her into the superb investigator he knew she could be. No question she had all the "tools."

Jason continued, "I want you to meet me at the Stockwell residence. I'll send you the address. It's in Briar Patch Estates. I'll get you up to speed when I see you."

"Briar Patch Estates, huh," she echoed. *"Well, La-Te-Da*...I'll see you in about twenty."

** ** **

Chapter Four
Into Thin Air

Jason arrived back at the front entrance, having just completed an inspection of the home's outside exterior. He had found nothing unusual or out of place. He heard an approaching vehicle and watched as the shiny black truck pulled into the driveway, parking adjacent to his Lexus. Sam stepped out of her 10-year-old Ford F-150 truck, which looked like it had just come off the showroom floor.

"When are you gonna trade that beast in for something more befitting the pretty young lady you are?" Playfully asked Jason, who teased her relentlessly about the truck.

"When? When it quits running, that's when!" She retorted. "So…where are we at?"

"Let's do another walk thru - Tara and I may have overlooked something last night - while I bring you up to date."

The detective detailed everything that had happened from the prior evening up to the assassination attempt earlier this morning.

"Holy Crap!" She blurted out. "Pretty much eliminates the Stockwell woman leaving voluntarily. She was definitely kidnapped. Probably for use as a pawn to be traded for information. Or not. Which means she's in mortal danger."

"That's my take," agreed Jason. "But *how* did the perps get her out without being noticed? This is an enclosed, gated community with the highest quality security money can buy. Only one way in or out…there are cameras all over the place and ongoing security patrols."

The pair arrived back at the front door. Jason continued, "Let's look around the pool patio and backyard...maybe something will point us in the right direction."

They commenced a detailed grid inspection beginning at the rear sliding doors, one on the left side and the other on the right.

Sam exclaimed, "Jason, come here!"

Jason hurried over to the far end of the patio where Sam was standing over an overturned deck chair behind a patio table. She was pointing excitedly at what appeared to be a piece of fabric caught on one of the chair legs. He took out his iPhone and a collapsible measuring tape he carried for just this purpose. Then he took a series of photos, using the tape to measure distances between the fabric and various points including the pool, table, and edge of the lawn. As soon as he finished this task, he picked up the piece of beige-colored fabric and sent Sam to retrieve a zip lock evidence bag from his car; she returned in less than two minutes.

"We've Got Our First Clue!" Enthused Jason. "We need to do a really detailed pattern search between here and the rear fence."

The pair split off, Jason on the right and Sam on the left, moving ever so slowly in a crouched position, expanding the search arc to cover every square foot in the greatest possible detail. After about 10 minutes, Sam suddenly straightened up, turning around to take another look at the ground she had just covered. Jason noticed Sam had stopped, and stood up himself, partially motivated by the need to stretch. Then Sam glanced his way, getting his attention.

"Jason! I think I've got something! Come over here!"

He reached into his pocket and pulled out his billfold, dropping it on the spot he was standing, then quickly walked over to Sam.

When he reached her position, she said, "Look at the grass between here and the patio...What do you see?"

Jason looked intently at the grass. After more than a minute he looked at her with a befuddled expression. "I'm sorry...I don't get it...*what am I supposed to see*??"

"The grass, *the grass*!! Look...*really look*...at the grass."

Jason continued to look with intensity. After a few more seconds came the *Eureka* moment. "Wait...what! The grass, the grass...*it's all bent,* like...like something's...*someone's* been dragged."

"EXACTLY!!" Exclaimed a now thoroughly excited Sam. "At first I didn't notice because the grass is short...but looking back from this angle, it's really apparent."

"Right!" Responded the equally enthused detective. "Now let's see where this leads."

They followed the slightly scrunched grass trail for another 25 feet where it came to an abrupt end about eight feet from the perimeter fence.

"Hmm...," muttered Jason when out the corner of his eye, he caught a bright glint near the shrub bordering the fence. He was about to walk toward the object when the familiar chill descended over him, stopping him in his tracks. The *movie in his mind* began playing...Jason walked over to the shrub to pick up what appeared to be, *actually was,* a cellphone. Just as he reached for it, he heard a rattling noise followed by a very large rattlesnake suddenly appearing, sinking its fangs into the meaty part of his hand between the thumb and forefinger. He saw himself fall to the ground, rolling over and over...

Real time resumed. Jason turned toward Sam. "DON'T MOVE!" He shouted. He reached down to his right leg, deftly lifting his pant leg with his left hand while simultaneously pulling his .32 caliber Beretta from its ankle holster. He raised it about a quarter of the way up firing two shots in rapid succession. A large snake flew up and out about a foot from a shrub, landing about three feet away from a very startled Sam, who screamed, "HOLY CRAP!!!" as she jumped back, putting another 3 feet between her and the now lifeless reptile. Jason holstered his gun, quickly walked past the headless rattlesnake, and retrieved the phone.

"*How* did you know that snake was there?" Asked a perplexed, but very impressed, Sam.

"Didn't you hear its rattle?" Asked Jason, seeking to quickly quash her rising curiosity with a rational explanation.

"No...," she answered tentatively...But damn good shooting, partner. I can always count on you to make the day interesting," she understated.

He held up the cellphone, turning his prize side to side to allow her a good look-see and remarked, "I'll bet..."

"...It's her phone," Sam said, finishing the sentence for him.

Jason placed the phone, which he had been carefully handling by the edges, in an evidence zip-lock baggie. They returned to the house, entering via the sliding glass door, and walked over to the kitchen bar; each taking a seat for a well-earned respite.

"OK," began Sam, "So we've effectively tracked her to the backyard, where she apparently vanished into thin air...which, based on where the trail ended...was a good thing - with her coming up just short of 'Rattlesnake City!' The question remains, *Where* did she go?"

"I've got a theory about that," proffered Jason as he got up and headed for the front door.

Sam stood up saying, "Hang on partner."

"What?" He asked.

"Maybe your billfold?" ...she said, grinning impishly.

"Oh, shit...Thanks, Sam," he replied, blushing.

** ** **

Jason pulled into *The Briar Patch Estates* Administration Building parking lot with his partner (he thought of Sam as his *partner*, even though technically she was his assistant) following close behind. They parked their vehicles and walked into the office where they were greeted by a friendly middle-aged woman sitting behind a rather large mahogany desk, pretty impressive for a reception area. Then again, this *was* "The Patch."

Ms. Congeniality glanced up at the pair and with a bright smile said, "Good Morning, how may I help you?"

To which Jason responded, "I'm Jason McVay and this is my partner, Samantha Talley." He pulled out his wallet, retrieved his Florida Private Investigator Identification Card, laying it on the desk for her perusal. As she looked it over, he continued, "We need to speak to your head of security. My firm has been retained by the Dynamadics Corporation to investigate the disappearance of one of their people who resides In Briar Patch Estates. If you check, I believe we have been granted access to whatever Briar Patch resources we might need."

The Receptionist handed back Jason's I.D. and said, "One moment, please." She picked up the desk phone, relating what Jason had just told her. After a few moments she said, "Yes, Sir," and abruptly hung up the phone. She looked up at Jason to inform him that "Mr. Dumont will be with you in just a moment, Sir." She had hardly finished speaking when the door behind her opened, revealing a short, bespeckled man with a full beard and a shaved head.

Striding over to Jason, he offered his hand, introducing himself, "Hello, Mr. McVay, I'm Robert Dumont."

Jason shook his hand, mentally noting the firm grip (he subscribed to the masculine notion that the firmness of one's grip was a good indication of character) and responded, "Mr. Dumont allow me to introduce my associate, Ms. Talley."

Dumont released his grip and offered his hand to Sam. Looking up at the much taller woman. he said, "Pleased to meet you, Ms. Talley."

She smiled, acknowledging with a slight nod as she extended her hand to the Security Chief.

"Please...," and with a sweep of his arm invited them to follow him to his office.

The office was but a short way down the hall. Upon entering, Jason was taken aback by its relative austerity...seemed out of character for the image-conscious organization. Maybe a personal reflection of the occupant? The incongruity really didn't matter...merely the result of Jason's obsession with observational minutiae.

Dumont settled in his chair and invited his visitors to have a seat in the two chairs facing his desk, which they promptly did, both pleasantly surprised at the unexpected comfort.

"I assume you're here regarding last night's incident at the Stockwell residence?" he stated.

"Correct," replied Jason. "As I'm sure you're aware, we have been retained by Dynamadics to investigate the disappearance of Diane Stockwell. Since this is a matter of national security, everyone involved must act with great discretion."

"Yes, I understand," replied Dumont. "I heard there was a shooting incident at the Dynamadics property earlier this morning...would that be connected to your investigation?"

"I really shouldn't say Mr. Dumont - remember 'discretion' - however, I can see you're a *professional,* so *Yes*, it is definitely connected. Of course, this *is* confidential."

Sam, looking on was thinking *look and learn girl! He's playin' this guy like a fiddle!*

"Of course, Mr. Stockwell. Goes without saying...and please, call me *Bob.* Now, how exactly may I help?"

"Well, I can see you have state-of-the-art security here, and I have no doubt it is most efficiently managed. My first question *Bob*...and please...I'm *Jason,* and my partner is *Samantha* - she likes *Sam* - my first question is about access control. I assume there is only one way in and out?"

"Yes, that's mostly correct, *Jason,*" he affirmed; then, elaborating further: "There is an alternate entrance/exit at the opposite end of the community. It's really just for emergency use, for instance, if the main entrance was somehow obstructed, or for hurricane evacuation. The gatehouse, however, is always manned. In fact, it's one of the check-in points that the security patrols must log into during the course of their shifts."

"And your security patrols," queried Sam, "I'm sure they are random...but could you tell us the frequency?"

"Sure," said Dumont, "during the day we have a single team patrol the entire community at least once every two hours; during darkness we increase that to once an hour. We use unmarked vehicles, and our associates wear civilian attire. Our aim is to be unobtrusive and as *discrete* (he gave Sam a wink and a smile) as possible. Normally, only associates manning the gates wear uniforms. I'm proud to say we probably have the best trained private security staff in the Orlando area. I know we pay the most, including Disney World. What you have to do if you want the *creme de la' creme.*"

"Well, I'm sure impressed!" Gushed Sam, unabashedly stroking the Security Chief's ego.

"As am I," Jason joined in, adding more fuel to the 'flattery' fire. Concluding his target was now sufficiently primed, the detective initiated his *coup d' etat.* "So, *Bob,* I really need your help. I've got a great lead on what may have happened. Unfortunately, it's highly classified, so while it's really unfair - what I'm about to ask - I'm counting on your trust and sense of patriotism to really help us out."

He continued, "I need copies of all your security and access logs for the previous 30 days. Oh, and I noticed a helipad on the way over...so those logs as well. I know it's a *big ask*, but I can tell you Dynamadics Corporation will be *very* grateful for your cooperation."

"Well, I don't know…I could get into serious trouble…might even lose my job if the wrong people found out."

Sam jumped in with feigned enthusiasm, "*Bob*, you're my key for this whole thing. I'm the *computer geek* who needs that data to put the pieces of this puzzle together…and I - both of us - give you our solemn word *no one will ever be able to trace anything back to you.*"

After a very long couple minutes of contemplative silence, Dumont looked from one to the other then said, "OK, I trust you. One caveat…when this is all over, you'll fill me in on all the details."

"You got it my friend!" Said Jason with all the enthusiasm he could muster.

"Give me a few minutes," he said as he left the office. In short order, he reappeared and handed a thumb drive to Jason. The three shook hands, with Jason gratefully patting him on the back as they left his office. Dumont walked them out to the parking lot, the two detectives each waving goodbye as they got in their vehicles.

** ** **

The Office Control System Manager confirmed, "Program One activated." The office lighting adjusted to the programmed level as smooth jazz softly emanated from the sound system.

The System Manager, in the British *butler accent* Jason had programmed (a nod to his sister's Housebot's voice) continued, "Jason is currently working the Stockwell Case with Sam. You have a message from Sam on your computer. There are no office security issues to report."

Maddy deposited her handbag in the top left drawer of the Receptionist Desk and walked over to the beverage dispenser requesting, "Iced Tea with crushed ice and a twist of lemon, please."

Annoyed with herself; she thought, *Damn, I did it again!* Both Jason and Sam unmercifully teased her about her politeness when dealing with the Artificial Intelligence functions. She couldn't help herself...that was just the way she was raised. Still, she was determined to stop. The three had wagered a dinner (at a restaurant of the winner's choosing) that she couldn't stop for an entire work week...beginning *today.*

Madison Winslow played a key role for *McVay and Associates,* she was the first associate Jason hired. The 5'2" petite black woman was an administrative whiz, having honed those skills during a 15-year stint with the FBI, followed by seven years with Michael McBride. After losing her Marine Corps son in the same incident that nearly killed Jason (a connection discovered after Jason joined the McBride Agency), she divorced her husband, who returned to his native Puerto Rico. She was well acquainted with fellow associate Samantha Talley, whose mom was one of her ex-husbands four sisters, hence Aunt Maddy. Small world indeed.

Maddy did a quick walk thru of the suite; first, Sam's office, her neatly cluttered desk a clear reflection of the girl's hyperactive per-sonality. She walked thru the adjoining door into Jason's office. Well appointed, the expansive office featured his ultra-modern glass desk (all the rage with the current crop of young professionals) with its beautiful oversized executive leather chair (a gift from his former colleague and mentor, Michael McBride). A large mural showcasing the Boston Cityscape with the Charles River in the foreground, add-ed a nice *New England* flavor. Two plush leather chairs done in a soft maroon color faced his desk. As she walked back to the Recep-tion Office, she briefly paused by the window overlooking Lake Eola with downtown Orlando in the background. The view justified the municipality's *City Beautiful* nickname.

She was about to sit down when her niece stepped in with Jason on her heels.

"Good morning, Aunt Maddy. I trust all went well at the dental ap-pointment?"

"It did," replied Maddy, "Good Morning to both y'all. Jason, you have voicemail from Ms. Wayne."

He said, "Thanks, Maddy," then to the beverage dispenser: "Coffee, light cream, 2 sugars...wait...Sam - coffee?" She assented with a nod, Jason continued, ..."and another coffee, black." He retrieved his coffee and walked into his office.

Sam picked up her coffee from the dispenser and took a seat in the reception chair nearest Maddy's desk.

"Aren't you going to ask me if I'd like a coffee, too?" Maddy asked Sam, feigning annoyance at the supposed slight.

"Why would I do that," she queried, "you have a nearly full glass of iced tea on your desk."

"*Quite the detective*," Maddy playfully retorted, assuming an air of haughtiness.

"And," Sam parried, "I'd wager a week's pay that you said *please* to the dumb machine."

"I can neither confirm nor deny your assertion," said her Aunt. They both burst out laughing. Maddy continued, "so...bring me up to date on the *Stockwell Caper.*"

As requested, Sam briefed her Aunt on all the happenings up to the present, including the attempted assassination at Dynamadics. She was able to provide a more detailed narration of subsequent events, having actually been there.

At first, Maddy was quite distressed about the shooting incident at Dynamadics, but quickly calmed down. She had come to believe Jason had some kind of *guardian angel* protecting him. Since she had been working with him, he had survived dozens of incidents that, on their face, appeared un-survivable. The irony.

Just as Sam finished updating Maddy, Jason came out of his office and began issuing instructions to his two associates.

"I've got to go back to Dynamadics and meet with Tara Wayne. Sam - you have that thumb drive that Dumont gave us - I need the two of you to breakdown everything on that drive, paying particular attention to all information about helicopters, especially comings and goings. When I'm finished with Wayne, I'll get in touch."

** ** **

Chapter Five
A Meeting Of The Minds

At Dynamadics main entrance, Jason was greeted by a large black man dressed in the *d'rigor* grey business suit of government agents. *Large* is perhaps an understatement. The gentleman stood about 6'10" and weighed somewhere in the vicinity of 300 lbs., making the 6'2" McVay feel quite small by comparison. In a high-pitched voice - a stark contrast to his size - the man introduced himself.

"I'm Special Agent Grande, Mr. McVay," (*of course you are,* thought Jason) "if you would accompany me...," and with a polite sweep of his right arm, indicated the lobby entrance through which Jason followed *The Hulk* to the nearest elevator. He noted an *especially friendly smile* emanating from Jennifer the Receptionist as they passed by her desk.

The elevator stopped at the fourth floor; the two men exited, walking briskly to the Executive Suite directly in front of them. Upon reaching the entrance, Mr. Big...uh, *Agent Grande,* turned and left. Erin, Tucker Henry's secretary, greeted him with a warm smile.

"Please follow me, Mr. McVay," she said, escorting him to a door opposite the CEO's office. Upon entering, he quickly realized he was in a conference room. Already seated at the large table were Tucker Henry at the head; to his immediate left, Tara Wayne sat with hands folded. To his right was a man - dressed in a grey business suit; seated to his right was an attractive young Asian-American woman, dressed in navy blue slacks and a sleeveless beige chiffon blouse, topped with a woman's blue blazer.

Tucker Henry, with a broad smile, invited Jason to "Please have a seat...can I get you anything?"

Jason demurred, sitting one place down from Tara.

The CEO commenced with the formal introductions. Indicating the man to his right, he said, "Jason, meet FBI Special Agent Owen Whittaker. Seated next to him is Special Agent Emily Cast. Agents Whittaker and Cast, allow me to introduce Jason McBride, a private investigator retained by Dynamadics."

The three individuals reached across the table to exchange handshakes, after which Tucker continued, "I'm going to turn over the floor to Agent Whittaker, he has some information for you."

Jason responded with a simple, "Of course."

Whittaker began, "First, let me express my admiration for how well you handled what was obviously a most harrowing situation. I understand Ms. Wayne would not be with us today if you hadn't acted so incisively. Our preliminary assessment is you - and Ms. Wayne - were targeted because of the disappearance of Mrs. Stockwell. Further, we believe her disappearance is, in fact, an abduction - and that abduction is directly related to *Project Expose'*. The intelligence community is well-aware of the Russians' desire to have this technology and that they are determined to obtain it, whatever the cost. Mr. Henry told us you were hired to locate Mrs. Stockwell, which at that point was being treated as a missing person case. Obviously, the focus has changed as it is now a matter of national security."

At this point, Whittaker sat back in his chair; Agent Cast taking over the narrative.

"Mr. McVay," she began, "we believe you and Ms. Wayne are still in great danger. That said, we also believe that by ceasing your investigation, the danger will also cease. It has been our experience that the Russians tend to ignore individuals they no longer consider a threat, believing this tactic saves valuable resources. With that in mind, we believe your best course of action would be to abandon the case. I can assure you the FBI, with its vast resources, is well-positioned to safely recover Mrs. Stockwell while thwarting the Russian attempt to access *Project Expose'*. What do you say? This is, after all, a matter of national security."

Jason looked from Tucker, whose face was an unreadable blank; to Tara, also wearing a neutral expression...but he caught *something* in her eye, *the way she gazed at him*...

"You know...I'm not sure. I'd like to confer with my clients before I give you an answer."

Agent Whittaker appeared to grimace slightly at his remark; Cast was more accepting and with a genuine smile said, "Sure, Mr. McVay, we don't have a problem with that."

Everyone stood, the two agents gathering their papers. Whittaker asked to use the Men's Room, and Tara directed him to the reception area. After he left, Cast took Jason aside.

She said, "Jason...*may I call you Jason*?" He assented with a nod. "I'm a friend of Laura Sparks. We worked together years ago when she was an FBI Special Agent. I know your sister as well. Anyway, we have stayed in touch over the years...and have helped each other out, trading CIA and FBI information for mutual benefit...you know how that works. Now I need your help. Something very wrong is going on...it involves Whittaker. Can we get together so I can explain? And sooner rather than later."

"Sure, no problem, Emily," he replied. "Any friend of Laura's..."

Before he could finish the sentence, she pressed her FBI courtesy card into his hand and whispered, "Here he comes...*call me,*" letting go his hand, she walked briskly to join Whittaker on the way out of the Reception Office.

Tara tapped Jason on the shoulder, "What was that all about?" She inquired.

"I'm not really sure," he replied. "Let me get back to you."

Tucker Henry joined the pair, suggesting they return to the conference table to parley. Back at the table, Tucker resumed his place at the head with the two investigators taking seats on either side of him.

"So...," opened Tucker, "Your thoughts? What was your take, Tara?"

"I think...my instincts tell me...something's off about this whole thing, Whittaker in particular. While I get his wanting us to drop out - this is really the usual territorial position the FBI takes with any case involving their agency - he seemed *particularly anxious* that we exit. Also, I picked up on a certain tension between him and Cast."

Jumping in, Jason added, "I agree with your assessment Tara." Glancing at each of them in turn he continued, "Emily Cast wants to meet with me. She hinted at a problem with Whittaker and I think it's *not* personal...more of a professional thing."

"Why would she trust you with such a potentially serious issue - she doesn't even know you?" pointed out Tara.

"Your right," he answered, *"but...Emily does know Laura.* The two of them have been friends a very long time."

Tara, noting Tucker's confused look, explained, "Laura Sparks is a former FBI Agent and is currently a CIA operative. She and Jason are also good friends." Glancing over at Jason, she amended her statement; "actually more than good friends...*really* good friends."

Tucker, with a knowing twinkle in his eye murmured, "Ah."

"So," resumed Jason, "I think I should meet with her and find out what's up, then we can devise a strategy going forward. What do you think Tucker?"

Jason and Tara simultaneously looked over at the CEO.

"Yes indeed," he agreed. "I leave it in your capable hands, Tara - keep me posted."

"Of course," acknowledged the Security Chief. "I guess we're done for now."

As if on cue, Jason's ringtone announced a call. It was Sam. He asked her to stand-by.

** ** **

Jason said a quick goodbye to the other two, and in an aside, told Tara he would be in touch.

Returning to his phone, he listened as Sam told him she and Maddy had put all the information obtained from Dumont's thumb drive into a narrative format.

"Great!" Exclaimed the detective. "I've got a couple of errands to run...listen, can you meet me at O'Doul's Irish Pub about five? We can mix a little business and pleasure (Jason knew this was one of Sam's favorite watering holes), I'm really anxious to see your report. Good work you guys!"

Jason left the Executive Suite, took the elevator to the ground floor, and crossed the lobby where he was once again rewarded with an inviting smile from the nubile receptionist, Missy Jennifer as he left the premises.

On the way over to his car, he passed the scene of this morning's *nastiness*, now encircled with the familiar yellow tape. He could clearly see the large hole punched in the oversized planter by the bullet meant for him/Tara; a reminder once again of the charmed life he led. As he got into his car, he noted Special Agent Grande standing next to a large black Lincoln Navigator, standard government issue for the various agencies. As he delivered destination instructions to the autopilot, he observed Grande disappear into the Navigator. *Hmmm, coincidence - or is Mr. Big up to something?*...the paranoid thought suddenly bouncing around inside his head.

After a 15-minute ride through surprisingly light metro traffic, the autopilot parked his car in its designated space and Jason left the vehicle for the short walk to the elevator. He exited on the fourth floor, unlocking his apartment with his iPhone. He entered his pleasantly cool abode and plopped into his comfortable recliner, finished in a supple creme leather - a housewarming gift from Laura. He pulled his phone from his pants pocket and instructed Siri to *call Laura.* After activating speaker mode, he put the phone on the adjacent end table. The phone rang on her end, immediately going to voicemail.

"HI Honey," he greeted. "I'm sure you're busy, but when you have a spare moment, give me a call. I need to ask you about one of your friends...Emily Cast. She's involved in a new case I'm working, which - of course - I'll tell you all about. Not urgent, but sooner would be better than later. Thanks, Love You."

He clicked off, got up and headed to his bedroom for a quick shower and change of clothes. After showering, Jason went into his large walk-in closet and emerged with a faded blue collared T-shirt emblazoned with an imprint of the spaceplane, *Explorer.* The now six-year-old garment was a gift from Laura. He was amazed it still fit; then realized all those hours of sweat in the gym actually had some payoffs. She had gifted him with the shirt shortly after her latest mission in the craft (highly classified; it had been kept out of public view). He selected a pair of light brown cargo shorts to complete the casual ensemble.

His phone's ringtone alerted him to an incoming call. It was Laura. After the usual platitudes... "How's the weather up there...keeping you busy," etc., he brought her up to date on the Dynamadics case beginning with last night's abduction; the assassination attempt earlier today; the meeting with agents Whittaker and Cast, concluding with Cast's suspicions about her partner.

For her part, Laura confirmed that Emily Cast was a good person, a dedicated agent with the highest ethical standards. She went on to say that if Emily felt there was an issue, he should take it as gospel. Laura said she was taking a week of leave time and had been planning a surprise visit. Now, she told him she was ready to come earlier if he needed help with the case. Jason said he looked forward to her visit and asked her to stand by for a possible earlier arrival;

there was a very good chance he would need her professional help. They exchanged a parting, "Love You," terminating the call.

Jason finished dressing, grabbed his wallet and phone, then headed out for the 30-minute trek to O'Doul's Pub.

** ** **

He pulled the Lexus into the Pub's parking lot, opting for a spot in the empty back row, which was his wont, given his paranoia with the dings and dents risk from the inconsiderate patrons who couldn't care less about their fellow patron's vehicle finishes. Jason climbed out telling the autopilot to secure his car. He spotted Sam's F-150 parked next to the handicap space at the end of the front row. Like her partner, she tried to minimize the chance of scratches, dings, and dents.

Upon entering, he surveyed the room and noted 3 of the 12 or so booths occupied; with an additional 8 patrons sitting at the tables set up between the wall booths and the large oblong bar in the center. Pretty sparse so far, but it was early. He spotted Sam on a stool at about the center. Seated on either side of her were two - and he hated thinking in terms of stereotypes - rednecks. One was short and pudgy, with a full beard; his weathered face topped off by a... have to admit it...cool *Texas Ten-Gallon.* The guy on her other side was taller and had a muscular build. A crooked nose and large scar on his left cheek dominated an otherwise nondescript face. Oh, there was that drooping handlebar mustache straight out of Tombstone, circa 1860.

Jason sidled up to the bar and sat on the empty stool adjacent to the *pudgy one*. He glanced over Shorty's head and caught Sam's eye. She smiled at him mischievously, and after a quick wink, turned to look straight ahead. The bartender came over to take his order; Jason asking for a bottle of *Blue Moon* craft beer..." with a glass, please."

The bartender quickly returned with his beverage. As he poured some beer into the glass, the Short One turned toward Jason and, obviously inebriated, informed him. "Check out the filly next 'ta me...now that's a tall drink-a-water!" Jason looked at him in silence. Shorty continued in a half-whisper, "Yeah, that dude (referencing his counterpart on the other side of Sam) been workin' her for a little while (came out: 'fur a whittle while'), "but - grabbing Jason's arm - I gotta tell ya...I don' tink da lady's imorested." Jason removed Shorty's hand from his arm, observing, "Looks like the lady can take care of herself."

"No, no... ya don unnerstan'," slurred the obviously drunk redneck, "dis guy, he *always* ges wha he wants!"

Jason glanced over at Sam, noting she was beginning to look pretty irritated. Turning his gaze back to Shorty, he repeated, "I'm telling you *she can take care of herself."*

"No, no," Shorty urgently whispered, again grabbing Jason's arm, "you don unnerstan..."

Jason again removed the drunken Shorty's hand... this time with considerable force.

"OW! You hurden' me..." blurted out Shorty.

A now thoroughly annoyed Jason glared at the drunken redneck, "*Listen To Me.* I'll put it in terms you can understand: "*Your friend would be better off trying to stuff a firecracker up a wildcat's ass than to mess with that woman!"*

He had hardly finished his admonition to Shorty, when...looking over at Sam, he saw Scarface grab her breasts. *Uh, Oh,* thought Jason. *This isn't going to be pretty.* Sure enough...

Sam suddenly stood up, simultaneously clasping her hands together, then in a sudden burst of power, rapidly raised her arms straight up between his arms, breaking their hold on her. Before the startled man could react, she reared back with her right arm. Then, her fist clenched, she brought her arm forward with incredible speed. Her fist impacted his crooked nose with such force blood sprayed everywhere as his body flew through the air, bouncing off an empty barstool before landing in a twisted heap on the floor. Scarface just lay there; his lights quite literally *punched out.*

Looking down at the unconscious man on the floor, the stunned on-lookers heard her declare, *"Don't you EVER do that to another woman again, YOU SON-OF-A-BITCH!!!"* She turned to leave, grabbing Jason by the arm; the pair bursting through the door and out into the parking lot, Sam urgently telling Jason to "Go to my place! We'll sort this out there."

They split up, heading to their respective vehicles. It took less than a minute for the F-150, tires screeching, to pull out on northbound Orange Blossom Trail, her partner following less than a car length behind her.

** ** **

Chapter Six
A Really, Really Bad Day

About 4 miles up the Trail, Jason followed Sam's F-150 as she exited to eastbound Exeter Road, taking them to her home in the still-under-construction Sunrise Park subdivision. Her brand new 2-bedroom loft townhouse, courtesy Richard Madison (Maddy's real estate broker brother) coming through once again for the Agency. The big bonus - he was helping her out with a great rent-to-own scheme...she'd have enough capital invested to assume an owner's mortgage in less than 5 years.

She pulled her truck into the garage with Jason parking in the driveway. Sam walked over to Jason, and he followed her into the house.

Glancing around the room Jason remarked, "Just like I remembered from last time...wait, what...*is that a new leather recliner I see?* In a nice creme finish, too. *Nice touch.*"

"Yeah," she replied, "remember last time I was at your place when I asked you about your cool creme leather recliner. The one you said was a gift from...what's her name - oh yeah, Laura (Sam knew full well who Laura was; this yet another example of their mutual teasing routine). Anyway, I got envious and so, well, *here we are.*"

Jason walked across the surprisingly spacious living area to the bar separating it from the more compact kitchen/dining area, helping himself to a seat at the bar.

"Crap!" Exclaimed Sam. "I left the report in the truck. Hang on, I'll be right back."

While he waited for his partner's return, he looked around her home again. *Yeah, she did all right,* he thought, *nice place, got class.* Looking up, he noticed sunlight was just beginning to penetrate the skylight, splashing over the balcony in front of the loft bedroom. To his left was a trophy case displaying at least a dozen trophies from past tennis tournaments. The girl had been a top tier amateur and in fact, could hold her own with more than a few pros.

Sam returned with the folder, unceremoniously tossing it on the bar. She walked past Jason to the fridge, retrieving two Heinekens along with a couple of frosted mugs.

"Thanks, partner," said Jason.

"My pleasure," she said. "Least I could do - your mug was half full when we left the pub."

"Yeah, about that...what the hell happened?" Quizzed the detective.

"Guy wouldn't leave me alone, couldn't take a hint...just that simple," she replied.

"Sort of brazen, what he did," Jason understated.

"Ya think?" Asked Sam, with more than a little sarcasm. "The son of a bitch," she went on; anger slowly rising as the moment replayed in her head. "I shoulda kicked him in the nuts."

"You clocked him, girl!" Jason reminded her. "Don't think the perv will try that stunt again anytime soon."

"I hope your right," she said. "My hand still hurts, woulda been easier to just kick him. Do ya think we'll get repercussions from O'Doul's?"

"No, absolutely not," affirmed her partner. "Terry O'Doul is a friend of mine - plus the bartender, Alfred, saw the whole thing. Not that it won't be the talk of the Pub for a few days...make that a few *weeks.* No...no need to cry over spilled perverts," he noted, tongue firmly in cheek.

Jason picked up the folder, quickly scanning each page of the report. Midway through page 4 he abruptly stopped; glancing up at Sam, left eyebrow arched, exclaimed, "Bingo!" He finished reading the page, then slid it over to his partner.

She read the page; then read it again, this time more slowly. "Wait, what," she said…"so *that's how they got Diane out!*"

"I *knew* you had the makings of a good detective," teased Jason. "Read those two log entries again."

"Right," Sam responded, reading aloud: "*2055 hours. Low flying helicopter over-flew this station* (the main entrance facility) *flying east to west.* Next entry, *2125 hours. Mobile Unit One reports a small helicopter at low altitude exiting the West end of Briar Patch property. Able to note only last four tail numbers: 4723; no running lights; flying in 'whisper mode'.*"

"You'd think someone…*Hello, Bob Dumont!*…might have thought those log entries were maybe *just a tad* unusual," observed the young investigator.

"A reasonable expectation, my friend," replied Jason, "but truth of the matter, 'the best security money can buy' - apparently doesn't rise to that level in the residential sector. Well, that's enough excitement for one night," he concluded. "Think I'll head out…need some serious down time after all of the day's excitement."

They both stood, Jason embracing his partner in an affectionate hug. She walked Jason to his car, waving goodbye as he pulled out of the driveway.

** ** **

No doubt about it, Jason thought as he waited for the Keurig to finish brewing his coffee. *Laura's right. It is most definitely a gift.* He recalled the previous evening's drive home.

Almost immediately after leaving Sam's house, the familiar chill settled over him, closely followed by *the movie in his mind.* He saw the on-ramp to the Orange Blossom Trail looming in the distance, when, without warning came a loud thud as a deer slid across the hood of his Lexus, crashing through the windshield, and impaling him with its antlers. The car skidded off the road, rolling over three times before finally coming to a rest upside down in a roadside revetment pond.

Real time resumed. Jason slowed the car, pulling off onto the shoulder and bringing it to a stop. Not a minute later a beautiful buck deer, sporting an impressive six-point antler rack, bounded across the road about 50 yards in front of him. Best part: Both he and the deer were still alive.

In less than 24 hours, he had avoided being shot, snake bitten, and getting gored. First time in over a year his foresight had activated; *now three incidents in rapid succession.* Maybe an omen? Jason experienced two emotions simultaneously: relief and gratitude, slowly being replaced with a vague sense of unease. Time to move on. He fixed his coffee, cream with two sugars, *just like Laura,* floated through his mind, bringing on a smile. *Strange how mundane things can trigger memories.*

** ** **

On the other side of town, in the suburban community of Winter Park, Agent Emily Cast sat at the kitchen table of the small 2-bedroom apartment she shared with her niece, a UCF student in her junior year. Carmody, the aforementioned niece, had already departed for the downtown campus, leaving Emily alone to struggle with her dilemma. She felt there was no time to waste.

Picking up her phone, she began texting: *Jason, we need to meet as soon as possible. I took a loss day at work, so I have the entire day free. We could meet at...*

** ** **

Jason carried his mug of coffee over to the kitchen table; sitting down to think about scheduling today's activities when his iPhone alerted him to an incoming text message. As he read the message, he quickly got a feel for how this day was going to go... *We could meet at Brunch 'N Lunch. It's a little hole in the wall place downtown on Orange Avenue - not far from our office building, great food - how's nine? Or whatever time works for you.*

Jason thumb-typed: *Nine is fine. And I know the place. You're right, the food is great. See you in a couple hours.* He tapped *Send* and laid the phone back down. He checked his watch; 7:35. Plenty of time. A fifteen-minute walk from his place.

** ** **

Agent Whittaker finished brushing his hair, adjusted the knot of his pale blue tie, then checked his suit jacket for any lingering lint. Satisfied with his appearance, he turned and walked out of the bathroom and over to the dinette table where he picked up his freshly cleaned Glock, dropping it into the belt holster at the small of his back. He stepped out the front door to await the arrival of Agent Grande who would provide the usual transportation to work.

Whittaker liked Agent Grande. D'Arby Grande had played four seasons - three as an all-pro - at tight end for the New England Patriots. A devastating knee injury prematurely ended his pro football career and the beginning of a new career as an FBI Special Agent. Whittaker had worked hard to cultivate the man's loyalty.

Special Agent Whittaker looked down the road to see the big Lincoln Navigator making its way to his house. He stepped off the porch and walked to the street; the SUV pulling up just as he arrived at the curb. Whittaker hopped in and greeted Grande.

"Good morning, D'Arby, ready for another exciting day with the FBI?"

"Good morning, Agent Whittaker. I guess so sir," replied Grande, with just a hint of sarcasm.

Owen Whittaker settled back for the 15-minute ride to the Orlando FBI branch office. Rather than trying to engage the taciturn Grande in any meaningful conversation, he considered his latest irritant, one Jason McVay.

Turning toward his *de facto* chauffeur, he inquired, "So D'Arby, what can you tell me about McVay's evening?"

"I can tell you this - it wasn't dull. He went to O'Doul's Pub arriving about 1715 hours. At about 1800 hours, he came out closely followed by his sidekick, Sam... something. Anyway, they both looked really agitated; jumping in their vehicles they headed north on the O.B.T. I followed at a discreet distance. They got off on Exeter Road and went to that new subdivision where she apparently lives."

"At about 2030 hours he left. I followed him to his place, where I kept watch for about an hour. Then I headed back to O'Doul's, and talked to an Al Wainright, the on-duty bartender. He stated that a male customer, who he couldn't identify, - *get this* - grabbed the breasts of the female customer - he identified as Samantha *something* - who apparently took umbrage; stood up and clocked the guy. I mean *clocked the guy!* He was out cold for nearly 10 minutes. Then she left, grabbing McVay on the way out...which brings us back to the beginning."

"Good work, D'Arby," praised Whittaker, "You don't have to submit a written report. Matter of fact, let's keep it between the two us for the moment."

"Tell me again why we're tailing this guy?" requested Grande.

"I can't really say much at the moment...let's just say I have a hunch...You'll have to trust me for now," replied Whittaker, as they pulled into the parking garage.

** ** **

At 8:50 AM Jason walked into Brunch 'N Lunch and immediately saw Agent Cast sitting at a table in the rear with her back to the wall - sort of standard procedure in the 'cops 'n robbers' world she lived in. He walked straight over, taking the seat she indicated.

"Good morning, Jason," she said smiling broadly. "Thanks for accommodating me on such short notice."

"No problem. Emily," he replied. "I took the liberty of calling Laura...and *not* just concerning you. Anyway, she holds you in the highest regard, both professionally and personally. That said, anything you have to say to me will be considered in that spirit."

Before Emily could reply, the waitress arrived to take their orders. She ordered the two-egg special; Jason opted for French Toast. They both requested coffee. As she scurried off to put in their orders and get the coffee, Jason remarked that she must be a college student, probably UCF. Displaying a penchant for wit, Emily allowed that his sleuthing skills were indeed impressive.

Jason laughed. "I can see why Laura likes you."

"Again," she said, "I really appreciate your willingness to help me. I have a serious work issue and could sure use some outside support. I'll get right to the point..."

She stopped mid-sentence as the twenty-something waitress returned with a carafe of coffee.

"Tell me young lady" ...looking at her lapel name tag, "tell me *Kathy*...do you by chance attend UCF?"

"As a matter of fact, I do," replied the waitress, "how did you know that?"

"Because he's a detective Kathy," said Emily. "Why, he even knew your name."

"But I'm wearing a name tag, remarked the young waitress...wait, *I get it,*" she said, smiling. "I'll be back in a few minutes with your orders," leaving them to their prior conversation.

"Nice girl," observed Emily. "As I was saying, the *situation* involves Agent Whittaker. This past Monday, the same day the Stockwell women disappeared, I overheard a very disconcerting phone conversation. Whittaker was in the Secure Interview Room, apparently believing he could have a safe conversation there. What he didn't realize...he had left open the interview monitoring app. That's an app we have allowing an agent to listen in on their partner's witness/perp interviews in the Secure Interview Room. I was in my car on the way home when I heard an alert tone, so I put the phone on speaker. This is what I heard."

Emily related that Whittaker asked, "if the package was secure and safe." He went on to say the "package needed to be handled carefully" at least until "final payment" was received. Moreover, Whittaker told the contact there were now some outside parties that would have to be dealt with. Finally, he told his unknown contact they would need to meet by the end of the day and that he would call later with the details.

"My god," said Jason. "Obviously, he's talking about the Stockwell disappearance...make that *abduction*...now, ...the question is how do we proceed? Do you think he suspects you're on to him?"

"I'm pretty sure he thinks I'm clueless. Being his partner, he has no choice but to keep me involved...he won't want to make me suspicious. He'll try to take control of the investigation under the pretense of 'the FBI always takes the lead in suspected kidnappings.'"

Jason offered, "I suggest we string him along...allow him to believe he's calling the shots. Meanwhile me, Sam, and Tara will conduct a shadow investigation with the primary goal of finding Diane Stockwell and secondly, keeping *Project Expose'* out of Russian hands. Do you believe he has any more accomplices in the Agency? What about that really big Agent - I think his name is Grande?"

"I'm not sure, but my gut says *no,*" replied Emily. "I've only had a few conversations with him. He's definitely on the quiet side, but I like him. D'Arby's new...this is his first field assignment."
"He's still in training status and Whittaker has been assigned as his training mentor. Ex NFL player, he played for New England I believe. With Whittaker, I'll let him think I'm following his lead...see if I can get him comfortable enough to be careless around me...maybe slip up."

"Good strategy," agreed the detective. "I've got a couple of ideas brewing...let me give you a call - say around eleven - to discuss today's agenda."

"Sounds great," said Emily. "I'll be at my place...remember, I've got the day off."

Kathy the waitress arrived with their food orders, along with a fresh carafe of hot coffee and left them to enjoy their meal.

** ** **

Jason entered the lobby of *Lake Eola Professional Tower,* walking past the FBI Regional Office suite on his way to the building's trio of elevators. He had just arrived from Brunch N' Lunch on the opposite side of the lake, really a misnomer - the *lake* was actually a pond formed from a sinkhole - the brief trip just what he needed after stuffing himself with French toast. As he walked into the elevator, he briefly reflected on his meeting with Emily...really bad news, really great company.

Exiting on the sixth floor he didn't have far to go before reaching the door to *McVay & Associates.* Stepping in, he greeted Maddy with a cheerful *Good Morning,* his secretary responding in kind.

"Is Sam here yet?" Inquired the detective.

"In her office," answered Maddy, "especially bright-eyed and bushy-tailed."

"Send her in after a couple of minutes...oh, how'd the Dentist appointment go?"

"*Sure*, to the first part," she said, "and *okay* to the second. Thanks for asking."

No sooner had Jason sat down, then his hyperactive partner burst through the door.

"Morning, Boss. What's up?" She inquired with her bright, toothy smile.

"Good morning...and don't call me *Boss.* Gotta say, you're pretty cranked up."

"*Right?* Don't know why...oh, my hand still hurts."

"Not surprised," Jason responded. "Listen, I want you to spend the day tailing Agent Whittaker...and don't get made! I'll fill you in later."

"OK, you're the ...*partner,"* she said, disappearing through the door connecting their offices.

Ten minutes later, Jason called Tara Wayne, arranging to meet her in 45 minutes at Dynamadics. Setting his phone on the desk, he walked over to the chair where he had left his briefcase. He looked inside to ensure he had the report folder with the Briar Patch Security Logs. After verifying the paperwork was there, he glanced out the window just in time to see Sam's truck appear from the parking garage below. A few car lengths ahead he saw a Lincoln Navigator. *Ah ha,* he thought, *five'll get me ten that's Whittaker's ride!* Jason grabbed his briefcase and walked out through the Reception Office. On the way to the door, he turned toward Maddy.

"I'm going to see Tara Wayne. Don't know how soon I'll be back...see ya later."

She acknowledged with a wave as he headed to the elevator.

Jason pulled out of the parking garage heading to I-4 and Dynamadics. As he entered the Interstate, he remembered he had promised Emily he would call at 11:00. It was 11:10. He reached into his pocket for his phone...but it was empty. *Oh, Shit,* he thought, realizing the phone was sitting on his desk. He took the next exit and circled back to the office. Jason was extremely annoyed with himself. He *never, ever* forgot his phone. Ten minutes later, he pulled into the parking garage.

** ** **

69

Ten minutes earlier...

At the same time Jason's elevator door closed, the door on the adjacent elevator opened. A tall, slim man with long scraggly hair and a drooping handlebar mustache stepped out of the elevator and briskly walked to Jason's office, entered, and stood directly in front of the startled secretary.

"WHERE THE HELL IS THE SAMANTHA BITCH!?" Loudly demanded the scar-faced one.

"I... I don't know," replied a rapidly panicking Maddy.

"You don't know. YOU DON'T KNOW!!!" Exclaimed the man with the scar and crooked nose. He pulled a pistol from his pocket, took aim, and shot Maddy in the face. "BITCH!" He yelled, putting the pistol away. He wheeled around and headed for the elevator.

Maddy slumped face-down on her desk, a pool of deep red blood forming, slowly spreading to the edges.

** ** **

Jason walked rapidly toward the elevator when he suddenly felt a wave of nausea, quickly followed by a chill enveloping his entire body. *SOMETHING IS TERRIBLY WRONG* ran through his panicked mind.

He exited the elevator, making for his office at a full run. He pushed through the still opening doors; grimly greeted by the horrific sight of Maddy slumped over her desk.
"OH GOD! OH GOD! NO!...NO!...NO!"

He rushed over to his beloved secretary.

** ** **

Chapter Seven
The Day Gets Better

Jason sat in the far corner of the waiting room pondering his next move. He glanced up at the officer standing watch by the I.C.U. door, a reminder of the continuing threat. Sam should be arriving any time now, she was about an hour out when he had called with the grim news; now, however, to his great relief, Maddy's condition had greatly improved. It turned out that at the moment the shot was fired, she had instinctively turned her head, the bullet barely penetrating her skull just above her left brow. The glancing impact had rendered her unconscious, having the same effect as a concussion. She regained consciousness less than an hour ago, at which point she had requested to see Jason.

Aside from a serious headache, which was diminishing as the pain meds started to take effect, she said that she felt OK, but was - understandably - in a state of high anxiety. She related the incident in detail; her description of the assailant left no doubt about his identity. Jason asked Maddy to *not* reveal the perp's connection to Sam in the belief that they could get this guy out of circulation quicker than the authorities. Of course, there was Sam's notorious temper to deal with.

Jason picked up his phone instructing Siri to *call Laura.* After two rings, he heard her sultry, husky voice: "Well, hello there...and welcome to *Girls Are Us...*how may I be of service?"

"Laura, I really hate to break the playful mood, but we have a very serious situation here; I need you to come as soon as possible." Jason brought her up to speed with an abbreviated version of events since their last call the previous evening.

Laura said, "I'll head straight for your place unless you call to say otherwise. Be on my way in a matter of minutes...just need to grab my *Go Bag.* Love you."

"Love you back," he replied, "See ya soon. Be safe."

Shortly after Jason disconnected, he saw Sam coming down the hall at a near run. In another moment she was standing in front of him.

"What the hell happened?" She asked, her intense anxiety obvious.

"Sit," He instructed, indicating the adjacent chair.

Jason took her through the sequence of events beginning with the shooting at the office up to his last conversation with Maddy in her intensive care bed.

"Can I see her?" Asked Sam, struggling mightily to suppress her erupting emotions.

"Sure, Sam," replied Jason, getting up and walking over to the officer by the I.C.U. door.

She watched as he spoke with the cop, who disappeared through the door. A few moments later, he returned; spoke briefly to Jason who in turn signaled for Sam to come over. She got up, walking briskly to the door where the officer directed her to Maddy's bed.

Sam rushed over to her Aunt's bed; Maddy lifting her head slightly, with a smile for her niece.

Unable to contain herself any longer, Sam broke down sobbing, barely able to say, "Aunt Maddy, I love you so much...I thank God for saving you...to let you stay in our lives!"

Jason waited patiently while Sam visited with her Aunt. About 15 minutes later, she emerged through the I.C.U. door and walked over to her partner.

"Gotta go," she said, "got some business to take care of."

"Sam..." Jason began...

"I know...I know what you're going to say, but I'm not gonna let you down...I've got a grip on this thing. You know as well as I do...*it's gonna be me or him.* It damn sure ain't gonna be me! I'll be in touch." She turned, and with head held high headed down the hall, quickly disappearing around the corner.

Jason pulled out his iPhone and called Emily Cast. After filling her in on all that had happened, including Laura's pending arrival, he asked her to find Sam and stick with her, helping in any way she could. He gave her Sam's address and phone number, then told her he believed Sam would head straight for O'Doul's Pub. Emily said she knew where it was and would go there first. Further, she advised Jason she had put in for - and had been granted - a week of lost time. Jason agreed that although that conflicted with their original strategy of having her monitor Whittaker, under the new circumstances it was the better course of action.

Before he left, he consulted with Maddy's doctor and was advised she should make a full recovery. If all went well, she could leave the hospital as early as tomorrow and be able to return to work in about a week.

$$** \quad ** \quad **$$

60 minutes earlier...

Sam stayed a discreet distance behind Whittaker's SUV as it traveled the long exit ramp from Florida's Turnpike to the Service Plaza, where he parked the vehicle directly across from the restaurant, got out and walked in. She parked about six spaces away and followed him in. He went straight over to a corner table where a rather tall man with thick black hair and beard to match beckoned him to sit. She discreetly used her phone to get his picture. Looking at the picture, she noted his prominent bushy eyebrows. Suddenly, her phone vibrated. It was Jason. As he talked, she turned, walking rapidly out the door and straight to her truck for the nearly hour long trip to the Orlando Regional Medical Center.

** ** **

Sergei Dimitrov studied the man sitting opposite him. Though he considered the FBI Agent a buffoon, he had, for the most part, hastened the day Russia would finally have possession of America's cloaking technology, allowing Mother Russia to take her rightful place at the table as a technological equal with the Americans, leaving the Chinese to grovel for little technology tidbits; hand-me-downs, if you will. Still, he was looking forward to the day he could put a bullet in the idiot's head.

Dimitrov, now a colonel in the SVR (Russia's CIA) had spent over twenty years to get to this point., He would now make his mark and achieve his goal of becoming the Director General of the SVR.

"You don't look so happy, my friend," observed Sergei.

"Well," replied Whittaker, "if your marksmanship had been better, we wouldn't be having this particular conversation."

"The man stumbled and pushed the intended target out of the way. Fortunate timing for them; not so much for me. A matter of luck," Sergei bluntly explained, plainly annoyed.

"Whatever," said Whittaker dismissively. "Take this," handing a cellphone to the Russian. "It's a burner. Bring it to the cabin. You'll be giving it to the woman when I call you later today with further Instructions."

"Yes, my liege," sarcastically acknowledged the Russian.

Special Agent Whittaker stood, wheeled around, and headed for the exit at a brisk pace.

** ** **

Sam pulled the F-150 into the same parking space she had used on her last visit. She got out, glanced around, noting only one other vehicle in O'Doul's parking lot, certainly not unusual for 2:30 in the afternoon.

Alfred Wainwright looked up just as the tall woman came in the door. *Oh shit,* he thought, *it's Sam what's-her-name, the man killer...* Sam walked up to the empty bar and with a friendly smile said, "Good afternoon, *Al...* right? I'm Samantha Talley; my friends call me *Sam."*

"I know who you are," nervously replied the bartender, "You're the lady what decked that guy last night."

"About that...," said Sam, "I need your help. Like what's the guy's name and where can I find him?"

Looking even more nervous, Al pleaded, "Look lady, I really don't want to get involved. Nuthin' personal, ya understand."

Raising her voice ever so slightly, Sam asked, *"Did you see what he did to me?"*

"I did! I did!" He admitted, "...and it was wrong, *real wrong,* but what you did was...*maybe* just a bit over-the-top? You really should let this go - *Sam* - this guy is *really bad news!* Are... *are you a cop?"*

"NO... *BUT I AM,"* announced Emily as she approached the bar, holding her FBI creds up for him to see.

"I don't want no trouble officer...I'm just a bartender," he said haplessly.

"It's *Special Agent...*and you're not in any trouble. We just need to find out who this guy is and where we can find him. Your name will *never* come up, *I promise."*

They could see the inner struggle in his eyes. That *deer caught in the headlight's* kind of look.

Finally, realizing there was no other way out, Al the Bartender gave it up. "His name is Demonia Nogudum. He came from one of those countries near Russia. He's a real bad hombre. He doesn't have real friends, just people that suck up to him...I really don't know why, they just do. Most people that know him, think he's a whack job. His nickname is *The Demon.* Get it, *The Demon...Demonia??"*

"Yeah, we get it," interjected Emily, "We just don't think it's funny. Where can we find him?"

"That," he replied, "I don't know. But he does 'errands' for this outfit in Kissimmee called Wildcat Courier Service...some say it's a front for a big drug operation."

"OK Al," said Sam, "we really appreciate your help." She dropped a hundred-dollar bill on the bar saying, "And we really need to keep this conversation between the three of us."

Nodding his head, he reached for the bill. The women turned and left the pub.

** ** **

As she exited the elevator, Laura retrieved her phone from her bag and opened the App, 'Entry Codes'; clicked on 'Jason's Home', then clicked 'enter'. She saw the green 'OK' icon flash once. As she reached his door, it swung open and she heard the System Manager greet her in his amusing British-butler accent, "Welcome home, Laura. I trust you had a pleasant journey. Please make yourself comfortable, Jason should be home within the hour."

She couldn't help smiling at Jason's quirky System Manager, the robotic system a reflection of its programmer's own quirky personality. Despite the urgent circumstances, she was happy to be here, once again with the love of her life. It was during these moments - just before she reunited with Jason - that she realized just how deeply she loved him. Laura yearned for the day when they could be together permanently. Of course, there were some serious issues - all involving her very unique status (*that is the understatement of the century,* ran through her mind) yet to be resolved. That's for the future. For the present, she was happy to just be with her man.

Laura dropped her *Go Bag* on the coffee table and took a seat on the comfy leather sofa she had helped him pick out. Glancing at her watch, she noted it was a little more than two hours since she had received his call. Most of that time had been spent securing her personal aircraft, then finding a scarce *Uber* ride to get here. Jason would predictably chastise her for spending her own money (he rarely let her pay for anything when they were together). Of course, it wasn't a problem. She was rich. *Very rich.* Jason was unaware, and she wasn't in any particular hurry to tell him. Fact of the matter, no one other than her cousin had any idea how wealthy she was.

Jason stood in the entryway, momentarily frozen. He glanced at his watch, then back at Laura, who was already rushing toward him. Before he could speak, she embraced him tightly; then came the long, lingering kiss as he heard in his mind, *I've missed you so...'me, too', he thought* in response. As they broke their embrace he said aloud, "How do you do that?"

"Part of the *extra-sensory thing* I guess," she offered with a mischievous grin.

"All the same, a bit spooky if you ask me," he replied, continuing the playful banter. "You made really great time getting here, just the trip here from the Airport takes thirty minutes."

"Everything just clicked...you know, just fell in place. Caught all the lights green, no luggage delay at the airport...that kinda stuff," she offered.

"Yeah...worked out perfect."

Changing the subject, she asked, "Anything new since we talked? I'm glad Maddy's going to be OK. I'm looking forward to finally meeting her. What's Sam doing? How about Emily...maybe you can have her team up with Sam."

"Way ahead of ya, hon. She's already with Sam. They're on the perp's trail as we speak. I expect to hear from her any time now."

"Good," acknowledged Laura. She reflected on just how aligned their strategic thinking was. "You know, before we do anything else, I could use a shower."

With a devious glint in his eye, Jason responded, "Me, too."

** ** **

Owen Whittaker walked through the Dynamadics lobby, looking around as if he owned the place. He stopped abruptly at Jennifer Devaroux's desk, holding his FBI creds out at arm's length for her to see. Using a tone of self-importance, he said, "I need to see a Ms. Tara Wayne...and I'm pressed for time, so if you would..."

"Of course, Agent...Whittaker," replied the put-off young receptionist. She looked at her computer screen and announced, "Ms. Wayne, there's an Agent Whittaker here to see you." After a brief pause, she glanced up at Whittaker, advising him, "Ms. Wayne will be right down." She pointedly turned away, avoiding any further eye contact with Agent *Rude.*

In less than two minutes the door to elevator #3 opened; Tara Wayne emerged, quickly walking over to Whittaker. Offering her hand in greeting, she said, "Agent Whittaker, good to see you. How can I help?"

As the pair walked back to the elevator, Whittaker said, "I need to interview John Stockwell, do you have a secure interview room available?"

Just as the elevator door closed, Tara replied, "Indeed we do. Would you like me to sit in?"

"No, but thank you," he said, condescendingly. "This part of the investigation is rather sensitive...kind of one of those 'need to know' things if you catch my drift. No offense."

"I do," responded Tara in an even tone, "and none taken."

The elevator door opened on the third floor. He followed Tara a short distance, stopping at a small room featuring a table with a single chair on one side: two on the other.

Tara said, "I'll get Mr. Stockwell. I should be back within a few minutes."

She turned to leave. "Thank you, I await your return." After Wayne left, Whittaker reached in his briefcase to retrieve his "bug" scanner. After a quick sweep of the small room, he was satisfied it was indeed secure. Wayne returned promptly with Stockwell in tow.

"Ah, Mr. Stockwell," said Whittaker, extending his hand. "I'm Special Agent Whittaker. I have some questions regarding your wife's disappearance."

Stockwell took Whittaker's hand, then followed him into the interview room. Turning toward Tara, Whittaker said dismissively. "Thank you for your help, Ms. Wayne, I'll take it from here." Tara nodded, turned, and walked away. Whittaker closed the door and curtly told Stockwell, "Sit down."

Stockwell quickly sat, nervously glancing about the room. "Sooo" ...he began.

"So," answered Whittaker, "We've arrived at a tipping point. My Russian friends are out of patience, and so, frankly, am I. You're worried. I get it. But we need the *Project Expose'* thumb drive, and we need it *NOW!"*

"I've told you we've got you covered...not to mention the quarter of a million dollars for your trouble. All you're doing by getting this to our Russian friends is simply leveling the playing field...they're *not* going to have a military advantage. When you think about it, the chances of conflict go down...they won't feel so threatened. Along with the money you'll get back - as promised - all your falsified college records...and a bonus - I will ensure your bogus records become 'genuine', wiping the implicating data from all national databases! Here's the problem; unless they have what they want within the next few days, Diane will be gone. Forever. And it will be on you."

Stockwell sat in stunned silence. He hadn't believed Whittaker would allow the Russians to harm his wife. Now, he felt trapped. There would be no dissuading the rogue agent. Still, he had to find a way out. He had been ready to exit the whole sordid deal - letting the chips fall where they may - at least he wouldn't be a traitor. Then they took Diane.

"Look, John," said Whittaker, "I know what you're thinking. I say let's turn this lose-lose situation into a win-win for everybody...including Diane!" Reaching into his pocket, he pulled out a Burner Phone and handed it to Stockwell. I'll call you on the burner with instructions soon. In the meantime, just be cool. No one should question you...this interview is normal for these circumstances. I'll submit a report to cover our 'conversation'. I'll be in touch."

They both stood and left the room, Stockwell back to work, Whittaker back to the Regional Office.

** ** **

Emily pulled her car in right behind Sam's truck. She watched Sam step out, shut the door, and walk down the driveway toward her car. Emily touched the 'down' button for her window; it began sliding down. Suddenly, she heard a loud crack, to her trained ear, unmistakably the report of an assault rifle.

"GET DOWN!!" She yelled.

Sam was already on the move, rapidly retreating; she moved for cover behind the shrubs fronting the walkway to her door as several more shots rang out. Simultaneously, Emily crouched as low as possible, slamming the shifter into reverse; tires screeching as she backed out, swinging the car 180 degrees. She shut it down, crawled over the seat and exited through the passenger door. Hugging the side, she quickly made her way to the back...and the trunk, which she had already opened with the interior remote switch on her way out.

While reaching into the trunk, in a low voice, Sam asked, "See anything...what's it look like?"

"I can partially see someone hunkered down in the front part of the house," Sam replied in the same low tone of voice. Two more shots rang out in quick succession.

Emily retrieved an AR-15 assault rifle from the trunk, flipping off the safety. "I'll give you cover fire so you can get back to the garage. Go out the back and try to outflank him; you should be able to get across the street at the house on his left side," Sam acknowledged with a nod.

The field of action was definitely in their favor. The house with the perp was in the first phase of construction; the exterior walls were up, but the windows had yet to be installed. The house on the left was at a similar stage; a big plus - a large backhoe and a crew pickup truck were parked in front of the second house, mostly obscuring the perp's view to that side. The other piece of good news, the site was devoid of workers...and so...onlookers.

Emily peered around the side, leveled her weapon, and began firing quick bursts. Sam ran the short distance into the garage, out the back door; then made her way to the other side of her house and to the front, where she paused in a crouch. More shots rang out as the perp returned fire in Emily's direction. Seeing Sam poised for the move across the street, Emily hand-signaled 'ready' and fired a continuous volley at the perp's position.

Sam sprinted across the street, veering to the right of the construction vehicles; slowing slightly as she circled around the house. She paused a beat before cautiously proceeding behind the adjacent house where the perp was holed up. Sam moved slowly in a half-crouch, holding her Beretta with a two-handed grip. Suddenly the perp came into full view with his back to her, using the front wall as a barricade and the empty living room window frame as his shooting portal. "DON'T MOVE A MUSCLE OR I'LL BLOW YOUR HEAD OFF!!" Yelled the young detective.

Taking his adversary at her word, he froze in place. "Now slowly stand, keeping your back to me and DROP THE RIFLE!" She ordered. He complied.

Emily, hearing Sam's commands, rose from her position by the car and ran across the street, her AR-15 in the ready position. She entered the open-door frame, immediately aiming her weapon at the perp's center mass. Recalling the bartender's description...the scar, crooked (now covered in a bandage) nose, and drooping mustache she knew she was looking at one Demonia Nogudum, the notorious "demon" himself. *How impressive,* she thought. *Actually, Not.*

Sam asked, "Emily, do you have cuffs?" To which she nodded in affirmation. "Good," Sam continued; then, to the perp: "Slowly turn toward me with your arms spread out." He did as instructed, coming to a stop face to face with his target. Sam saw the venomous hate in his eyes as he clenched his jaw tightly.

"Sam, WATCH OUT!!" yelled Emily, seeing him go for the pistol in his waistband. He yelled, "Bitch!" and was able to get off two quick shots as he raised his weapon, which missed their mark by a wide margin. Sam didn't miss. The three shots she fired struck him in the center of his chest. He fell straight back, landing with a dull thud, the light gone from his lifeless eyes.

The women looked at each other in silence. Emily pulled out her phone and dialed 911. Sam holstered her pistol, took out her phone, and called Jason.

** ** **

Chapter Eight
Guns n' Roses

Jason set his phone down on the table. He thought, *At least the call wasn't the mood-buster it could have been, so there's that.* Glancing over at his lover, he remained silent for a moment.

Laura, with a concerned expression, looked back at her mate. She knew everything Jason was about to say, having mentally eavesdropped on the conversation. Ever since she had mind-melded with him all those many years ago, she had had the ability to read his thoughts, but until this moment she had never used it; this being a major violation of her kinds' ethics. Jason now had that same telepathic ability; he just didn't know it. One day soon, she would teach him how to use this gift; more importantly, how he could prevent her from intruding into his mind; unintentional or otherwise. For now, she would listen.

Jason related the events leading up to the death of Demonia Nogudum, beginning with Emily meeting Sam at O'Doul's Pub earlier in the afternoon. The pair were now awaiting the arrival of the police and would get back in touch after they were done with that part. Sam had assured Jason that she and Emily were OK. Both women firmly believed an evil presence was now gone forever.

"*Quite* an eventful day," he understated. "Say...would you be interested in a fine meal at an amazing eatery in the company of your loving and devoted servant?" He asked playfully, attempting to lighten the somber mood.

"*With great pleasure, my love!*" She enthused. "But I haven't *a thing* to wear." She knew that wasn't true; *her* walk-in closet was replete with all manner of clothing: from mostly casual shorts, blouses, and jeans to a selection of dresses, including formal evening gowns.

"Look real hard," he implored, "I'm quite sure *my lady* can find *something.*"

She slowly walked over to Jason - her quickening arousal palpable - half-whispering, making her naturally husky voice as sultry as possible..."If you say so big fella." She embraced her lover, pulling him in for a long, lingering kiss. Coming up for air, he gently pushed her away pleading, "I need to fuel the machine woman; the last time I ate was breakfast...let me get my strength back. You know what they say, 'Well fed, good in bed!'" He pleaded, tongue in cheek.

She was having none of it. "You made that up Jason McBride," she said with an impish smile.

"Guilty as charged," he admitted.

Laura walked toward her closet, letting her robe fall to the floor on the way. Jason accepted that this particular battle was already lost.

** ** **

Immediately after she finished with the 911 Operator, Emily called Jason's sister, Sandy McVay, who she knew professionally through Laura, but until now had been unaware she was Jason's sister.

"Hi Sandy...I'm in a bit of a jam and need a favor." She continued, "It's a pretty big Ask." She went on to explain in a short - but still detailed - version of the events leading up to this moment. Emily told Sandy she needed her help in keeping the incident low profile as possible. In fact, best if the CIA Agent could keep her out of it altogether.

Sandy replied, "Give me a few minutes, I'll get back to you." The phone went quiet. Emily sat back, watching Sam pace back and forth as she talked with Jason.

After about five minutes, her phone vibrated. It was Sandy. "Hey Sandy," she answered.

"OK Emily," said Sandy. "I've got it handled. I just got off the phone with (CIA) Director McBride. By a stroke of luck, she and Sheriff Brown happen to be friends. Anyway, she told him that you're part of a CIA/FBI task force and your identity needs to be kept confidential. So... *you were never there.* And be assured that Sam will be treated with respect, *'handled with kid gloves'* I believe is the phrase she used. A Lieutenant Morrison will be the lead investigator and should be there shortly. Check in with him and then get out of there."

"Thanks Sandy," replied a grateful Emily. "I owe you big time!"

"Not to worry...we girls will always have each other's back. Gotta go, I'm in the middle of dinner with Stafford." (Stafford Var, her longtime boyfriend and Laura's cousin).

"Of course," said Emily. "Thanks again; enjoy the rest of your evening," ending the call. She heard the sound of approaching emergency vehicles in the distance.

** ** **

Agent Whittaker parked the Navigator in his designated parking space and made for his apartment's rear door, entering his access code as he walked. The door opened and he immediately picked up the scent of pot roast cooking. *Ah,* he thought, *the Housebot's on the job.* This 'bot was the latest generation, the kind you could actually program with a personality, which he had declined to do. It came with the rental, so why bother? Still, he was happy to have the multi-talented device...robotics had come a long way in twenty years. Plus, he had made a good investment back then; his thousand shares had gained value more than twenty-fold; it could conceivably repeat that gain again by mid-century, a mere two years away.

He took off his jacket and tie, setting his holstered gun on the table. Whittaker instructed the Housebot to serve his meal, along with a glass of red wine. The Agent suddenly felt all of the day's annoyances settle upon him; the Stockwell "interview," manipulating the Talley woman, and, worst of all, dealing with that pompous Russian ass. He settled down at the bar; voice commanded the TV to turn on, then tune to the Channel 9 news. *"...in the first of two violent crime stories,"* announced the anchor, *"Orlando Police received a call around noon about a shooting at the Lake Eola office of a prominent local detective; it appears to be related to a second shooting later today that resulted in the death of the suspect. A Lieutenant Morrison of the Orange County Sheriffs' Office stated that eyewitness accounts placed the deceased suspect at the scene of the earlier shooting. For more, we go to our on-the-scene Reporter, Sharon Blake, at the Sunrise Park subdivision. Sharon..."*

"Holy Shit!" exclaimed Whittaker loudly, quickly putting two and two together.

** ** **

Diane Stockwell wasn't one to easily panic, but now, nearly forty-eight hours since her abduction, she was beginning to feel...well, just a bit uneasy. Once again, she reviewed what had happened, in the hope she might recall some tiny detail she missed to help her figure out *exactly* what was going on, particularly her role in this thing. Undoubtedly, it had to do with *Project Expose'*...it didn't take a genius (which she actually was) to figure *that* out.

Given the circumstances, she had so far been treated well. The cabin that served as her "jail" was well-furnished with a comfortable sofa, coffee table, and loveseat. A small desk and chair sat facing a large window that was covered by a heavy drape. Adjacent was a small kitchen with a table and four chairs. An electric range and microwave lined the wall next to a well-stocked refrigerator. A pantry closet, also well-stocked, was across from the refrigerator.

The cabin's rear wall was dominated by an open-hearth fireplace. A flatscreen TV (she was allowed use) was mounted above the fireplace mantle. The upper level featured a full-length balcony fronting a loft bedroom furnished with a queen bed, dresser and a small, but adequate bathroom. A rather quaint spiral staircase provided access to the ground floor.

Her captor had said she would be safe and comfortable as long as she followed two rules:

(1) She should not attempt to leave the cabin. To do so would surely result in her death.
(2) Although her captors were masked, she should avoid looking at them. As long as she was unable to identify them, she wouldn't pose a threat, allowing for her eventual release.

So far, she had been compliant, but she was becoming increasing antsy.

Diane didn't have a whole lot to work with - but there were a few clues. For example: she knew her captors were Russian and that there were at least three in the contingent guarding her. Further, she knew they believed she wasn't too smart, also a common assumption within the Dynamadics social community. Ironically, she picked up that little tidbit by eavesdropping on one of their conversations - in Russian - which she spoke fluently. Unfortunately, nothing pertinent to her situation had so far been discussed. On a more positive note, she was beginning to believe that her husband had been coerced and was not the traitor she had assumed him to be.

Glancing at her watch, she noticed it was slightly after 6:00 PM. *Hmm, I wonder what's going on in* the *world,* she thought; picking up the remote, she selected Channel 9 for the local news. The TV came on, catching the anchor in mid-sentence... *"In the first of two violent crime stories..."*

** ** **

"Good evening, Mr. McVay," welcomed the maitre'd. "Good to see you again, Sir."

"Thank you, James," replied Jason. "As always, a pleasure to be here. I look forward to another superb dining experience."
"Right this way, Sir," said the maitre'd, "we have your usual table ready," leading the couple to a table in a corner of the rooftop terrace. A vase laden with a dozen red roses sat at the center.

As he slid out the chair for Laura, Jason inquired, "How is Brent doing?" (Brent, James' son and quarterback for the Weston High Huskies football team, had suffered a severe concussion while playing in the state championship game).

"He's doing well; thank you for asking," replied James, "and looking forward to the start of the fall semester at U. of F. which doesn't sit so well with his sister, a junior at F.S.U." Jason laughed at the reference. "Glad he's well...as for the rivalry thing, good luck with that!"

Smiling, James set an open menu in front of both diners. "Enjoy your dinner. The wine steward will be over momentarily." With a slight bow, he returned to the maitre'd station.

Laura looked around, taking in the spectacular view of the surrounding Disney parks lying under a beautiful star-studded sky. The appropriately named Starlight Terrace was the feature attraction of this, the newest Disney hotel, *The Centennial.* The hotel's name referenced the not-to-distant centennial of the Disney World complex. At forty stories, it was one of the tallest structures in the Central Florida region. It had rapidly become one of the most popular fine dining sites in the area, usually requiring reservations weeks in advance. Jason, who had done some investigative work for the CEO, had negotiated lifetime "instant" reservation privileges for the Starlight Terrace in lieu of monetary payment. This unusual feat was considered a monumental *coup* by all his business associates.

Laura reached across the table, gently enfolding Jason's right hand with both her hands. They locked eyes as he heard in his mind, *I love you more than words can say, so I'm saying it this way...the most intimate way there is. I want to spend the rest of my life as your mate.*

HOW ARE YOU DOING THIS?? Jason thought in response. *You're - just a little bit - scaring me. I love you more than anything, but this isn't natural. Goes way beyond my "future vision." You have to explain what this is...this mind thing...*

...I understand my love. I promise you will know all about me soon. Until that time, I ask for your trust...and your patience. I'll Always Have Your Back!

Jason thought, *That's good. You know I'll always have my "front!"* Laura let go of his hand, laughing aloud at the obvious reference to his "future vision."

Laura looked Jason up and down, thinking to herself, *all this...and a sense of humor, too!*

They spent the next two hours happily discussing aspirations, places to go, things to do together... and the prospect of children.

**** ** ****

The doorbell rang, prompting Jason to glance at his watch. On its face, he saw Sam and Emily's image super-imposed over the time: precisely 7:00 AM. He immediately stood up and walked over to let them in, announcing their arrival on the way over.

"They're here, honey."

"Great!" Answered Laura as she hovered over a frying pan filled with bacon, the delicious odor permeating the entire apartment.

Jason hugged each woman in turn. "Something sure smells good," commented Sam; Emily quickly following up, "Smells like *Brunch 'N Lunch* to me; didn't realize I was hungry 'til now."

"Welcome to my humble abode," he said, looking from one to the other. "Please...make yourselves at home...*mi casa, su casa!*"

"Why thank you, kind sir," said Sam light-heartedly, as she took a seat at the breakfast bar.

Emily pulled out the chair next to Sam. She sat down; looking around she said, "You have a really nice place here Jason. I'm impressed.

Most men I know don't rise to this level of sophistication in home decor."

"I'm afraid I can't take credit for most of what you see," he confessed. "The lady in the kitchen is really the responsible party."

"Nonsense," said Laura, taking off her apron as she approached the bar. "I merely made a few suggestions...the actual scheme is all Jason."

..."And that's why I love the woman," he said, smiling broadly. The group shared a good laugh.

Everyone enjoyed their breakfast, talking about anything that was wasn't work-related, concluding with Emily's observation: "If I didn't know better Jason, I'd be thinking, 'well, that's how an old married couple acts' and I mean that in a *good way.*"

"I know, Emily," replied Laura. "You just never know what might happen," a mischievous twinkle in her eye. Jason looked in her direction, nodding ever so slightly.

Laura retreated to the kitchen, returning in a few moments with a platter of assorted pastries and a fresh carafe of hot coffee.

"Enough pleasantries," pronounced Jason with faux sarcasm. "Time to get down to business."

The next hour was spent with Sam and Emily revisiting - in great detail - the events beginning with Al the bartender and culminating with the death of Demonia Nogudum, a.k.a. *Scarface.* Emily related her conversation with Jason's sister, who contacted Director McBride; setting in motion a *fix*, giving Emily the cover she needed. There was no way Whittaker could know of her involvement in the incident; simultaneously protecting her career while allowing her continued participation in the corruption investigation of Whittaker.

Jason issued the day's "marching orders." Emily was to set up a meeting with Grande, then rendezvous with Jason and Laura at Dynamadics for a 1:00 PM meeting with Tara; Jason and Laura would be spending the morning with Maddy. Sam was charged with investigating the suspicious helicopter activity discovered in the Briar Patch Security Logs. Then, if everything went smoothly, the Team would get together at O'Doul's Pub around 4:00 PM to review and assess the day's work.

** ** **

Sergei Dimitrov picked up on the first ring. "Yes, Owen," he answered with as much of a neutral tone as he could muster.

"You sound out of breath," observed Whittaker.

"Just finished my daily five-mile run...you should try it sometime," he sarcastically replied. Getting right to the point, he continued, "What do you need?"

"Did you happen to watch the morning news?" Queried Whittaker.

"No," he said, then in a tone one would use with a child, "*I just finished a five-mile run.*" "Right," Whittaker curtly replied. "Well, *if you had bothered,* you would have seen the story about yesterday's twin shootings: the first involving a whack job shooting Jason McVay's Secretary at his office; the second incident with the same whack job being shot and killed in a protracted gun battle with - get this - one Samantha Talley!"

"So... who the hell is Samantha Talley?" Asked the Russian.

"Samantha Talley *is McVay's* sidekick...his assistant investigator," explained Whittaker in a decidedly exasperated tone.

"And I should have known that...*how?*" Retorted the equally irritated Dimitrov.

"Never mind," said Whittaker. Point is the *connection* of the shooting with McVay's camp. Thing that bothers me...no way she could take out a guy armed with an assault rifle and fifteen magazines of ammo with just a pistol. Something doesn't add up...when I get to the office, I'm gonna check it out - what with the McVay connection. Oh, the other thing I called about... yesterday you mentioned something about resolving the McVay issue."

"I did," affirmed the Russian. "I really can't get into it on the phone - encrypted line or not - but if *you* were to perhaps watch the TV news at noon...well..."

"I'll definitely put it on my agenda," confirmed the FBI agent in a more friendly tone. "Oh, and I will be in touch with new instructions this afternoon...you will be at the cabin, right?"

"As you wish," answered Dimitrov in a mockingly subservient tone, before abruptly hanging up.

** ** **

Sam and Emily thanked Jason for his hospitality, with a nod to Laura for the great breakfast. They left together for the parking garage to retrieve their vehicles and head out to their respective assignments. Sam noted it was 8:00 AM. She thought, *right on schedule...*

Laura put the last of the breakfast dishes in the dishwasher, unnecessary - the Housebot would take care of that along with laundry, floors, dusting, etc., what Housebot's do. She felt a little silly, but it was just in her nature to be considerate...even with Artificial Intelligence creations. Jason came out of the bedroom wearing chocolate brown slacks and a collared short-sleeve jersey in a subtle orange color, replacing the T-shirt and shorts he had worn at breakfast. Laura passed him on her way to the bedroom, also wanting to change from her shorts and Jason's T-shirt she had "borrowed." Ten minutes later she came out, wearing black dress slacks and a sleeveless white chiffon blouse with a plunging neckline.

Jason looked her up and down, pausing at the neckline. With one eyebrow arched, he said, "You look great, honey...your blouse doesn't leave a whole lot to the imagination, though...I'm just thinking about the Dynamadics meeting."

"No," replied Laura, "You're thinking about all your male acquaintances checking me out."

"Well," he said, "maybe a little...just sayin'."

"It's gonna be OK," she said with a smile, "plus, *I am on vacation...*sort of."

"Fair point," he replied, glancing at his watch. "It's almost nine. We should get to the hospital."

They headed out the door, walked over to the conveniently open elevator for the ride to the garage level. As the door opened, Jason felt the familiar chill descend and the *movie in his mind* began playing. He saw the two of them walk over to his Lexus and get in. They fastened their seatbelts and Jason pushed the Start button, at which point everything went to a blinding white as the vehicle was engulfed in a huge fireball. Then everything went black.

Real time resumed. Jason grabbed Laura by the arm. "STOP!!" He yelled. Alarmed, Laura broke his panicked grip on her arm and instinctively grasped his right hand with both her hands. Instantly, she saw everything he had just seen. She released her grip and looked Jason in the eye.

"We're OK," she said, "let's think this through."

After a minute, Jason exclaimed, "I've got it! *We know it's an ignition-activated device.* I'm going to unlock the car with the remote and then press the hood release, leaving the hood ajar. Then I'll re-lock the car and call 911 to report a possible car bomb. After they respond, I'll tell them I noticed the hood ajar and immediately called 911. Everything is plausible, given what's been happening to all of us the past couple of days."

"I agree," said Laura. "Perfect plan. Let the bomb squad do their thing. No doubt someone is out to get you...us...before we can un-cover what's going on with the whole abduction thing."

Instead of calling the press-monitored 911, Jason decided to use his Sheriff's Special Access card, insuring some confidentially, at least for a while. He dialed the number on the card; explained who he was and what his suspicions were. After a brief hold, he heard, "This is Sheriff Brown, Mr. McVay, what's going on?" Jason quickly explained the situation. Brown advised that the bomb squad was on the way and he, along with a Detective Morrison, would be close behind.

Within ten minutes, the Orange County Sheriff's Bomb Squad arrived, followed by four Orlando Police vehicles; their occupants quickly dismounted, setting up a secure perimeter around the complex's parking garage. The Bomb Squad was able to deactivate and remove the device in about thirty minutes.

Sheriff Brown took Jason aside to tell him he had been in contact with CIA Director McBride and was aware that Special Agent Cast, along with Jason's agency, was involved in a highly classified operation involving Dynamadics. He assured Jason he would keep all the mission operatives out of view so they could successfully complete the operation. Jason expressed his sincere gratitude, shook hands with the sheriff, and excused himself. He walked toward Laura who was shaking hands with Detective Morrison. He turned to leave, nodding at Jason as the two men passed each other.

"What was that all about?" asked Jason.

"He's arranged a ride to the hospital for us and will have your Lexus brought over later."

** ** **

Chapter Nine
Getting Our Ducks In A Row

"**G**ood morning, Rasheen," Whittaker said as he approached the Receptionist's desk. "What's new?" *Dumb question,* he thought, it's only just past eight in the morning.

"Good morning, Agent Whittaker, nothing new yet, but the day's young," replied Rasheen.

Whittaker continued down the center aisle toward his office. Upon entering, he set his briefcase on the corner table. Before he sat down, he stuck his head out, looking in the direction of Grande's desk. The big man glanced up, making eye contact.

"Agent Grande...a word," he said quietly. Grande immediately got up and walked into the Senior Agent's office. "Close the door," he ordered. "Have a seat, it hurts my neck, having to look so high," chuckling briefly at his attempted humor. Grande remained expressionless.

"I have an assignment for you. Locate Jason McVay and maintain close surveillance until he's in for the night. Anything out of the ordinary, contact me immediately; otherwise just document his activities *for my eyes only,* the surveillance being part of a confidential investigation."

"If I may, sir," requested Grande, *"what exactly constitutes* 'out of the ordinary?'"

"I think you can figure that out for yourself," replied Whittaker; intentionally vague.

"All right then," affirmed the big man, "will that be all?"

"That's it, Agent Grande," said Whittaker, "good hunting...*and don't get made!*"

Grande got up, literally ducking out the door with an uneasy feeling that he was on the edge of something, *something not so good.*

** ** **

Emily sat thinking about what she wanted to say to D'Arby Grande, when her ringtone announced an incoming call. It was Sam.

"Hi Emily," said Sam, "Just arrived at Wildcat Courier Service. What a dump. Obviously, a front...probably money laundering. Matter of fact, looks like the office could be a converted laundromat...wouldn't that be a hoot? There are two other cars parked out front, plus a van with a Wildcat Courier Service decal on the side. Oh, - get this - one of the cars is a spanking new Mercedes Benz sedan...maybe the boss is here. Next door is a pretty big nightclub, with a huge parking lot. In between the two businesses is what looks like a rudimentary helipad. This place is about a mile and a half south of downtown Kissimmee."

"Good luck," offered Emily, "I was just getting ready to call Grande and set up a meeting."

"Right," acknowledged Sam, "Well, I'll let you go...keep me posted."

"And you likewise," replied Emily. "Bye." Sam said her goodbye and they both clicked off.

** ** **

"Hello," said Grande, when his car's hands-free speaker activated.

"Hello, Agent Grande. This is Emily Cast. I'm hoping you're willing to meet with me. All I can say at the moment is that it is urgent I see you as soon as possible. It could quite literally be a matter of life and death!"

"Certainly, Agent Cast," he replied in his unusual high-pitched voice. "Time and place?"

"How about the Starbucks on Semoran at University Boulevard? Say about 9:30. And please, call me Emily. Oh, be sure to keep this confidential. You'll understand why after we meet."

"Sure thing, Emily. And please...It's D'Arby. See you at Starbucks; Semoran and University, 9:30," he confirmed.

"Thanks, D'Arby. I'll see you soon." The speaker returned to music as the call disconnected.

D'Arby felt trepidation; he had the sense he was approaching a crossroad in his new career. He liked Agent Cast and respected her investigative ability along with her substantial experience. To him, she was the antithesis of Whittaker.

** ** **

Sam entered the office and walked to the counter. She quickly surveyed the interior; besides the counter were two desks, the one on her left was occupied by a fifty-something guy with a distinctive, precisely sculpted goatee. He was busy with paperwork and hadn't bothered to look up. On her right was a larger desk that looked older than her. There were three men seated around the desk in worn out, very plain wood chairs. All three had shaved heads. Two appeared to be in their twenties; the other one looked to be around forty. They were engrossed in what appeared to be a poker game, ignoring the potential customer at the counter.

"Excuse me," announced Sam. "A little help please."

The older of the three poker players looked up. "Lady, we don't open until nine. There's a sign outside the door sayin' that. Come back then."

"Oh, I'm *Not* a customer. I'm an Investigator retained by Dynamadics Corporation. We're investigating the disappearance of a Dynamadics Executive's wife."

The single occupant of the left side desk abruptly stood and stepped over to the counter. With a decidedly cold stare, he demanded to see some I.D. Sam pulled her Florida Private Investigator license from her pocket along with a *McVay & Associates* business card which she handed over with a smile. *Mr. Goatee* looked over her creds, then handed them back.

"So, what exactly does Wildcat Courier Service have to do with some missing person from Dynamadics? We're a *courier service.* We move papers and packages...*not people.*" The sarcastic comment seemed to amuse the card players, who broke out laughing; ending abruptly when they noticed the icy stare aimed in their direction.

"I won't take up much of your time, I just have a couple of things that need to be clarified, Mr. ...?"

"Bilitnekoff," he answered, "I'm the Manager here."

"OK, Mr. *Bilitnekoff,* I need you to help us understand..."

Holding up his hand Bilitnekoff said, "Hold on lady...let's step outside where we can talk without interruption."

"Fine," replied Sam, turning to the door. Once outside, they walked over to a picnic style table a few feet from the company van. They sat on benches across from one another.

"So," the detective began, "Can you verify that Wildcat Courier has a long-term lease on a helicopter from United Air Rentals located at Orlando International Airport? Tail I.D. of said helicopter being JCT2914723?

"Yeah, we lease a helicopter...I'll take your word on the tail number. What's that got to do with anything?" he tersely asked.

"It seems," began Sam, "that this past Monday - the night of the disappearance in question - a helicopter with the tail number I gave you was identified by security personnel at Briar Patch Estates as having passed directly overhead around the time of the subject's disappearance. What can you tell me about that?"

'Well...let me think...that was Monday night you say?"

"Correct," responded Sam, seeing the question had caught him off guard.

"Umm, well...I remember a helicopter ride to Tampa was scheduled for our Company Director, Mr. Dimitrov on Monday night. I'm not sure why exactly; it was of a personal nature."

"*Why* would the helicopter fly over Briar Patch? That doesn't seem a logical flight path to Tampa," said Sam.

"Perhaps the pilot was momentarily disoriented...," offered the flustered Manager.

"Perhaps," replied Sam, "but *Why* would they be flying so low...low enough that the tail number could be easily read from the ground. More to the point...*Why* would they be flying In *Whisper Mode?*"

Realizing he had been outflanked by the detective, the simultaneously embarrassed and angry Manager said, "You need to speak to Mr. Dimitrov," instantly realizing he had just made a huge mistake.

"You're right," said Sam. "Where can I reach him?" she asked.

"Uh, he's out of town today," replied Bilitnekoff. "I'll leave a message for him. I know he'll be back here tomorrow."

"Thanks for your help, Mr. Bilitnekoff." Sam, standing up, turned to head for her truck.

Bilitnekoff went back inside, took out his phone, hit a speed dial number and said, "Sergei, *We Have a Problem...*"

** ** **

The Starbuck's parking lot was nearly empty; Emily saw only three other vehicles, one of which appeared to be leaving. She parked in the front row, walked the short distance to the entrance; the door automatically sliding open to admit her. She felt the welcome rush of cold air on her face. Only 9:20 AM and already 87, hot, sticky degrees outside. Orlando in the summer. The price they paid each year for the glorious Orlando winter.

She walked up to the service counter, counting only four other patrons as she arrived. A slightly overweight, but very pretty college-age girl greeted her with a bright smile.

"Good morning, what would you like?" Asked the young Hispanic woman.

Glancing at the associate's name tag (Rita), Emily, returning her smile said, "Good morning, Rita. I'd like a mocha latte and one of those cinnamon buns just behind you."

"Sure thing...be ready in just a few minutes," confirmed Rita.

While waiting for her latte, Emily felt a *whoosh* as the door slid open; simultaneously, Rita looked up...*really looked up*...prompting Emily to turn around. There stood Agent Grande, all seven feet of him. Emily stepped to the side to allow the big man access.

Grande looked at Agent Cast, and said, "Good morning, Emily," then turned to face Rita.

The young waitress seemed momentarily taken aback by the outsized man in front of her, but quickly regained her composure. With that same bright smile, she said, "Good morning, sir. What can I get for you?"

Looking in Emily's direction he asked, "What did my friend order?"

"A mocha latte...with a cinnamon bun," replied Rita.
"I'll have the same...hold the cinnamon bun," said Grande. "Would you like regular, large, or..."

"...*Extra*-large," said Grande, finishing the sentence for her.

Of course, thought Rita before confirming, "One extra-large mocha coming up. If you'd like, I can bring the orders to your table," she offered.

"That would be great," said Emily.

Emily walked to the rear, Grande close behind, selecting the last table by a window. She deferred to her companion, allowing him the preferred seat facing front.

Grande looked around, commenting on the place being nearly deserted.

"Time of day," explained Emily. "Two hours ago, you'd be hard-pressed to find a seat, even with all the take-out business they do. They have a pretty good sit-down breakfast menu."

"So, D'Arby," continued Emily, "I'll get right to the point. I believe Agent Whittaker has gone rogue. He's involved in the Stockwell abduction. We - me and Jason McVay - believe he's helping the Russians obtain very critical, top-secret technology from Dynamadics, which would make him a traitor. I know he's been assigned as your training mentor. I also know you're a patriot, and I'm not referring to your NFL days. In my view you have all the tools to be an exceptional agent. I'm not trying to butter you up. That's just what I believe. Otherwise, I wouldn't put my career at risk by having this conversation with you."

Grande raised his hand to indicate "stop." Looking Agent Cast in the eye, he said, "Emily, you have no idea how good you just made me feel. I'm 100% on your side! This past week has been horrible for me, I knew something was very wrong with this guy, but I didn't know what to do...I'm the new guy, fresh out of the academy, trying to make a good impression. But...I know right from wrong, and what Whittaker's having me do is dead wrong!"

Grande went on to detail his assignments from Whittaker, particularly the instructions to shadow Jason and keep his reports between them.

For her part, Emily told Grande all they had discovered and what more they suspected.

"D'Arby, you're in a great position to help us get Diane Stockwell back safe and sound, not to mention bringing this son-of-a-bitch down. He has no idea I'm anything more than his ignorant partner who has taken leave time, which I'm sure he interprets as a convenience; allowing him the excuse to use you - who he thinks he can manipulate - in my place."

Emily went on to tell D'Arby about her involvement with Sam Talley in the Nogudum shooting incident and how the CIA was covering up her involvement.

"I know Sam tangled with that Nogudum character at O'Doul's Pub. Obviously, he took umbrage with the public beating he took from her. That's one tough little lady," said Grande.

"Really not so little," corrected Emily, "she's six feet tall and over 150 lbs. of mostly muscle."

"You're absolutely right," agreed D'Arby, "just from *my perspective....*"

They finished their lattes. Getting up to leave, they exchanged their personal cellphone numbers. Emily told D'Arby what to report to Whittaker about Jason's movements. For his part, he assured Emily, he would keep her up to date on anything unusual with Whittaker.

As they left, Rita said, "Y'all have a really great day!"

D'Arby turned to look back and with a smile cheerfully said, "I will now!"

** ** **

Whittaker glanced up at the clock, noting it was almost 10:00 AM. He had just got off the computer and was puzzled why information about yesterday's shooting incidents was so restricted. It was very rare that FBI special agents couldn't get details about any domestic shooting incident. Classified as "Eyes only - Need to Know" by the CIA reduced most agents to the same access level as the media. As he sat at his desk sulking, he felt his personal phone vibrate. Pulling the phone from his pocket, he looked at the Screen. It was Sergei Dimitrov.

** ** **

Having spent more than an hour answering the various investigators' questions, Laura and Jason were looking forward to their visit with Maddy. Jason was assured his car would be released soon then delivered directly to him.

Jason thanked the Officer for bringing them to the hospital, then turned to Laura. "We're going to have to make a mad dash for it," he said, referring to the tropical downpour going on outside.

She acknowledged with a nod. Grabbing the door release, he shouted, "LET'S GO!" Quickly as he could, he squeezed his 6'2" frame through the door opening, with the not much shorter Laura sliding across the seat and exiting right on his heels. He grabbed her hand as they ran in tandem across the ten feet to the covered entrance. They looked at each other - both soaking wet, despite the relatively short distance - breaking out in laughter.

"What the hell?" Said Laura, "It's only 11:00 O'clock in the morning."

"I know, I know," Jason replied. "Just Florida in the summer. These things can happen at any time. Don't worry, the sun will be back in no time."

They entered the Lobby, going to their respective restrooms to dry off. They rendezvoused at the reception desk, and after the perfunctory protocols were met by an Orlando Police Officer (even though the original threat - Nogudum - was no longer with us, *the two of them* were now considered at risk) who escorted them to Maddy's private room. He stopped at the door, allowing the pair to pass in front of him.

"Jason!" Exclaimed Maddy as she elevated her bed to a sitting position. He came over and affectionately kissed her on the cheek.

"Maddy, let me introduce my friend..."

"...Laura," interrupted Maddy, "You're even more beautiful in person! Jason has told me so much about you...I'm truly delighted to finally meet you, though I wish the circumstances were different."

Laura walked over, cutting in front of Jason, and took Maddy's hand with both her hands. Suddenly, Maddy sat bolt upright, wearing a very startled expression.

It's all right, Maddy heard in her mind, *I have a gift, you might say a kind of ESP. I want you to know I share Jason's feelings for you...I'll always look out for you.* Maddy instantly relaxed, a bright smile replacing her initial shocked expression.

Out loud, Laura said, "It's an honor to meet you, Maddy. Jason thinks the world of you."

"Girl, I don't know how you did that," said Maddy, *"but it don't make no never mind to me,* I'm just glad you're here...with Jason." Turning toward Jason, she queried, "Friend - what do you mean...*Friend?*" a mischievous glint in her eyes.

The three of them spent the next hour talking about Jason and Maddy's experiences working together at the agency in Boston, punctuated with much laughter. Jason said they had to leave for the meeting with Tara and that he would keep her updated. Maddy told the pair she expected to be released in a couple of days and would see them then.

** ** **

Chapter Ten
Twists And Turns

Sam climbed in her truck for the drive to the next stop on her itinerary: Mr. Robert - *please call me Bob* - Dumont, Security Manager of Briar Patch Estates. She really needed to talk to the Security Officer who *actually saw* the helicopter. Bob could facilitate that. She glanced at her watch and noted it was exactly 9:00 AM. *Ah, she thought, now I could go in all legal-like to conduct business*, briefly smiling at the thought. Sam cranked the ignition, threw it into reverse, and was about to turn the truck around when she saw one of the skinheads come out the entrance yelling for her to "Wait!!"

She buzzed down her window. The guy - who she recognized as the oldest one of the 3 card players- told her that Mr. Bilitnekoff had found the paperwork that would "straighten this whole thing out." Sam shut off the ignition, climbed out, and headed toward the entrance when she suddenly felt a sharp sting in her left shoulder. Glancing over, she saw what looked like a dart embedded near her rotator cuff. She started feeling woozy before everything faded away...

** ** **

Tara answered her phone on the first note of her ringtone. It was John Stockwell.

"Yes, John," she answered, "What's up?"

"I need to see you right away," the tension thick in his voice, "...and in private."

"Certainly, John," she replied. "Come right up." Tara instructed Siri to "get Jennifer." A second later the Receptionist appeared on the

105

screen. "Jennifer - short of a 'three-alarm' emergency, hold all my contacts until I say otherwise."

"Yes, Ms. Wayne," she acknowledged, clicking off.

A minute later, Stockton appeared at her door, looking like a man headed for the execution chamber. She waved him in and slid the door shut behind him, engaging the "do not disturb" icon on the small screen just below the "Chief of Security, Tara Wayne" nameplate.

"Have a seat, John," she said indicating one of the large leather chairs in front of her desk. "I have to say, you don't look too good. Did you hear something about Diane?"

'Well...yes and no," he answered. "It's a long story...and not a good one. I'm not the man you think I am...at least when it comes to honor and loyalty. I've been thinking long and hard; I'm going to try to do the right thing - even at Diane's great peril."

Tara folded her hands, resting them in her lap as she leaned back slightly in her chair with an expression of concern. She listened with rapt attention as the overwrought Stockwell related how he was being blackmailed by Agent Whittaker.

Whittaker had somehow discovered Stockwell had submitted forged documents about his doctoral degree in Aerospace Engineering from M.I.T. as part of his application to Dynamadics all those years ago. He expressed deep remorse for his deception and that he was now ready to accept the consequences. He went on to say Diane had absolutely no idea about his transgression. Further, he stated he was very sorry for the dangerous situation he had placed her in, saying he hadn't realized just how much he loved her until this tragic moment. Stockwell pledged to do everything he could to save his wife and thwart the Russian attempt to steal *Project Expose'*.

Tara got up, walked around her desk, and stood in front of the distraught man. She put a hand on his shoulder, looked him straight in the eye and said, "John, we've known each other a long time. I believe you're a good person at heart. You've made a terrible mistake...I won't pretend there won't be consequences. I *can* promise you this - I will do all in my power to help you. At the very least, you'll regain a measure of self-respect in the knowledge that you're a patriot, *not a traitor.*" She could see the tension beginning to recede, evidenced by his more relaxed facial expression.

"Thanks for that, Tara. You *are* a good friend. As I said, I'll do all I can to help," he reiterated.

"What I need you to do now," instructed the Security Chief, "is go back to your office, lock yourself in - speak to no one - and write down everything you know about the plot and what they are expecting from you. I'll need you to come back up, this time to the Conference Room, to speak with myself and Jason McVay, a private investigator and two of his associates. Our discussion will be private - at this point we're not involving the authorities. I'll call you when we're ready."

Tara turned around, returning to her chair. Stockwell stood up and looked directly at her. "Thank you, Tara. I'll be waiting for your call." He turned, making a hasty exit.

** ** **

They exited through the hospital's front entrance, Laura immediately spotting Jason's shiny black Lexus waiting in one of the two *Police Only* parking slots.

"Look Jason, your car...just like they promised," pointed out Laura. They hurried over; worried the rapidly darkening sky would again catch them in another tropical downpour. They got in quickly. Jason looked around, then said, "I'll be damned, they detailed the car." He pushed the start button, backed out, and headed for the exit.

"Hungry?" Asked Jason. "We've got just enough time to grab a bite before the meeting."

"I *could* eat a little something...do you have a place in mind?" Queried Laura.

"I do," answered Jason, before turning up the radio's volume.

"...and the storm has just been upgraded to a hurricane with winds of 85 mph. Hurricane Miguel is currently on a track toward the Tampa - St. Pete - Clearwater area...but that could change in the next 24 hours. Watches and warnings will be issued within that timeframe. We return you to "Smooth Jazz All The Time," for your continued listening pleasure."

"Great!" Said Laura sarcastically. "Just what we need in the middle of an abduction/espionage investigation."

"We'll work around it," said Jason, "this isn't my first "rodeo in a hurricane." Plus, these things don't exactly follow their predicted paths half the time," he assured her, albeit with trepidation.

In less than 15 minutes they arrived at Brunch 'N Lunch, just in time to get an upfront parking spot as a previous patron pulled out. They finished parking and went in. The place was chock full of the noon lunch crowd. Jason stood on tiptoe to see if he could find an open table. Suddenly, he felt a gentle tug on his sleeve. Looking down, he saw a pretty, young waitress smiling up at him. It was *Kathy,* the UCF student who had waited on him and Emily a couple of days ago.

"Follow me," she said, guiding them to the last table on the window side; a bus boy was just finishing up. As they took their seats, Kathy handed each of them a menu.

"Well, hello young lady!" Enthused Jason. "Laura, this is Kathy, who I had the pleasure of meeting when I was here with Emily."

Laura glanced up at the waitress with a friendly smile saying, "Nice to meet you Kathy...and thank you for coming to our rescue, table-wise."

"My pleasure, Miss Laura. I'll give you folks some time to look over the menu...Coffee?"

"Please," replied Jason with Laura nodding in agreement. The waitress turned and left.

"Nice girl," observed Laura, "she's already earned herself a good tip."

"She's working her way through UCF; she's a Junior," said Jason, recalling the $40 tip he left last time...more than the tab itself. Maybe overly generous, but she could use the money.

Kathy returned with a carafe of coffee and took their identical orders for the BrunchBurger with fries and a side order of onion rings. Not healthy they knew, but they allowed themselves a culinary wickedness moment at least once during their "together" times. They told Kathy they had an appointment and were in a bit of a hurry...to which she replied, "no worries."

While waiting for their lunch, they discussed the failed car bomb and the prior assassination attempt at Dynamadics - not to mention the wounding of Maddy and subsequent gun battle involving Sam and Emily versus *Scarface* at her townhouse. Said gun battle now jokingly referred to by Sam as the *Gunfight at the O.K. Corral.* While acknowledging the continuing danger they faced, Laura pointed out Jason's two extraordinary advantages: his defensive future sight and...*Her.*

Kathy arrived with their burgers. "Here's lunch," she said. "Oh, did you hear the latest on the storm? They just upgraded it to a category 2 hurricane. I think they named it *Miguel.* Might reach us by this weekend...or not. Anyway, Enjoy!" she said as she turned to leave.

And *enjoy* they did, wolfing down the burgers, most of the fries, and all of the onion rings in just over 5 minutes. They were due at Dynamadics in 30 minutes.

** ** **

Emily locked her apartment with a click on her smartphone and walked the short distance to her car which she had left on the street. She climbed in, deciding to review the case file on the Stockwell abduction during the trip to Dynamadics. She engaged her safety harness, entered the vehicle control code, and instructed the Autopilot to take her to Dynamadics. The Autopilot confirmed the destination and informed Emily they would arrive in 25 minutes. She glanced at her watch and noted it was 12:30 PM. Not much time to spare. She picked up her phone and told Siri to "Call Sam." The phone rang four times, then went to voice mail.

"Hello Sam. I hope you've had a productive morning. I'm happy to report that the meeting with D'Arby Grande went well...actually *great*. Anyway, ring me up when you get a moment. I'm headed for the Dynamadics meeting. Talk to ya later. Bye."

Emily reflected on her earlier meeting with the oversized FBI Agent. She was indeed happy that her intuition had proved correct. He was definitely one of the good guys. She promised herself that she would do all she could to help him; to mentor him with his career.

** ** **

John Stockwell glanced at the digital clock on his desk - set in a beautiful chrome frame with a photo of the Spaceplane *Explorer* in the corner opposite the clock. Last year's birthday gift from Diane brought on an intense wistful feeling. He noted it was now 12:50. He expected to be summoned to the Conference Room any moment. He was ready. With great care, he had scrubbed his brain for the smallest detail of what had happened since his first meeting with the FBI traitor, Whittaker. He picked up his notepad for one final review.

** ** **

Jason pulled the Lexus into the same *Visitor Parking* slot he had used on his last visit to Dynamadics. "12:45 PM / 93 Degrees" was prominently displayed on the large digital clock above the building's front entrance. They got out of the car and Jason instructed the Autopilot to "secure the vehicle." "Look at that," observed Laura, "ten minutes to spare."

"I don't see Emily's car," said Jason as he scanned the visitor parking area. As if on cue, his phone vibrated. He checked the screen and saw "Emily Calling." "Hey, Emily," he answered..." where are you?"

"Hi Jason," she replied. "I'm about five minutes out...meet you in the lobby?"

"Sounds good," he affirmed. "See ya in about five," clicking off. Turning toward Laura, he remarked, "She's gonna meet us in the lobby." They went through the front entrance and were met by the recently promoted *Sergeant* Thomas, the on-duty security officer the day of the now infamous assassination attempt.

"Mr. McVay," he said with a bright smile, "really good to see you again." Thomas extended his hand and firmly gripped Jason's hand in a sincere handshake.

"Likewise, *Sergeant* Thomas," replied the detective, "and congratulations on your promotion. Certainly, well deserved." Turning toward Laura, he said, "Sergeant Thomas was on duty the day of the shooting; his quick response saved a lot of lives, including *yours truly*!" Turning back to Thomas, he said, "Sergeant Thomas, this is my associate, Laura Sparks."

"Happy to make your acquaintance, Ms. Sparks. Mr. McVay gives me too much credit. If anyone was a hero that day, *it was Jason McVay!*"

Just as Jason got ready to respond, Emily came through the entrance.

"Ah, Agent Cast," said Thomas, "Once again, welcome to Dynamadics. If you would step over to the Reception Desk, we can get you all checked in." Emily replied, "Thank you Sergeant." Turning toward Jason and Laura, she continued, "...shall we," indicating the Reception Desk.

Jennifer, our bubbly young Receptionist, looked up, her usual bright smile on full display. "Welcome back to Dynamadics. Ms. Talley is awaiting your arrival in the Executive Conference Room. Please... go right up," she said, with a nod toward the elevators.

** ** **

The trio, led by Jason, exited the elevator, walking the short distance to the Executive Office Suite, where the door slid open on their arrival. Erin, the Executive Secretary stood and smiled. "Good afternoon, everyone. Ms. Wayne is in the Conference Room."

Jason replied, "Good Afternoon, Erin." Looking to his left, he continued, "If memory serves, we want to go this way."

"Correct, Mr. McVay. The right side brings you to Mr. Henry's Executive Office."

Laura and Emily followed Jason to the Conference Room. He knocked gently, then opened the door. Tara was seated at the head of the table. She motioned for them to enter.

"Come in, come in," said Tara, "Can I get you anything? Water and coffee are by the table."

"I'm good," said Jason as he took the first chair on the left side. "Likewise," said Laura, taking the seat next to Jason. Emily chose the seat opposite Jason on the right side, saying she was also good. Jason introduced Laura and Tara. They reached in front of Jason to shake hands.

"Good to finally meet you Laura," Tara said, "Jason is always talking about you."

"Don't know why it's taken so long," remarked Laura. "I finally get to thank you in person for helping Jason get his start here in Orlando...what...almost four years ago."

"You're welcome, but it's been Orlando that's benefitted from his practice locating here," replied Tara. She continued, "Well, guess we better get down to business. Oh...where's Sam?"

"She wasn't scheduled to be here. She's caught up investigating this "*Wildcat*" outfit."

"Right...you did tell me that," she confirmed. "Now, I've got an investigation 'game changer'...and it's a lot to take in." The team looked from one to the other in eager anticipation.

Tara outlined what Stockwell had told her in his remorseful confession: the blackmail being used to obtain his cooperation; Diane's kidnapping - an apparent insurance policy; and his pending turnover of the thumb drive. Jason, Laura, and Emily - the three of them - all displayed expressions of shock at this totally unexpected development. They momentarily sat in silence, digesting what they had just heard.

Finally, Jason spoke up, "So you're telling us that Stockwell suddenly had this *epiphany*...this sudden moral 'course correction'...in spite of the clear danger to his wife, not to mention himself?!"

"Let me stop you right there, Jason," interrupted Tara. "I've known John Stockwell a long time. And... if I do say so myself, I'm a pretty good judge of character. It's my belief that he's a good guy at heart - this whole episode is way out of character for him - he just couldn't live with it anymore...despite the danger to Diane. He sincerely wants to *right that wrong* now."

"That's good enough for me," affirmed Jason, Laura and Emily nodding in agreement. I, *we*...have total confidence in your judgement."

"So," queried Laura, "where do we go from here? It would be productive to question him - get more detail...something he might have forgotten could come to mind...especially considering how focused he is on atoning for his initial poor judgement."

"Agreed," replied Tara. "He's willing, *actually anxious*, to help anyway he can. He's waiting to be summoned as we speak."

"Does he know I'm an FBI Agent?" asked Emily.

"I'm not sure," replied Tara, "doesn't matter...like I said he's willing to do *whatever*. If y'all are ready, I can have him up here in five minutes."

"Let's do this!" exclaimed Jason, excited anticipation in his voice.

** ** **

"What the hell!" Exclaimed Whittaker, "*Why* did they do that?" Noticing some curious glances coming his way, he said, "Hold on." He got up, quickly walking over to the office door which he promptly shut. He looked at his phone as if he were looking at some kind of idiot, then said, "So, *what do we do now?*"

"What do we do now?" Parroted Dimitrov on the other end of the call, "What we do now *is turn the situation to our advantage.* What's that old American saying...something about turning lemons into lemonade? Didn't you learn anything about adversity in FBI school?"

"It's *Academy,*" interrupted Whittaker, "not school...*Academy.*"

"Whatever," said Dimitrov dismissively, "point is, we now have a new advantage...we've got the girl's phone!"

"Sure, great," sarcastically replied Whittaker. "So what, all the conversations are encrypted ten ways to Sunday on a locked phone?"

"True," agreed Dimitrov, "but I happen to have access to the best hackers in the world. It's only a matter of time before we'll know who she's called and what they said."

Somewhat placated, Whittaker said, "Yeah, I forgot your people's hacking ability continues to be a thorn in our side. We've still got to deal with McVay."

"That's in the works," replied Dimitrov. "Bilitnekoff's boys are on it. He will become irrelevant in short order...what's that noise in the background?" Queried the Russian.

"Oh, that's a weather alert," answered Whittaker, "something about an approaching hurricane. Have the Stockwell woman call her husband on the burner at 5:00 PM sharp. Gotta go."

** ** **

Stockwell came in and stood at the end of the table opposite Tara.

"Have a seat John," Invited Tara.

Stockwell sat down, looking furtively toward the other end of the table, as if his inquisitors were about to pounce - which they were - but in a more benign way than he ever would have imagined.

"John," began Tara, "this is Jason McVay and his associate, Laura Sparks." They both nodded in his direction. "On my left is Emily Cast, an FBI Special Agent. I am telling you up front she is *Not* here in that capacity, rather consider her a part of Jason's team."

"The goal here," she continued, "is first and foremost to secure Diane's safe return. Second, to secure *Project Expose'* and bring the perps to justice; last, to give you the opportunity to redeem yourself and rebuild your life. No promises...but if we can achieve the first two, the third should fall in place for you...and Diane."

After Tara's opening remarks, Stockwell visibly relaxed; the tension in the room melted away. "Thank you, Tara," said Stockwell, "thanks to you all for this opportunity to set things right; I feel blessed and ashamed at the same time. My biggest concern is getting Diane back unharmed. That said, I'm ready for your questions, I'll tell you all I know."

The team spent the next hour interrogating John Stockwell. He did, indeed reveal all he knew...a virtual treasure trove of information. Actually, his presentation was so well prepared they only rarely asked a question, and then only to clarify a particular point.

Stockwell outlined how he had been blackmailed by Whittaker, and in fear of losing everything he had, capitulated to their demand of turning over *Project Expose'*. He remarked that he was blindsided by Diane's abduction; sure it was insurance he wouldn't waiver. He told the team that he was awaiting further instructions from Whittaker later today.

The team decided to let that play out in order to devise a rescue plan and terminate the threat. And bring the traitor, Whittaker to justice...a priority for Special Agent Cast. Jason said he, Laura, and Emily would be heading for O'Doul's Pub for a pre-planned rendezvous with Sam to compare notes, after which they would call Tara. She had already assumed the task of staying with Stockwell as he awaited contact with Whittaker. Tara adjourned the meeting. Jason, Laura, and Emily headed for the elevator, then the lobby.

** ** **

Chapter Eleven
The Approaching Storm

Sam slowly regained consciousness. She had a splitting headache which was further aggravated by vibrations from...opening her eyes, she realized she was in a helicopter. And handcuffed. She looked down at an unending canopy of trees; a small clearing suddenly becoming visible just ahead. Glancing around, she saw the pilot in the front; seated next to him was a guy she recognized from Wildcat Courier...the oldest of the card players, the one who had beckoned her to return. Sitting next to her in the other rear seat was a big, burly guy with a thick black beard. He smelled bad...*real bad.*

As the chopper gently touched down, the pilot cut off the power. The smelly guy reached around her to open the door and in a thick Russian accent ordered, "Let's go bitch." She stepped out - kind of tricky with her hands cuffed behind her back - onto the grass. Another guy - this one wearing a mask, grabbed her roughly by the elbow and walked her over to a four passenger ATV, forcing her onto the back seat, then walked around to the other side. Sam quickly scanned the clearing, which was pretty ordinary except for a stand of Royal Palm trees - this particular species rare outside of south Florida. Just before everything went dark under a blindfold, she could just make out the last four digits of the chopper's tail number: *4723.*

Sam sensed two more getting onboard, so she had three escorts. One was easy to identify by the smell. Oh My God - *the Smell!* The one next to her belted her in; the ATV taking off with a jolt. After bouncing around for what she estimated to be about five minutes, the ATV came to an abrupt halt.

** ** **

At Dynamadics, the trio bid goodbye to Sergeant Thomas, exited the main entrance and walked briskly to Jason's car, stopping there to discuss what to do the rest of the afternoon.

"Never saw that coming," observed Jason, referencing John Stockwell's change of heart.

"For a fact!" Exclaimed Laura. "This changes our whole approach."

"That's for sure," chimed in Emily. "Gotta say, *I'm really worried about Sam.* I've got a bad feeling she's in some kind of trouble."

"I'll second that," said Laura, eliciting a troubled expression from Jason, who was well aware of her extraordinary - almost supernatural - intuitive abilities. Now *really concerned,* Jason said, "I'm reluctant to do this, but I'm going to initiate the Emergency Contact protocol."

The *Emergency Contact Protocol* was one of several processes developed in response to the "Citizen's Privacy Law" enacted by Congress about eight years earlier to ensure citizen privacy from the ever more intrusive commercial interests; media - especially electronic media; and, of course, government. Electronic tracking, especially location tracing of cellphones, was effectively terminated. Only certain government agencies were allowed to "track" criminal suspects and other nefarious folk - and then, *only after rigorous vetting by the courts.* Unfortunately, there were unintended consequences resulting from this mostly benign law...as Jason McVay & Company could now readily attest.

Jason had been trained in this procedure while working in Boston. In actual practice, the process was easy to initiate and worked flawlessly. In order to take advantage of this option, one would have to acquire a specially modified cell phone, which, of course, Jason had done. Several years ago, he had purchased ten of these phones - at no small expense. In the event he or Sam (or any other future field investigator) couldn't be contacted, a signal would be sent to the field agent's phone, producing a very loud tone, akin to an "amber alert". If there was no response (by voice only) within five minutes, the field agent's phone would be electronically disabled - rendered useless for all purposes, including hacking.

Jason took out his phone, opened *Messages,* selected *Sam's Phone,* typed in a 10-digit code then selected *Send.* His screen displayed: *Are you SURE you want to send this message?* He selected *Yes;* then selected *Send.* He saw *Message Sent* appear on the screen.

A moment later, another message appeared on his screen: *The party contacted has 5 minutes to respond with a voice call. No response will result in the permanent electronic termination of the phone. This process is irrevocable.* The screen went blank. Jason put the phone back in his pocket. Both women glanced at their watches.

"So," Jason began, "if we don't hear back, here's what I think we should do. Emily, you go to Wildcat Courier - *be VERY careful* - to see what you can find out. The two of us will head over to Sam's place - I have her code - to see if we can find anything. Give me a call when you're done at Wildcat...If I don't hear from you in two hours, I'm sending the Calvary."

At the five-minute mark Jason heard an alert tone. He retrieved his phone. The screen displayed: *Action Complete,* then went blank. Jason looked from Laura to Emily then said grimly, "OK, then. Let's go." Emily headed for her car. Jason and Laura climbed in the Lexus.

** ** **

Sam was helped out of the ATV and walked a short way when her "escort" paused their movement saying, "Stairs." At the top of three stairs, she was paused again as a door was opened. After a few more steps, she was stopped once more and instructed to "hold still" while the handcuffs were removed. Next, the blindfold was pulled off. She was told to sit on the loveseat beneath her. Looking around, she realized she was in a cabin, most likely a vacation rental. Sitting on the sofa directly opposite was a very pretty, slim blonde woman who she immediately recognized as Diane Stockwell. The masked man standing over her announced: "Two rules. The door is unlocked. Do Not Go Outside. If you do, you will be killed. Second, avoid anything more than a glimpse at any of us. Any attempt to identify us means you will not leave this place alive."

"What about the big guy with the beard?" Asked Sam. *"He's* not wearing a mask."

"Don't worry about him," replied the masked one, "he's an exception to the rule."

Right on cue, the guy with the beard, but sans a mask, came in with Sam's briefcase and tossed it over to the coffee table, where it landed with a thud. He turned; following his compatriot out the front door; loudly shutting it behind them.

"Jesus!" Exclaimed Diane.

"What?" Asked Sam.

"The Stench...what the hell is that *smell?"*

"I know," said Sam, "it's the big guy with the beard...I'd give him my next paycheck if he'd just take a shower!" Both women laughed. She got up and walked over to Diane, hand extended. "I'm Samantha Talley...Sam for short. I work for a detective agency retained by Dynamadics."

Diane stood, firmly gripping the other woman's hand. "I'm Diane Stockwell...I'm sure you already know that. I can't tell you how happy I am to see another friendly face, the dire circumstances not with-standing!"

** ** **

Emily was on the southern beltway approaching the Kissimmee off-ramp when her ringtone alerted her to an incoming call. Looking up from the file she had been reading, she said, "Activate speaker." She continued, "Hello, yes," ...then getting this unexpected response; "Hello Agent Cast, this is Director Upton. What are you doing at this moment?"

Taken aback by the "out of the blue" call from FBI Director Upton, she nervously answered, "I...I...um...I'm in my car headed for Wildcat Courier Service in Kissimmee."

"Listen to me carefully Agent Cast," instructed the Director, "safely pull over to the shoulder and stop the vehicle. On your phone go to the Security App. When prompted, enter your FBI Agent I.D. Number, then the code word: 'axlerod' in lower case. Then enter today's two-factor security code. When you've finished all that, a list of five choices will be displayed. Select 'Director's Private Line' and press *Send.* We will be reconnected on a secure, encrypted line. Got all that?"

Still recovering her composure, Emily responded, "Yes Sir." She instructed the Autopilot to pull onto the shoulder and stop the vehicle. She moved the case file from her lap and retrieved her phone. Though still somewhat rattled, Emily implemented the Director's instructions, quickly recalling her training for this particular protocol - designed to ensure total security at both ends of the line. Immediately after pressing *Send,* Director Upton came on the line.

"Agent Cast, are you on?"

"Yes Sir," she replied.

"Good," he acknowledged. "I know that you are assigned to the Diane Stockwell abduction investigation along with Agent Whittaker. I also know you are involved with one Jason McVay and his private agency who are simultaneously investigating the Stockwell abduction at the behest of the Dynamadics Corporation."

"I have recently been briefed by CIA Director McBride, whose agency is coincidentally engaged in an ongoing action involving Dynamadics and Russian espionage, *which specifically includes Wildcat Courier Service.* We are in the process of coordinating our two investigative efforts. Director McBride had high praise for Mr. McVay - which is sufficient character reference for me; she informed me of your involvement in the unrelated shooting incident and her effort to keep you out of the publicity. Incidentally, she commended your actions...from the Bureau's standpoint, *the incident never happened.* She did, however, say you had some very pertinent information concerning Agent Whittaker."

"I do, Director," she confirmed, "and I'm afraid it's not good." She went on to relate her and Agent Grande's initial suspicions about Whittaker, confirmed today by John Stockwell.

"Would that be the D'Arby Grande that played tight end for the Patriots?" Queried Upton.

"One and the same," confirmed Emily, "and, if I may say so, in my humble opinion he has the makings of an exceptional agent."

"You *may,*" said Upton...and duly noted. Please describe your current relationship with the McVay Team and where things stand up to this minute."

As requested, Emily detailed everything: Whittaker compelling Grande to tail McVay; this morning's attempted car bombing; her meeting with D'Arby and subsequent plan for him to keep tabs on Whittaker; finally ending with the suspected abduction of Sam.

The Director instructed her to continue working with McVay and Grande, allowing McVay to continue taking the lead on the investigation. Because of national security concerns, Upton said he and Director McBride agreed the CIA would be the lead agency, pooling the resources of both agencies. He cautioned Cast that she was involved in an "unofficial" capacity. That said, both agencies would unofficially "have her...everybody's...back." He concluded by saying she should share this conversation with McVay. He requested they all stay away from Wildcat until he conferred further with CIA Director McBride. The call was then terminated. Emily said, "Siri, call Jason."

** ** **

"I see you travel light," joked Diane.

"Yeah," replied Sam, "My escort didn't give me a lotta time to pack." Looking around, Sam continued, "Not bad accommodations for an abductee. Not bad at all."

"I know," agreed Diane. "I was kinda surprised myself. Not at all like you read in the crime novels...you know, all hog-tied, gagged, and stuffed in some dark, dank closet." They both giggled at the vision. "Even better," she continued, "plenty of food...meat, fruit, cereal, eggs...even ice cream. And beer. There's a case of beer with more on ice."

"No shit!" Exclaimed Sam. "I'll bet we're the most pampered abductees in the history of kidnapping!' Another round of giggles ensued.

"So that's a good sign...right?" Asked Diane, with just a hint of angst.

"I honestly don't know," replied Sam, "but I think it's a good sign." (Actually, she had serious misgivings about their captors allowing them to leave alive, but she didn't want to alarm Diane, at least not at this point). "I see there's a loft bedroom up there."

"Yeah," confirmed Diane, "It's only a Queen...but I think we can both fit OK. Wait a minute...stand up for a second. Whoa, you're taller than I am - and I'm 5'11."

"Not by much," observed Sam, "I'm 6' even. Not to worry...we'll be fine," she assured Diane.

"Well, You're *a tall drink of water,*" teased a grinning Diane.

"Right," said Sam, "As if *you* never heard that remark!"

"All the time," affirmed Diane. They enjoyed a laugh over the shared pet peeve.

"You're beautiful...still have that girly figure," observed Sam. "I can see why you were such a successful model."

"Thanks," said Diane, "kind of you to say. Just *how much* do you know about me?"

"Professionally, quite a lot," replied Sam, "personally, not so much...but I've got a feeling we're gonna get to know each other real well."

"So," said Diane, "*professionally* speaking, *how much* do you know about me?"

"Well, for starters," replied Sam, "I know you're a whole lot smarter than you let on. C'mon, *You're a card-carrying Mensa member.* Why you would want to keep your *gift* so secret is beyond me. And I say that with respect. I just feel that you super-smart folks have an obligation to make society better...wait, I'm sorry. I have no right to judge you...I'm sure you have your reasons. And be assured, none of us will *ever* violate your right to privacy."

Sam sat in silence. After a minute, Diane said, "Sam, come over here," indicating the vacant end of the sofa. Sam got up, went over, and plopped down. "You're not the first person to tell me that - and you're absolutely right. I was blessed with good looks and more than my share of brain power. I've always felt guilty about that, even knowing that it's just the 'luck of the genetic draw'. If we get out of this mess, I'm gonna change that."

Sam sensed a strong connection emerging between them. "I'm the product of a military family. My dad was a Marine. My brother *is* a Marine. In fact, he was just promoted to Brigadier General. He was...*is* my boss's best friend. I served three years in the Corps before bouncing around as a physical trainer while trying to break into the Women's Pro Tennis tour. I was good, just not good enough. Eventually, Jason - my boss - offered me this gig, and well, here I am."

"You already know I grew up in a military family," said Diane. "We're both military brats, so we've got that in common. I gotta say, you're *exactly the kind of person* I would want to be stranded with, so given our terrible circumstances, I'm thankful for that."

"We're gonna get out of this," vowed Sam, "we're gonna be one hell of a team!" The two women stood up and hugged: each energizing the other with confidence and determination.

** ** **

"Goodbye Emily," said Jason, looking over at Laura who followed up with, "Bye Emily, talk to you later." Emily responded, "Bye guys...I'm headed home. Call if you hear anything...or if you need me." They heard *easy listening* music softly playing in the background as the car's radio reconnected.

"Knock me over with a feather!" Declared Jason, "I knew this caper was a pretty big deal...but the directors of two really big agencies getting *personally involved...*sure gives me pause."

"Me, too," agreed Laura. "I was especially surprised at Upton giving you *carte blanche* with the investigation...he must have a lot of faith in you."

"Actually, he's got a lot of faith in Kaitlyn McBride, who's got a lot of faith in my sister...you get the picture."

"Yeah, I do," replied Laura, "still - well deserved...*faith really does flow downhill!"* They both broke out in laughter.

"Five minutes to arrival at destination," announced the autopilot. Jason could see the exit to Exeter Road - and Sam's townhouse - looming in the distance. "Return to manual control," ordered Jason.

"Returning to manual control in three...two...one; auto-control disengaged," confirmed the autopilot.

As Jason resumed driving, they heard..."*We are interrupting this program for a Hurricane Miguel update. The eye of the storm is about 50 miles southwest of Tampa Bay where it is expected to make landfall about 11 PM Friday as a category 2 hurricane. It is projected to follow a northeast trajectory; taking it through west central Florida, the Ocala National Forrest and into northeast Florida; exiting the state in the Jacksonville area. A Hurricane Warning for the Tampa Bay area is expected to be issued at 6:00 PM, EST. Stay tuned for further updates. We return you now to the regularly scheduled program."*

Just as Jason passed the *Exeter Road - Exit 1/2 Mile sign* he felt the now-familiar chill come upon him. Braking hard, he immediately pulled the car onto the shoulder. A startled Laura watched him rapidly descend into a trance-like state.

The *movie in his mind began* playing. Jason saw his car come off the exit ramp onto Exeter Road; travel a mile; turn onto Sunrise Way; and at the third house down, turn *right* into the driveway of Sam's residence. He got out of the car, shut its door and turned toward the path leading to the front door. Suddenly, he felt a strong impact - as if he had just been shoved from behind. Then everything became blinding white before turning black. Real time returned.

Laura watched, fascinated, as he instantly returned to his normal self. "Are you OK?" she asked, knowing exactly what had just happened. He nodded in response. "Future Vision," she stated, again getting an affirming nod.

"There's a guy ready to ambush us at the house directly across the street from Sam's. Yeah, same house as last time...except this time there's "crime scene" tape around it. Here's the plan: I'll let you off at the corner of Sunrise...there's two houses - under construction - before you reach the third one with the perp. He's gonna be set up in the windowless living room; when he hears the car, he'll stand up to take his shots. You can easily get the drop on him from the back. I'll give you time to set up, then turn onto Sunrise and go to Sam's. Wait for me to open the car door...then do your thing. Take him out if you have to."

"Got it," said Laura. She reached around to the small of her back and retrieved her Beretta.

Jason shifted the car back to *Drive,* re-entered the road, then onto the exit ramp for Exeter Road. He slowed as he approached the intersection of Sunrise Way, coming to a stop.

"Ready?" he asked. Laura nodded. "Go," he said. She left the vehicle and headed toward the house at the corner before disappearing from view. Jason turned onto Sunrise, then into Sam's driveway. He took a deep breath, then opened the car door.

Laura wasted no time getting to the target's house. As she took up her position, she saw the perp stand up and level his long gun just as Jason pulled into Sam's driveway.

"MOVE A MUSCLE AND I'LL BLOW YOUR GODDAMN HEAD OFF!!!" yelled Laura.

Taking the woman at her word, the guy froze in place. "Now...SLOWLY Place The Weapon On The Ground...DON'T TURN AROUND!" she commanded. Jason arrived at the front of the house, his own Berretta drawn and pointed squarely at the perp's chest.

"I've got him covered. Laura...Here..." he said, tossing over a pair of handcuffs. She holstered her pistol and picked up the cuffs. Instructing the perp to "get on your knees and clasp your hands behind your head." She carefully walked up behind him: grabbing one hand, swinging his arm down; then quickly repeating the process before deftly cuffing him. She helped him stand up and marched him out what would eventually be the front door. Before escorting him across the street, Jason quickly surveyed the area to confirm they were alone. Fortunately, there were only two completed and occupied homes on the street: Sam's and one 2 houses down - whose "snowbird" owner was up north for the summer; the other nine houses were in various stages of construction.

They brought their captive into the house and thoroughly searched him; said search yielding a wallet, cellphone, notebook, a nine-millimeter Glock, with two fully loaded magazines, and a penknife. Oh, particularly interesting, a small pill container. They further trussed him up with rope, gagged him, then took him into the garage where they secured him to a bolted workbench with another pair of cuffs before returning to the house to discuss their next move.

** ** **

Chapter Twelve
Questions...and Answers

Jason walked over to the refrigerator. He looked back at Laura, who was seated at the breakfast bar. "Want a beer?" He asked, opening the fridge door.

"Sure, thanks," she replied, pulling her phone from her pants pocket.

"Only thing she's got is Heineken...is that OK?" He queried.

"Sure, fine, whatever..." answered Laura absently as she brought the phone to her ear. "Hello Emily...got a little update for you," she understated. Laura detailed the recent events leading up to the present moment. When she finished, Emily responded with "REALLY! I can't believe it! Sam was spot on with the 'O.K. Corral' reference. Maybe she should consider moving to a more sedate neighborhood," she said, laughing.

Jason came over with two bottles and took a seat at the bar opposite Laura. He overheard her ask Emily to call his sister, Sandy and bring her up to date on the latest happenings; also requesting Sandy set them up with a local CIA "safe house" where they could stash their perp. Finished with the call, Laura laid her phone on the bar, then reached for her beer.

"The safe house is the way to go," observed Jason. "I had the same idea in mind...shouldn't be a problem...Sandy is a ranking Senior Agent with a lot of authority. Not to mention how close she is with Director McBride. Now, let's talk about the *'elephant in the garage.'*"

"Don't forget, Mr. McVay, *I'm also a CIA Senior Agent*, and am known to have the Director's ear as well," she said in an exaggerated miffed tone.

"As I am aware Agent Sparks," confirmed Jason, "But at the moment *you* are on vacation. No slight intended, milady," he said, clasping his hands together and bowing his head. "Please forgive me."

"Well...just this once," said Laura. They both laughed as they clinked their bottles together. "Now, about the interrogation...," she said.

Jason suggested, "I think we should just try to get the basics, let the pro at the safe house do the heavy lifting."

"Agreed," affirmed Laura. She set her beer down; walked over to the coffee table, picked up the items Jason had found during his shakedown and set them on the bar. Laura lined them up: a wallet, cellphone, a pocket-size notebook, a penknife, and a pill container. They set about examining the items individually. The wallet contained a Florida Driver License in the name of Nikita Vaslov; a Russian Diplomat's I.D. with the same name (*Uh,oh,* thought Jason); three credit cards; a Diplomatic Firearm Permit (for the Glock); a photo of a rather pretty woman; and a ticket for an upcoming Orlando Saints soccer game. Laura thumbed thru the notebook; unfortunately, the writing was in Russian. The pill container held a single white capsule. Laura said simply: "Cyanide."

"So why would a Russian diplomatic attaché' have a cyanide capsule?" Queried Jason. "More to the point, why would someone of *his rank* be the one trying to assassinate *us?*"

"Exactly," replied Laura. "Why indeed? Let's see what he's willing to give up."

They gathered his belongings and went into the garage, finding their prisoner still firmly secured to the workbench. As they approached the man, he began trying to talk, but the gag thwarted his effort. Jason stepped over and rudely ripped off the gag, leaving bits and pieces of Vaslov's lip stuck on the duck tape.

In flawless English he proclaimed, "You can't hold me like this...I'm a senior diplomat...*I have diplomatic immunity!* I demand to be put in touch with the Russian Consulate in Orlando *immediately!*"

"Seriously?" Asked Laura. She picked up his diplomatic creds, glanced at them, then with an icy stare said, "Mr. ...*Vaslov*...you just tried to kill us! You can stick your *diplomatic immunity* where the sun never shines!"

"You can't prove that" said Vaslov. "I never fired a shot."

"Not for lack of trying," interjected Jason. "If Agent Sparks hadn't got the drop on you, well..."

"I have nothing more to say," stated the Russian. "Contact the Consulate."

Jason and Laura looked at each other, nodding in silent agreement. Jason reapplied the duck tape gag, then joined Laura on the way back into the house.

** ** **

John Stockwell sat at his office desk, beads of sweat breaking out on his forehead. It was precisely 5:00 PM. His ringtone sounded, prompting him to sit bolt upright. He glanced over at Tara who nodded at him. He answered the phone, putting it on speaker. "Yes?" he said nervously.

"Mr. Stockwell are you alone?" asked the thickly Russian-accented voice.

"I am," lied Stockwell.

"You better be," warned the caller, *"your wife's life depends on it."*

Stockwell looked over at Tara with a terrified expression. She looked back, shaking her head slightly while moving her hands up and down slowly in a "calming" motion. Stockwell began to regain his composure.

"You'll be receiving instructions in the near future with the details of the thumb drive hand-over and release of your wife. You now have one minute to speak with her."

Diane suddenly appeared on the phone's screen. All things considered, she looked well. "Are you OK?" Asked her anxious husband.

"I'm OK and being treated well. Please do as they ask and everything will be all right. And please tell Maddy's niece that I look forward to working with her when this is over. Love you."

The call was terminated. Stockwell looked over at Tara with a quizzical expression. "Who is *Maddy's niece*?"

"I don't know," answered Tara, "...wait, yes I do. Maddy is Jason McBride's secretary. Her niece is...Oh my god, *they've got Sam!*"

** ** **

The pair had barely come back in the house when Laura felt her watch vibrate. A quick glance revealed Emily Cast calling. She continued over to the bar and picked up her phone. "Hello Emily," she answered. She listened intently for a couple of minutes, occasionally acknowledging with an "uh, huh", "OK", and "great;" finally ending her part of the conversation with: "got it...thanks so much, we'll be in touch...gotta go," ending the call. She opened the *Notes* app on her phone and quickly began thumb-typing.

Laura looked up at Jason. "Your sister - *my partner* - came through big-time. She's got us set up with a safe house in Altamonte Springs where we can stash this clown. And here's the best part...one of the agency's best interrogators just happens to be there. Actually, he's on vacation and is being allowed to use the vacant house so he can save some money. Nice perk, huh? Anyway, he'll be staying on to help us out."

"How lucky are we?" Asked Jason rhetorically. "Better get our 'diplomat' ready for transport."

** ** **

Diane handed the burner phone back to Dimitrov. Putting the phone in his pocket, he said, "If everyone does as they are told, then you should be back home with your husband by tomorrow night. In the meanwhile, relax. Watch TV. Talk to your new friend. Your ordeal will soon be over...*and you'll be considerably the richer for it.*" He turned and abruptly left.

Sam, who had watched the phone call to John Stockwell unfold, got up from the loveseat, walked over to the fridge, and asked Diane if she "wanted a brew," who answered with an enthusiastic *"please."* Sam grabbed a couple of cold ones and headed over to join Diane on the sofa. She handed Diane her beverage then plopped down on the opposite end. "So...," Sam said, "'*considerably the richer for it'*...what the hell is that all about?"

"I'm not exactly sure," answered Diane. "My guess is the Russians are paying him a large sum of money to placate him and at the same time have something else to hold over him."

"What about me?" Asked Sam.

"Oh. You'll have to negotiate your own financial settlement," said Diane with a straight face. Then she broke out laughing, followed in short order by Sam.

"No, silly," said Sam, regaining her composure, "I mean where do I fit in their scheme? I don't see the point...*and I'm a trained detective.*"

"Yeah, right," agreed Diane. "*What* would be the point? Wait...maybe you were a 'panic grab'; not planned...a spur of the moment thing...maybe a poor decision by someone further down the food chain and now they don't know what to do with you."

"Sounds pretty plausible to me...the more I think about it, *more probable than plausible.* You missed your calling girl, you shoulda been a detective," opined Sam. "And for the record, I'm kinda worried about the '*They don't know what to do with you*' part."

** ** **

"That's the address," said Laura, spotting the *1275* on the mailbox. Jason pulled the Lexus into the driveway, parking behind a Honda SUV. He scanned the nondescript ranch style home fronted by a small, but neatly trimmed lawn. A young man stuck his head out the front door inviting the trio to "come on in." In the back seat, Laura looked at their captive warning, "You know the drill, Vaslov...let's go." She shoved him toward the door Jason had just opened. Vaslov got out; Laura nimbly sliding out right behind him, keeping her Beretta discreetly by her side. She closed the car door and the three walked to the front entrance, their host politely holding the door for them.

After Laura was in, he shut the door, went straight to Vaslov, quickly applying a cuff to his right wrist. The young agent went down the hallway - Vaslov in tow - and disappeared into a room. In just over a minute he returned, offering his hand to Jason.

"Hello, Mr. McVay," he said, introducing himself. "I'm Jaydan Sanders; pleased to meet you."

Jason quickly appraised the young man standing before him: Jason's similar height, but slimmer; blonde hair and a most unusual shade of blue eyes accenting a rather handsome face. He took the young man's hand, replying with a smile, "Likewise; your reputation precedes you."

Jaydan turned toward Laura, looking at her with a surprised expression. He stared at her in silence, as if he was trying to place her. "I *know* you from somewhere," he said, "I... I just can't recall where...do you remember me?"

"I don't," lied Laura, "perhaps at Langley...I'm assigned to the Director's Office. I'm..."

"*Laura,*" he interrupted, "Laura Spade."

"Sparks," she corrected, "Laura *Sparks*. And I'd certainly remember meeting a handsome young man like yourself," she said with a coy smile. Laura offered Jaydan her hand.

Blushing, he shook her hand. "Pleased to meet you Ms. Sparks, *again...Or Not.*"

Laura thought back to the last time she had seen Jaydan fourteen years ago. Amazingly, he didn't look a day older. But then, neither did she...

Jason, bemused with their repartee said, "Well, Jaydan - and please, call us Jason and Laura, we're not *that much older* than you - what's next?"

"What's next," parroted Jaydan, "is pretty cut and dried. I need to know everything that happened leading up to his capture; then everything that's happened with him from that point until now, including the results of whatever interrogation you've already done. Next, tell me the most salient points you need to know."

Jason and Laura took turns relating the ambush scenario, leaving out the *future-vision* part; the items recovered, including the encrypted phone, and the basic garage interrogation. They detailed the kidnappings - emphasizing Sam's recent abduction - the *Project Expose'* information the Russians were after, and the upcoming "hostage exchange" in the works. Jaydan said he'd get on it immediately as they exchanged phone numbers.

They thanked him profusely - especially for his giving up vacation time - to help them out.

"Call us as soon as you have something...Thanks!" Said Jason as they walked out the door.

** ** **

As Jason backed the car down the driveway, Laura pulled out her cellphone instructing Siri to "Create a conference call to include myself, Emily, and Tara." The robotic voice responded, "One moment please." Laura put her phone on speaker. They heard ringing. On the second ring Emily answered: "Hello Laura."

Laura said, "Hold for a conference call Emily." The ringing in the background stopped as Tara picked up. Laura told the women it was imperative they meet as soon as possible. She suggested Brunch 'N Lunch since it was centrally located for the three of them. The two women agreed to a 7:00 PM arrival time, concluding the call. Jason glanced at his watch, noting that the timing was ideal from their Altamonte Springs location. He un-muted the car's radio for some background music during their ride to the restaurant. Instead of some easy-listening music, he heard: *"A hurricane warning has been issued for Clearwater, St Petersburg, Tampa, and Pasco County. A hurricane watch is in place for Lake, Orange, and Seminole Counties, to include the Ocala National Forest. Hurricane Miguel is expected to make landfall near St. Petersburg in the next 24 to 36 hours as a Category Two hurricane. The next advisory will be issued at 10:00 PM. We now return you to the regularly scheduled program."* The music resumed; Jason glanced over at Laura muttering, "Great."

They arrived at Brunch 'N Lunch with 5 minutes to spare. "Look," he told Laura, "There's Tara's Lincoln. The place looks smacked...we might be waiting a while for a table. But first...we've gotta find a parking spot."

He was just about to pull into the traffic lane when Laura exclaimed, "Wait! That SUV (pointing at a car parked in the spot just in front of them with its backup lights on) is looking to back out." Jason shifted into reverse. He backed up while simultaneously lightly tooting the horn. The SUV's driver took the hint; backed up and pulled out, vacating the spot for them. An arm suddenly appearing out the window waving in appreciation.

"Are you kidding me?" said Jason, glancing at Laura. *"My Pleasure,"* as he adroitly pulled into the newly vacated prime spot.

"Wait," said Laura. "Are you kidding *me?* The same thing happened last time we were here. Talk about the luck of the Irish."

"Technically," observed a grinning Jason, "luck of the *Scottish*...but point taken." They got out of the car and walked the short distance to the door. Upon entering, they saw just a single person waiting for a table...*Tara.*

"Hey Tara," greeted Laura, "how long you been here?" Jason, smiling, nodded at Tara.

"Maybe 5 minutes," she replied. "Did you see Emily?"

"No," they both answered simultaneously, then laughed. Jason continued, "She may be trying to find a parking spot - we got lucky - it's tough this time of day. Well, I'll be damned," he swore in surprise. He waved his arm at the young waitress standing next to the donut display case. "Kathy!" He shouted. She turned, recognizing Jason immediately, then quickly walking over. "Well hello *stranger,*" she said, smiling broadly.

"*We've GOT to Stop Meeting Like This,*" said Jason; the two of them breaking out in laughter.

In an aside, Laura told the bemused Tara about the pair's quirky relationship. They watched as the waitress summoned a busboy. After a brief discussion the busboy disappeared into the far end of the restaurant. In less than two minutes, the busboy peered around the corner at the back. Kathy grabbed three menus at the greeting station, glanced at the trio saying, "This way please." A moment later, they were being seated at a choice window table - the busboy busily wiping the just-cleared table. Jason gave him an appreciative nod. Turning to Kathy, he said, "Once again, you've worked your magic!" Turning to the others he continued, "This pretty young lady is Brunch 'N Lunch's best kept secret."

Blushing, Kathy said, "I don't know about all that, but I do know that you and Miss Laura will have coffee...and you, ma'am?" She asked Tara, who replied simply, "Yes, coffee please." Jason informed the waitress they were waiting on Emily's arrival, who she remembered. Kathy promised she would keep an eye out, then turned and left.

Tara observed, "Nice girl. The second *Jason crush* I've seen in as many days. Don't you find it annoying, Jason?"

"No, *he* doesn't," interrupted Laura, with a look of faux petulance ... *"but I do."* Everyone broke into laughter.

A moment later, Kathy the Waitress reappeared with *four* coffees and Emily right on her heels. *"Look who I found,"* she announced. Emily took the vacant seat next to Tara as Kathy set the tray of coffees down and handed her a menu. "I'll give you folks some time and come back for your orders," abruptly disappearing around the corner. The table went quiet while everyone perused their menu's dinner selections.

Kathy returned shortly to take their orders. As soon as she departed, Jason briefed Tara on their confrontation with the would-be-assassin ending with his capture. Tara brought her colleagues up to date about Diane Whittaker's phone call with John; concluding with Diane's reference to "Maddy's niece" that Tara interpreted as code for *they've got Sam.* Her companions nodded in agreement. Emily was about to ask a question when Jason interrupted her. Pulling his phone from his pocket, he said, "Excuse me, I've got to take this." He got up, disappearing around the corner, presumably headed out the front door.

After Jason left, Emily asked Laura, "So... did you guys find out anything significant from our Russian friend?"

"Not much," she replied, "He gave us his name which matched his I.D., then screamed diplomatic immunity. I'm pretty sure he knows by now what he can do with his *diplomatic immunity."*

"So," inquired Tara, "are we to assume that he will now be *professionally* interrogated?"

"Indeed," replied Laura. "He is currently in the custody of one Jaydan Sanders, among the best of the Agency's interrogators."

Tara perked up. "That name sounds familiar...hmm...is he by chance related to *Baylin Sanders*?"

"Sure is," confirmed Laura. "He's Baylin's nephew. How do you know Baylin?"

"I've known him for years...I was assigned to his security team when I worked for NASA. His work was highly classified...he was NASA's top R&D scientist at the time. As I recall, he had a lot to do with stealth technology. Anyway, a really nice guy...we became friends and have stayed in touch over the years. Small world, huh?"

Just then, Jason reappeared, looking pretty amped up. "That was Jaydan," he announced, - looking from Tara to Emily - "our interrogator. *I've got some news.*"

The detective reported Vaslov admitted to being involved in securing the *Project Expose'* technology along with the related blackmail / kidnapping plot. The Russian had gone on to say that Sam had indeed been abducted and was confined in the same location as Diane. He allowed that Sam's kidnapping was *not* part of the original plan but rather a stupid blunder by one of his comrades. He assured Jaydan that the women were uninjured and being treated well. Further, he said it was their intent to release the women unharmed once *Project Expose'* data was turned over. Vaslov had implied that his return to his comrades was now a condition of the affair's successful resolution.

Kathy appeared with their dinners, and intuiting the group's desire for privacy, quickly served the table and left. The four discussed the related events in between bites; all of them suddenly realizing they were hungrier than they had thought. Laura suggested they reconvene at Jason's apartment in the morning to strategize over breakfast with unanimous agreement.

As they left Jason gave Kathy an affectionate hug, thanking her once more as he pressed a hundred-dollar bill in her hand. Laura, catching a glimpse of the denomination, looked at him, eyebrow arched.

Catching her eye, he grinned sheepishly and said, "...*What?*"

Everyone said their goodbyes; Tara and Emily left to have drinks at a local watering-hole; Jason and Laura drove the short distance around Lake Eola back to his apartment.

** ** **

Jason lay in bed, feeling the warm glow of the two Cabernets he had imbibed. He saw the outline of his lover as she approached, her naked body sensuously revealed in the soft glow of moonlight streaming in the window. He felt her welcoming warmth as she snuggled up to him. They intertwined fingers, joining in a long, impassioned kiss, before losing themselves to the intimacy of the night.

** ** **

Chapter Thirteen
A New Twist

Jason rolled over, fully expecting to bump into his mate, but no, her side of the bed was empty. He sat bolt upright, glanced at his watch and saw it was now 6:15 AM. *Shit,* he thought, *I over-slept.* Which was true. It was a rare day he slept past 5:00 AM, weekends included. He climbed out of bed, grabbed his robe, and headed to the bathroom for a quick shower.

Laura was opening a package of bacon when she suddenly picked up a subtle scent of bayberry. *That's Jason,* she thought, as he embraced her from behind.

"Well, good morning sleepy head," she said, turning around for her first kiss of the day.

"So *why,*" asked her lover, "did you let me sleep in? We have company coming."

"Not anymore," said Laura. "They aren't coming, and you needed the extra sleep."

"What do you mean, *they're not coming?*" inquired a perplexed Jason.

Laura explained that Baylin Sanders - Jaydan's uncle - had arrived in a private Agency jet and was being picked up by Emily, who would then drive him over to meet with Tara at Dynamadics.

"That explains breakfast, but aside from being Jaydan's uncle, *who* is Baylin Sanders and why is he meeting Tara at Dynamadics?" Asked Jason.

"Baylin Sanders," she began, "Is the foremost aerospace scientist in the United States, if not the entire world. Think Spaceplane *Explorer.* Most academics consider him the Stephen Hawking of Aerospace Science. He's the guy that developed the cloaking technology *Project Expose'* is designed to protect; which, I am very sure has to do with his sudden appearance."

"Is that all?" said Jason, feigning sarcasm, but truly impressed with his reputation.

Just then, Jason heard his phone's ringtone. He stepped over to the bar and picked it up. "Good morning, Tara," he greeted, putting the phone on speaker as he laid it on the bar.

"...and Emily is bringing him over as we speak. I'm sure Laura can fill you in on who exactly Baylin is - Jason glanced at Laura, who nodded - and what he has to do with *Project Expose'*. Reason I'm calling...I need you guys to meet us in my office...say in about an hour?"

"Copy that," replied Jason. "Gotta go now...see ya in an hour." He terminated the call and looked over at Laura who was now putting the bacon back in the fridge. "By the time you're dressed, I'll have the coffee ready...to go of course." Jason headed to the bedroom to dress as Laura set about making the coffee. She turned on the TV, catching Weatherman Sam Spade in the middle of today's weather forecast.

"Miguel should make landfall on the Pinellas County coast around 3:00 PM as a Category 1 storm with winds of 80 mph gusting over 100. The current track takes it on a course through Lake County, then curving slightly northeast through the Ocala National Forest before exiting somewhere just to the south of Jacksonville. On its current projected path, the center should pass just north of metro Orlando. By the time it reaches our area, it should diminish to a tropical storm. But make no mistake, this is a dangerous storm not to be taken lightly. While the government has recommended sheltering in place, if you must travel, exercise extreme caution. All tolls have been suspended until further notice."

Laura clicked the TV off just as Jason appeared. "Let's go!" He exclaimed, both heading for the door; him with a briefcase, her with the - *arguably more important* - coffee.

** ** **

Whittaker was sitting in the exact same booth at the same Florida's Turnpike Plaza they had occupied during the previous meeting. He looked out the window at the lowering sky. The landscape trees in the parking lot that were bending slightly in response to the steadily increasing wind. He glanced at the entrance and saw Dimitrov walking toward the table. It was exactly 8:00 AM. *Always on time,* thought Whittaker... *I'll give him that.*

"Dobroye utro (Good morning), Sergei," Whittaker greeted in Russian, trying his best to sound friendly.

"Dobroye utro," Dimitrov responded with a slight smile, "I didn't know you spoke Russian."

"Hemhoro (a little)," replied Whittaker. They both chuckled. "Anyway," he continued, "I hope today our mutual efforts will finally bear fruit."

Before Dimitrov could respond, their waitress arrived to take their orders, pouring coffee for each man as they quickly perused their menus. She took their orders then abruptly departed.

"My kinda waitress," said Whittaker, "gets right to it...remind me to leave a good tip. So, you were about to say..."

"Da...Yes," replied the Russian, "I was about to say...I think we may have a weather problem to deal with."

"Yes, there is that, but we now have something new in the mix. Do you know a *Nikita Vaslov*?" Inquired Whittaker.

"I do," answered Dimitrov. "he's a low-level security operative of the Kremlin, why do you ask?"

"Because" explained the Agent, "he's presently in the custody of the CIA somewhere in the Orlando area having been captured by our favorite detective, Mr. McVay, who he was apparently trying to assassinate."

"And you know this how...?" Inquired the Russian.

"That's not important," responded Whittaker, "*what is important* is that he's revealed we have the Samantha woman in our custody. He has proposed a trade - McVay's partner for him. At first blush, I viewed this as a terrible complication. After some thought, however, I believe we can turn this new circumstance to our advantage."

Dimitrov was lightly rubbing his ample beard as he contemplated what Whittaker was telling him. Their waitress appeared with their orders, inquired if there would "be anything else;" after their mutual "no, thank you," turned and abruptly left.

"I think I see what you're getting at," observed Dimitrov. "Rather than being a liability for us, the woman becomes *an insurance policy.*"

"*Da, My friend!*" Exclaimed the rogue agent. "Exactly right! We use her to ensure the turnover/exchange doesn't become an ambush."

Both men smiled, each pleased with the apparent fortunate turn of events. Over breakfast they discussed the details of the pending turnover/exchange, believing the end was now finally in sight. But there was that damn storm to think about.

** ** **

"Gotta say, I'm impressed!" Exclaimed Sam, wiping the sweat from her brow. "Look at you, *fifty* sit-ups and you've hardly broken a sweat."

"Thanks Sam, but number one, it takes *a lot* to get me sweaty and number two, I've been - like you - an exercise nut all my life. Plus, I'm skinny. I'll bet you've got twenty pounds on me, and you're only a little taller. *Wait* - no offense...you're in *great shape*, solid as a rock!"

Sam laughed. "None taken. I know where you're coming from. We both have plenty of Incentive to stay trim; me for work, you for...well, cause it's the right thing to do. Holy crap! Look at that thing!"

Diane turned around and saw the image of the giant storm on the TV. It was depicted just coming ashore in the St. Pete area of Pinellas County. The weather guy intoned: *"...is still strengthening but should slowly begin to lose its punch as the eye moves over land. Current wind speed near the eye wall is 110 mph with gusts in excess of 125 mph. Miguel is now projected to move in a near straight line on a northeast course that will take it through Lake County, the Ocala National Forest, into Union County, then Flagler County before exiting just south of Jacksonville. The good news is the brunt of the storm will barely brush the Orlando metro area and by that time will have been downgraded to a tropical storm."*

The two women looked at each other, both considering the integrity of a log cabin.

"Shit," said Diane, "what are we gonna do?" Looking anxiously at her friend.

"Actually," replied Sam, "I *do* have something in mind..."

** ** **

Jason pulled into the spot next to Emily's car, already parked in one of the *Reserved – Visitor* spots close to the Dynamadics main entrance. He glanced at his watch, noting it was 9:07 AM. "Damn, we're late," he observed.

"Don't fret big guy," teased Laura, "I think they'll still let us in."

He chuckled. "Yeah...but you know how I am about being late."

"It's gonna be OK, I promise," she teased. They both laughed.

They got out of the car, immediately feeling the wind, which annoyed Laura, whose hair was being seriously blown asunder. Jason, looking skyward, remarked that it looked like a squall was imminent, prompting the pair to make a dash for the door. Upon entering, they were met by Security Sergeant Thomas.

"Good morning Mr. McVay...Ms.Sparks," greeted a broadly smiling Thomas. "Long time, no see," he joked.

"Yeah, right," replied the detective, "and Good morning to you. It's getting pretty gusty out there," he continued as Laura stood to the side effecting what repairs she could to her wind-blown hair.

"The hurricane is supposed to just miss us, but it's still gonna be nasty," said Thomas.

With a nod, Jason headed to the Reception Desk, closely followed by Laura, still fussing with her hair. A smiling Jennifer warmly greeted them. *She should be a model,* thought Jason.

"Good morning Mr. McVay, Ms. Sparks," she said, "please go right up."

"Thanks Jennifer," replied Jason, "have a nice day." The pair turned and walked to the elevator.

Exiting on the fourth floor, they headed to the now-familiar Executive Office Suite. Entering the Reception area, they were directed to the Conference Room. Jason opened the door for Laura. Stepping in behind her he noticed Tucker Henry at the head of the table. Seated in her usual place on his left was Tara. On Tucker's right was a rather good looking casually dressed man who he guessed to be about his age. *Must be Baylin,* he thought. Emily occupied the seat next to him. As Jason and Laura walked to their seats next to Tara, both the new person and Tara stood up.

Tara proceeded with introductions: "Jason, I'd like to introduce Baylin Sanders. Baylin is an astrophysicist working for NASA. As a matter of fact, he's the head of R & D there. Baylin; this is Jason McVay, our lead investigator. I believe you already know Laura." The two men reached across the table to shake hands.

Jason said, "It's a pleasure, no - *honor* - to meet you, Baylin. Your reputation precedes you."

"Thanks, Jason...a pleasure for me as well. It may interest you to know that I am *well aquatinted* with your sister, Sandy. For many years. Laura as well."

"Indeed," responded Jason. Pointedly looking at Laura, he continued, *"I did not know that."*

Seeing Jason's irritation, Tucker Henry jumped in. "Don't be upset with Laura...or Sandy for that matter. They were simply observing CIA protocol. You see, in addition to his NASA job, Baylin is, like Laura and Sandy, a *Senior* CIA Agent. As a matter of fact, he is here today in that capacity. The three of them were part of a now disbanded, super-secret team of 6 select CIA and FBI Agents called *Serendipity.* What they did is classified at the highest level...suffice it to say they quite literally *saved the Earth.* The entire team was awarded the *Medal of Freedom."*

Jason glanced at Laura, then reached across the table to shake Baylin's hand once again. "I had no idea, Baylin, you have my sincerest respect and appreciation for what you - glancing back at Laura - *what all of you did,* whatever *that* was...again, thank you!"

Laura said, "Out of respect for you, Director McBride authorized us to bring you into the loop, albeit in a limited fashion. You are now part of a group of 35 people...*on the entire planet...*who are aware of Serendipity's previous existence. And Emily, Director Upton - himself a Serendipity alumnus - authorized your inclusion. Needless to say, this information can never be revealed under any circumstances." Both Jason and Emily nodded in silent assent.

Tara glanced at Tucker, saying, "With your permission I'd like to turn the discussion over to Baylin?" the CEO nodding in affirmation.

Once again, Baylin stood. "Thanks Tara," he began, "the reason I'm here is to implement a new strategy. We are going to turn over *Project Expose'* to the Russians. Not, however, in its present form."

Baylin informed the group (Tucker and Tara of course already aware) that *Project Expose'* was designed to disable the cloaking technology the Russians had recently stolen by remotely disabling the ability of pilots to switch cloaking on and off. Langley has determined they are now mere months away from being able to incorporate this technology into their military aircraft. Further, a CIA/FBI task force has concluded the Russians will inevitably obtain this technology, no matter our Intelligence agencies on-going efforts to prevent it.

He went on to say that Jason's sister Sandy, who happened to head the aforementioned joint task force, suggested that instead of wasting resources on preventing the inevitable loss, they instead turn it into an intelligence coup.

"The short version," continued Baylin, "Is that we *change the coding of the software.* More precisely, we add a layer of *hidden code* to the original *Project Expose'* software."

"Wait," interrupted Emily, "I'm certainly no computer genius, but the Russians *must have* at least *one* among their computer scientists - who will discover our subterfuge."

Tucker Henry immediately jumped in: "Not to worry, Emily! What they *don't have* is Baylin Sanders! This is the man who created the very technology they stole. And now *he is going to add the hidden coding.* Case closed."

Before Emily could acknowledge, Baylin said, "Thanks for your vote of confidence Tucker. But, as I have to constantly remind people...that was, and continues to be, a *team effort.* I am confident we will be able to conceal this new coding from our Russian counterparts."

Baylin explained Sandy's idea. She had proposed that *Project Expose'* be altered in such a way that our military could "see" their cloaked aircraft without the Russians' knowledge. In other words, their pilots would believe their craft were invisible, when in fact they were not, at least to the American military. Baylin said that he would have to create corresponding software to allow our military to secretly communicate with the new hidden coding in the *Project Expose'* software.

Baylin stood, saying, "You folks will have to excuse me, I've got to get down to the Software Development Lab to help the team finish up the *Project Expose'* coding modifications."

The rest of the group stood as Baylin went around the table shaking hands with the men and hugging the women before leaving. As they again took their seats, Jason observed, "That's the first honest to God hero I've ever met! He's given much to his country...indeed the world."

"*You have no idea...,*" said Laura under her breath.

Glancing in Laura's direction, Jason asked, "What?"

"Oh, I was just agreeing with you," Laura replied with a smile.

The next twenty minutes were spent discussing how to make sure the exchange of the modified *Project Expose'* thumb drive and the women captives went smoothly - at the same time careful not to arouse the Russians' suspicion it was *too easy.* Now they had a hurricane to factor in. That would have to be played by ear. Tucker said he would act as liaison with CIA Director McBride, bringing her up to date after the meeting. Jason said he and Laura would head over to see Agent Sanders at the safe house; Tara would be joining John Stockwell; and Emily would remain with Baylin. Their assignments established; the group adjourned to begin their various tasks.

** ** **

Jason and Laura dashed out the front door, making a beeline toward the car. Despite the short distance, they were pretty wet. On the way to the safe house, they stopped by the local Outback Restaurant and picked up the five "to go" steak dinners they had ordered earlier at Dynamadics. Just in the nick of time, too...most every business was closing in response to the oncoming hurricane. Though mass power outages were a thing of the past - all homes and buildings were individually powered by solar energy with back-up generators - travel still remained a very real danger. *Everybody* was preparing to hunker down.

After a short drive from the restaurant, they pulled into the safe house's driveway, immediately seeing Jaydan holding the front door open. After another mad dash, they were safely enclosed in a dry sanctuary. The wind was fairly howling now with the rain pelting the front window.

"We come bearing gifts!" Exclaimed a grinning Jason as he set the large Outback take-out bag on the foyer table. The couple stood by the door, not wanting to drip all over the house.

"Very cool," enthused Jaydan. "Hang on a second, let me get you some towels," he said, disappearing down the hall. He quickly returned, handing a large towel to each of them. "Now it's getting nasty," said Jaydan, stating the obvious.

"It is," agreed Laura. "How's our guest doing?"

"He's been quite the chatterbox, actually," allowed Jaydan. "Oh, and he's *not* who he says is. And now that I think about it, explains his sudden 'chatterbox' turn. Langley called to tell me our Nikita Vaslov is actually one *Vladimir Kaslov;* a very high-ranking Russian Security Agent. Apparently he's willing to tell us anything - as long as we promise to keep his true identity from Sergei Dimitrov. He doesn't know it, but when Langley informed me who he really was, they instructed me to not expose his real identity to *anyone* outside the agency."

Jason asked, "Anyone besides me getting hungry?"

"That's a big 10-4!" Enthused Jaydan. "I'm ready when you are," he confirmed.

"NO!" interrupted Laura. "We're gonna wait for Emily to get here;" putting the issue to rest.

** ** **

Chapter Fourteen
Stormy Weather

John Stockwell, hearing a light tapping noise, glanced up to see Tara standing at his already open office door.

"Have a moment?" Inquired the Security Chief.

"Yes, yes," he replied, "please... come in." Tara strode into his office; Stockwell indicating a chair facing his desk. "I just finished reading Baylin Sander's coding changes to *Project Expose's* software programming. Brilliant. Talk about a 'Trojan horse'. If he hadn't outlined it for me, I *never* would know that coding existed within the program...and I'm pretty damned competent when it comes to computer coding, if I do say so myself! Thank you for getting the document to me so quickly. I can't get over it...just brilliant. Brilliant!"

"Should come as no surprise John," observed Tara. "The man is a genius after all. The same guy that gave us the stellar drive *and* the cloaking technology *Project Expose'* is based on."

"I know Tara," he acknowledged, "still...for a tech geek like me, it's simply awe-inspiring."

Just then, the ringtone of the Whittaker-supplied burner phone announced an incoming call. He glanced at Tara. She nodded, indicating she knew who was calling.

Stockwell answered, "Hello...yes, I'm alone...hold on while I shut my door (Tara got up to close the door). Yes, of course, it's very bad here as well. Certainly. I understand. I'll be waiting for your call. No, I think I'll wait out the storm right here. All right then." Stockwell laid the phone on his desk. "That was Whittaker. I'm sure you've already surmised there won't be any exchange meeting before the storm passes."

"No surprise there," said Tara. "I think I'm gonna stay put as well. I don't relish being out in this weather. Plus, all the comforts of home are here anyway (she was referencing the on-site Guest Quarters with all the creature comforts one might need)."

"Before I head back to my Office," she continued, "I want you to know Baylin Sanders thinks highly of you...I think he used the term 'cutting edge' to describe your work...and while you did exercise poor judgement, in his view you are well down the path to redemption. Keep that in your mind as we work toward resolution of this nasty business."

"Thanks for that, Tara. I promise you...all of you, I will do all I can to make things right."

"I'm sure you will," responded Tara as she looked out the window at the intensifying storm. "There goes Emily's Traverse (a smaller version of the Lincoln Navigator). I hope they get to Orlando International before they close the airport."

** ** **

"Damn," said Emily, glancing at the warning on the car's view screen: *The LENR PowerPac Requires Maintenance.* "Talk about bad timing..." The LENR PowerPac being the nuclear power source for this vehicle - for *all* vehicles - a version of the cold fusion system first used to power the spaceplane *Explorer.* It was nearly twelve years since the last internal combustion engine had been in use. And the PowerPac performed almost flawlessly. Almost. But even then, it was inevitably a computer glitch causing the problem.

"Not to worry," said Baylin, "the vehicle has enough stored energy to function for another 10,000 miles." He should know, being the guy who developed the first LENR drive for spacecraft that led to its adaption for all transport vehicles.

"You're right Baylin," sighed Emily. "Just me being edgy when any little thing goes wrong."

"I get it Emily," replied Baylin. "It's part of the baggage we *perfectionist personality* types have to accept. Acknowledge that some things are simply out of our control. Always apply critical thinking to any situation; invariably you will come to a well-reasoned conclusion."

"Easy for you to say, smart guy that you are," teased Emily. "But thanks - that's certainly sound advice - and appreciated."

The autopilot informed them that they would reach their destination within ten minutes. The pair's safety was never an issue; all modern vehicles were equipped with state-of-the-art autopilot systems featuring radar guidance and obstacle avoidance systems allowing for navigation even in total darkness.

"You're smarter than you think, Emily," opined Baylin. "I took the liberty of reading your FBI Performance File. I'm impressed. So is Director Upton. Your career is on a very bright path, but you didn't hear that from me. Speaking of *bright paths*, you should know that Agent Grande has been reassigned to the NASA Security unit, effective immediately. And yes, it is most definitely a promotion."

Emily, in an almost child-like manner, clapped her hands in glee. "Sorry," she said, "I'm just really happy for him."

"He still has much to learn, but his strength of character is as big as his size. He'll be the perfect fit for our team. No pun intended," he added with a smile.

"Arriving at destination," announced the autopilot. The NASA jet suddenly came into view, sitting on the tarmac adjacent to the VIP Hanger. The car came to a stop just short of the left side wing tip. Baylin tapped his watch and the plane's access ramp came down as the interior lighting illuminated. He reached over, placing his hand on Emily's shoulder.

"Gotta go, Thanks for your help. Keep up the great work Special Agent Cast!" Before she could reply, he grabbed his *Go Bag,* opened the door, and made a mad dash through the driving rain, quickly disappearing into the craft. She heard the low rumble of the jet as it taxied to the runway. A moment later she saw the planes marker lights fade from sight as it soundlessly lifted off into the storm.

She directed the autopilot to "take me to 1275 Randall Drive, Altamonte Springs."

** ** **

The two women were focused on the flat screen as weatherman Sam Spade informed them, "*...the storm has weakened slightly since making landfall. Windspeed is currently 90 mph with occasional gusts up to 115 mph...*" Just then they heard the front door open, with all five of their captors crowding into the cabin. Three of them stood by the far wall while their apparent leader walked over to address them in his heavily Russian-accented voice: "We are here to have meal. Our cooking stove is not work. We will make our dinner; eat, and then return to our cabin. You will stay seated where you are until we leave. Don't look at us at table. You may continue to watch TV."

He walked into the pantry. Two of the others walked over to the dining table and took a seat. The third Russian - the odiferous one - joined his comrade in the kitchen, passing directly in front of the women seated on the sofa. Diane began gagging, prompting Sam to break out in a laughing fit. Diane, between gags, elbowed Sam in the ribs several times.

The "spokesman" (apparently his comrades couldn't speak English) demanded to know "*What* so funny?"

"Oh nothing," said Sam as she pinched herself in an effort to get under control. "We're just really nervous because of the storm." About the same time, Diane discreetly covered her nose with the gagging finally abating. Sam envisioned "waves" of stench, much like one would see in a cartoon, wafting off *Smelly Guy,* eventually suffocating the women with the horrific odor. She felt another laughing fit coming on - fighting it off by biting her tongue so hard she actually drew blood.

** ** **

They could hear the rain pounding against the front of the house. Laura set her phone back down on the kitchen counter. "That was Emily," she announced. "She'll be arriving in five minutes."

"Thank God!" Exclaimed Jaydan. "I'm so hungry my stomach's growling in three different languages!"

"Amen to that," Jason chimed in. "Let's remember, it's not Emily's fault...so *no teasing.*" Laura's ringtone activated. It was Emily. She put the phone on speaker.

"I've just turned onto Cassidy, but the water's almost up to the car door. It's terrible out here. I hate to ask, but can someone meet me at the car? I can only carry one thing and I don't want to come back out."

"Sure," replied Jason as he grabbed a poncho, "I'll be out as soon as you pull in the driveway." He dropped the poncho over his head then looked out the window just as Emily's car slowly pulled into the driveway. Then it happened. The chill descended as everything froze. The *movie in his mind* began playing. Jason saw himself open the front door and make a mad dash for the passenger side just as Emily emerged from the driver side door. Suddenly, he heard a loud crack; glancing up just in time to see a huge Oak tree coming down on him and Emily before everything went black.

Real time resumed. Jason turned toward the bar where Laura's phone lay and shouted, "EMILY, GET OUT OF THE CAR *RIGHT NOW - RUN TO THE STREET, DO IT THIS INSTANT!!!*"

He turned back to the window in time to see the car's interior light come on as Emily emerged from the door. Suddenly they saw a bright white flash followed by a tremendously loud boom causing the house to shake on its foundation.

"What the hell!" yelled a wide-eyed Jaydan as Jason tore out the front door which violently slammed shut. He and Laura quickly went to the door, both pushing mightily to open it. As they forced the door open against the hellish wind, a thoroughly soaked Emily ran in quickly followed by an equally drenched Jason a full minute later, holding two wet, but intact carry out bags. Jaydan took the bags from the dripping Jason and set them on the table.

"Oh my God!" exclaimed Emily. "I almost got killed!" She ran over to Jason, who was picking bits of tree bark off his Poncho. She grabbed him in a tight embrace profusely thanking him for the life-saving warning. After she let go, he remarked, "You were pretty nimble climbing over that tree trunk, girl! I don't think I've ever seen anyone move so fast in a hurricane."

Everybody laughed as the tension began to subside. "Jason, *how* did you know that tree was coming down?" Inquired a curious Jaydan.

"Didn't you hear that crackling sound just before the loud crack?" Asked Jason, stealing a glance in Laura's direction.

"Yeah, I heard it too, but wasn't really sure what it meant," added Laura as she glanced back at Jason, a knowing glint in her eye.

"All right, then," said a seemingly placated Jaydan. "So... *can we eat now?*" he pleaded.

"Sure," replied Laura. "Emily, why don't you and I get the dinners ready to serve while I bring you up to date on our *guest,* who at the moment is tied up in the bedroom," both women laughing at Laura's corny pun.

Jason smiled as he looked at Jaydan who was good-naturedly shaking his head. They watched the women head into the kitchen, Jaydan looking forward to *finally* eating.

** ** **

The two women slowly moved closer together on the couch. In a low whisper, Sam said, "*Smelly Guy* is sitting the furthest away...lucky for us...I can barely smell him at this distance."

"Don't you start," replied Diane as she nudged her friend in the ribs.

"Ouch," whispered Sam. "I wonder what they're up to...jabbering away in Russian."

"*I speak Russian,*" whispered Diane.

"*Really*?" Asked a newly perked-up Sam.

"Da... *yes...,*" confirmed Diane. "So...be quiet, grab the remote and lower the sound on the TV."

Sam lowered the sound level and the women sat back - Sam paying attention to the weather guy on TV while Diane cocked her head in the direction of the kitchen table. After about 15 minutes had passed, the men stood up, putting their masks back on. Four of them headed out the front door. The lead guy came over to address his captives.

"We are leaving to go to our guard posts outside cabin. Each side of cabin is being watched. As you know, strong storm is upon us. We Russians are not afraid of a little heavy weather. This cabin will continue to be guarded as before. I am sure you not so stupid to try escape. You would, of course, die. Just stay warm and cozy in cabin...I assure you it is of strong construction and quite safe. We will be just outside if something happens to cabin, but as I say is not likely. I leave you now." The Russian turned and left; the door banging shut behind him.

A curious expression crossing her face, Sam looked at Diane. "So... *what did they talk about?*"

Diane teased, "A little of this...a little of that. No, I'm kidding. What they're going to do isn't what they told us. The leader guy said he was going to tell us they'd be watching the cabin as before and would reassure us we would be safe during the storm. Actually, only *one guy* is going to be posted...on the front porch. The rest of them are going to be in their next-door cabin, nice and dry and cozy. They'll do shifts of one hour on and four hours off. They think we'd be too afraid to try and escape in a hurricane."

Sam sat in silence for a moment as she pondered what her friend had just told her. Then she spoke, looking Diane right in the eye. "Diane, I believe we're in mortal danger. I'm gonna make a run for it. I've figured out where the helicopter is from this location...between a mile to a mile and a half from here. I can get an idea when the storm will be letting up enough for the helicopter to fly and time my run accordingly."

"You can pilot a helicopter?" Asked an incredulous Diane.

"Sure," she replied, "I learned during my Marine Corps service. It's been a while, but you know, it's like the 'riding the bike' thing. Plus, it's a pretty basic model...I won't have any trouble."

"I'm going with you!" Exclaimed Diane.

"No, No!" Responded Sam. "It's way too dangerous. If anything goes wrong, they'll kill us on the spot! I'll have a better chance alone. No offense, but I've got the training and experience."

"That's true, but you yourself said I was in great shape...*and* I'm a marathon runner," pleaded Diane. "Plus, they're *not going to kill us.* During their conversation, *Smelly Guy* asked what to do *if* we tried to escape. The lead guy said *under no circumstances were we to be harmed.* This order apparently came from the top...he was very emphatic about it. I guess we under-estimated just how valuable we are - *alive.*"

"Well, that's good to know," said Sam. "I'm still reluctant to put you in any kind of danger, but under these new circumstances...if you're that determined, well I guess OK, then."

"Thanks, Sam! I really need to do this...it's really important to me."

** ** **

"I must thank you for such a wonderful meal, you have treated me well under the circumstances. I hope somehow I can have our side respond in kind. This espionage thing is, after all just a business, yes?"

"You tried to kill us Vladimir Kaslov a.k.a. Nikita Vaslov," observed Laura.

"Nothing personal, I assure you, just business. Nasty business, but again, *just business.*"

"Moving on," interrupted Jaydan, "what can you tell us about our women's location?"

"Ah," responded Kaslov, "I can assure you they are safe...and if I may say, quite comfortable in a luxury cabin located in the Ocala National Forest. They have been treated well. I am prepared to provide you all the necessary details of the plot and its principals as soon as I have confirmation of my agreement with Director McBride."

** ** **

Chapter Fifteen
Run Like The Devil

Diane, putting the last of their supper dishes in the dishwasher, asked her friend, "I'm gonna have a coffee...would you like one?"

Sam, intently watching the storm details unfold on TV, glanced up at Diane. "Sure, sounds great," before turning her attention back to Sam Spade's ongoing hurricane coverage. As Diane set about brewing their coffee, she continued mulling over their upcoming escape attempt. While she had great confidence in Sam and her ability to handle this kind of situation - the woman was a Marine combat veteran after all - she questioned her own resolve. One thing for sure, at the end of this day she'd know a lot more about her strength of character.

Sam watched the weather graphics depict the storm's intensity as it cut a path through the central part of the state. The other *Sam* - the weather guy - outlined the storm's timetable, *"...reaching maximum intensity during the overnight hours before rapidly diminishing just before sunrise."* Diane arrived with their coffees and took a seat next to her buddy.

"So..." began Sam, "looks like we're gonna catch a break with the storm. The timing should work out great. In another four hours - about midnight - the eye should pass over us and then the storm's gonna pick up forward motion, mostly moving away right about daybreak. We've got to set a timetable...leave in the darkness, just as the storm starts to let up; then it will get light as we make our way to the chopper. By the time we get there, it should be daylight!"

"Sounds good," Enthused Diane, "But how are you gonna be able to find the helicopter?"

"My watch," Sam answered.

"Your watch?" Queried Diane with a puzzled expression, "What do you mean...*my watch*?"

Sam smiled mischievously. "My watch has a feature within the compass app called *Tracer. Tracer* keeps track of all my movements for the past 48 hours. When I activate the app, I'll be able to retrace yesterday's ride in their ATV from the chopper to the cabin."

"I'll be damned," said Diane. "That is definitely some pretty cool *cloak and dagger* stuff!"

"Speaking of *stuff*...we need to get some things together. Look around for flashlights, hunting knives, things like that," suggested Sam.

"How about ponchos or some other rain gear?" Asked Diane.

"No," replied Sam, "that would only slow us down...we're just gonna have to get wet. Plus, if the timing works out, the storm will be letting up right around daylight."

For the next 15 minutes, the pair scavenged the cabin. Diane found a hunting knife in a utility drawer and a pair of small, but very bright, flashlights in the cosmetics cabinet in the loft bathroom. Sam discovered a pocket-sized tool kit that contained both a common and Phillips screwdriver, 2 pairs of pliers, including needle nose, a small mirror; and a bonus: the kit was equipped with an interior light. Sam placed her items on the dining table next to a medium sized carving knife enclosed in its own protective sheath. Diane came downstairs and put the hunting knife and mini flashlights next to Sam's stuff. They stood on opposite sides of the table looking over their escape paraphernalia. "Let's sit down," suggested Sam. They walked the short distance to the sofa and plopped down. Sam glanced at her watch.

"It's 9:30," she announced, "time we get our act together." Diane nodded in response. "Here's what we're gonna do...," continued the detective.

Sam outlined her plan in some detail, explaining her reasoning as she went along. She asked Diane to interrupt her at any point if she didn't understand or if she saw a possible flaw. Sam said they would make the attempt at 5:00 AM sharp. The timing was critical. The storm was predicted to begin diminishing around 4:00 AM as it pulled out of the area. While it would stay relatively windy, the rain would stop. Tomorrow's sunrise was scheduled at 6:20 AM which meant it would begin to get light around 5:30 AM.

At 5:00, Diane would create a distraction at the front door, allowing Sam to come up from behind and disable the guard. Diane raised her hand - already alarmed with the prospect of Sam not being able to disable her larger adversary. Sam assured her friend that she was confident of success - with the caveat that Diane did her part. Next, the pair would head to the ATV, making their escape in the vehicle. If everything moved on schedule, by the time they reached the helicopter the rain should have stopped with the winds dropping off to a more reasonable 20 to 30 mph. At this point, Sam would have sufficient daylight to fly under *visual flight rules* so she could get them to Orlando and safety.

"Good plan!" Exclaimed Diane. "Gotta be honest, though. I'm still nervous about your taking out the guard on the front porch."

"I understand," responded Sam, "It is unnerving. First, if by *taking out* you think I intend to kill him, I assure you that is *Not* the case. I'm just gonna knock him out. Then you're gonna tie him up while I gag him...next we go the ATV and *get out of Dodge!* The only way I would ever kill anyone would be to save my own neck, or someone else's."

Diane stayed silent for a moment as she processed all this in her mind. *Sam knows what she's doing. She's got tons of training and experience.* She spoke up, "OK, then. I'm good with it. I'm confident in your ability...and *you* should know that *I've got your back!*"

"Thanks, partner," Sam replied, "I know you do!"

They both sat in silence as the wind howled outside with the rain pounding the cabin. On the TV, Sam Spade, the weather guy, had removed his suit jacket and loosened his tie as he kept up a running commentary about the ongoing Tropical Storm *Miguel,* only moments ago downgraded from hurricane status.

"We should try and get some sleep," suggested Diane.

"Fat chance," replied Sam with a wry grin. She looked at her watch, setting the alarm for 4:45 AM. Looking over at her friend, she instructed, "Set your watch alarm for 4:45 AM."

The two women turned their attention back to Sam Spade, holding forth: *"the storm continues on its predicted path and is picking up forward speed even as the core winds, now down to 40 mph, continue to slowly fall off. The good news is by noon tomorrow we should be enjoying a sunny, albeit breezy day."*

Both women sat with eyes shut, but neither was sleeping. Sam was worried about her partner...and yes, Laura. Diane again thought about John with the dawning realization that she did indeed love her husband.

The sudden vibration on her wrist jolted Sam awake. She had fallen asleep despite her earlier prediction, apparently more tired than anxious. Sam looked over and saw Diane stand up and stretch. "Hey Sam," she said, "sleep well?"

"Must have been more tired than I thought," replied Sam, "how about you?"

"Been awake about an hour...before that I nodded out on and off."

Sam stood up and glanced around the room. Their adrenaline kicking into high gear, now both women were wide awake and fully alert. They walked in tandem over to the dining table. Sam picked up the sheathed carving knife, portable tool kit and one of the two mini flashlights. Diane grabbed the hunting knife and remaining flashlight.

"OK," instructed Sam, "here's what we're gonna do: I'm going out the kitchen window and around to the front porch, where I'll come up on the perp from behind and take him down with a choke hold. Once he's out, tie his hands then feet with the rope we left by the cabin door. I'll gag him. Timing is critical. When I go out the window, allow *exactly one minute,* then make just enough ruckus to get him over to the door...that's when I'll jump him. Come out the door with the rope ready to tie him up. Oh...if it looks like I'm having trouble, feel free to jump in!"

"Got it!" Exclaimed Diane.

"Part two," continued Sam, "we make a beeline for the ATV, crank it up and get the hell outta Dodge. Plan B, if the ATV doesn't start right up, we *Run Like the Devil...*just follow me!"

"Got it!" Repeated Diane.

The two women looked intently into each other's eyes, then silently embraced. "We got this!" Pronounced Diane.

"Showtime!" Exclaimed Sam, releasing her embrace and heading to the kitchen window. As Sam climbed out, Diane looked at her watch, noting the time as she went to the cabin door.

Sam hit the ground and quickly made her way to the front of the cabin. Just as the weather guy had predicted, it was now raining lightly, and the winds had dropped significantly. *God Bless Sam Spade* flashed through her mind.

As soon as Diane reached the front door, she began rapping and yelling - *but not too loudly* - that they needed help. Outside, Sam peered around the corner in time to see the guard stand up and walk the short distance to the door. Sam deftly leapt onto the porch; in just over a second, she reached her quarry. She jumped on his back, applying a vice-like grip around his neck, simultaneously wrapping her legs around his midsection.

The surprised Russian quickly straightened up to his full 6'4" height. *Damn,* thought Sam, *just our luck it was the biggest guy's shift.* He began pulling on Sam's arm encircling his throat with both meaty hands. Intent on quickly choking him out, she used all her strength to further tighten her grip as he began spinning around in an effort to shake her off him.

Diane burst through the door just in time to see the big Russian turning around. A second later, he moved toward the front wall and with the full weight of his body, slammed the clinging woman into the wall with such force Diane thought he had broken a number of Sam's ribs.

Sam felt excruciating pain shoot through her rib cage but held on for all she was worth. Diane rushed toward the pair to help her friend when the guy toppled over on top of Sam. He suddenly went still. Sam rolled him over, all the while maintaining her tight grip. After a few moments, she released him, nodding at Diane who immediately began tying his hands. Finishing that, she began tying his feet while Sam gagged him.

"Are you alright?" Anxiously asked Diane.

"I'm okay," lied Sam, ignoring the sharp pain in her side. "Let's go!" The two ran over to the ATV. "SHIT!" Exclaimed Sam, "They took the damn key...it's too risky to take the time to hotwire it. We've gotta make a run for it!" She took off at a full sprint into the woods with Diane right on her heels. Once the underbrush began to get thicker, they were forced to slow down; it was just too dark, and first light was at least 15 minutes away.

They had each turned on their flashlights, which helped some, but the undulating shadows caused by the still-brisk wind kept them at a slower pace to avoid sudden pitfalls. They heard a loud crack behind them; probably a large tree toppling over. This speculation proved accurate. Unfortunately, the tree in question had crashed onto the porch of the cabin housing their Russian captors. Startled awake by the crash, it was only a matter of minutes before the women's escape would be discovered.

** ** **

After a few moments of confusion, Asimov, the Lead Guy, called for quiet. He asked if everyone was OK, then began issuing rapid-fire instructions: sending one man to check on the cabin sentry, another to check out the damage to the cabin, and *Smelly Guy* to check on the ATV. After freeing their subdued comrade, they gathered weapons, grabbed a couple of portable searchlights, and headed to the ATV where *Smelly Guy* sat in the driver's seat, at the ready. The crew had been sleeping with clothes on, so they were ready to go.

Asimov looked at his men and laid out the plan: He and Pavlov (the guard subdued by Sam) would pursue the women in the ATV. *Smelly Guy* objected, correctly pointing out that he was the best trained for this type of mission. Asimov said, "You're right. Unfortunately, if we find ourselves having to sneak up on the women - well..." *Smelly Guy* got up and stepped out of the ATV, hanging his head in disappointment; muted chuckling erupted among his comrades.

"We will capture the women in short order," predicted Asimov. "After we return to the cabin, I will inform Sergei of the new situation. I remind everyone, despite of what they've done, *no harm is to come to the women.* Is that understood?" The entire crew assented with nods.

** ** **

Sam bent over in pain. *Probably bruised ribs,* she thought. *Maybe broken. No matter. Gotta push through this. Are you a pussy? Or are you a Marine?* She stood up and looked Diane in the eye.

"You're hurt?" said an alarmed Diane.

"I am... ribs," confirmed Sam. "No matter...gotta keep going, I'll fix it later."

Diane looked at her friend, with a concerned, but knowing, expression. Then she nodded.

They heard the ATV fire up. "They're coming for us," said Sam. She glanced at her watch face. "We're a little more than a mile from the chopper. This way," she indicated, pointing to their left. "Let's go!"

The rain began to let up and first light was emerging. They heard the ATV in the distance, prompting them to increase their pace. Diane's left foot suddenly dropped into a small hole, causing her to crash headfirst into the ground. She yelped in pain. Sam stopped and turned around, seeing her companion writhing in agony. She suspected the worse.

When she reached Diane, she focused her flashlight on her foot. What she saw confirmed her fear. Sam inspected the site carefully. "Your foot is caught in a rabbit hole. I've gotta get it out of there."

Diane, grimacing in pain, nodded at Sam.

"This is gonna hurt girl," Sam warned.

"I know," replied Diane, "just do it!"

Sam placed her hands near Diane's ankle and on her calf. With a sudden forceful yank, she pulled Diane's foot clear. Diane let out a scream, then harshly whispered, "I'm sorry..."

"No need to apologize...I know how much that hurt," said Sam. She carefully inspected Diane's ankle, already purple and swelling up. "Try to stand up Diane," she encouraged. Her friend stood up but almost fell over when she tried to take a step. Tears welled up as the injured woman attempted to fight off the pain.

"You've got a bad ankle sprain," observed Sam, "maybe a break. Either way, you can't go on."

"Right," agreed Diane. "Leave me here. We know they won't harm me. Actually, may work out to our benefit. They're gonna have to get me back to the cabin which should give you time to reach the helicopter. If we're really lucky, they won't assume that's exactly where you're headed. They don't know you have piloting skills."

"Good point," agreed Sam. "I should get to the chopper in 10, maybe 15 minutes. You hang in there. After I get outta here, we'll be coming back for you!"

"I know you will Sam." The pair hugged briefly. "Now...get going, your ride is waiting on you!"

Sam smiled at her friend, then turned and ran, disappearing into the brush. Diane gingerly sat down, turning on her flashlight so her pursuers could readily locate her. In a few minutes she heard the approaching ATV and saw the light from the bouncing vehicle illuminate the surrounding brush.

** ** **

"Look!" Shouted Asimov. "Over there!" He turned the ATV slightly, heading toward the flashlight beam waving frantically in the distance. A figure propped up by a tree came into view. "It's the *Diane* woman," he said in Russian. They pulled up next to her. Asimov shut down the ATV. They climbed out of the vehicle, Asimov's companion leveling his pistol at her.

"I'm not armed!" Shouted Diane as she raised her hands in the air. "I think my ankle is broken."

"Noaoxon hE ctpearn B hee! Til meank, 4toC heN hE tak?" Asimov said to his partner in Russian.

Diane instantly translated the Russian to English: "Wait, DON'T SHOOT HER! You're a medic, what's wrong with her?"

The Russian Crews' medic holstered his pistol, went over to her and examined the ankle.

"Y hee BblBnxhyta AoAb]kkA," the medic informed Asimov; Diane once again translating: "She has a sprained ankle."

"AoAb]kkA? (A sprained ankle)" Repeated Asimov. "Da (yes)," confirmed the medic.

Asimov looked down at Diane as the medic removed her shoe and began wrapping the ankle. "My medic informs me that you have a - how do you say - *a sprain ankle*. We will get you back to cabin. This *try to run away*...very foolish. You maybe could be killed."

"What about my friend Sam?" Asked Diane, fully expecting to be interrogated as to her partner's whereabouts and destination.

"Your friend," said Asimov, "is...*what is American saying*...oh, I know! She is of little *consequence.* It is *You* who is important to us."

Diane was amused by the Russian's pride in his knowledge of English, cleverly coming up with the *consequence* expression. They loaded her into the front passenger seat, Asimov choosing to sit directly behind her. His companion cranked up the ATV and they began the short trek back to the cabin. The rain had stopped, the winds had further relaxed and it was now daylight.

** ** **

Sam emerged from the brush and saw a road about thirty feet in front of her. She looked at her watch and activated the *Tracer* app. The map display indicated the helicopter was located in a clearing about 150 yards north - to her right. She glanced around, pleasantly surprised at just how quickly the weather had improved. With sunrise coming in 20 minutes, there was plenty of daylight. Sam thought about Diane. She was worried about the ankle sprain. Hopefully, someone on the Russian crew had at least some rudimentary medical skills. Less concerning was Diane's safety...as the primary bargaining chip...matter of fact, now the *only* bargaining chip; Sam was confident they would be taking good care of her friend. With a renewed sense of optimism, she turned north and began jogging toward the helicopter and freedom.

The chopper was exactly where indicated on the *Tracer* map. She went to the entry port only to find it locked. No matter. She reached into her pocket and retrieved the tool kit, selecting the common screwdriver. In a matter of moments, she jimmied the entry and climbed into the pilot's seat. Sam looked over the controls and did a pre-flight checklist in her mind. It had been a while, but she thought, *just like riding a bike.* She hit the ignition and the chopper sprang to life. With a smile, she lifted off on a northeast course. A few minutes later, she was over the cabin. She hovered for a moment as several of the Russian crew scurried around the yard. No Diane. Most probably in the cabin, hopefully being attended to.

She dropped to within 20 feet of the ground. She saluted the three Russians in the yard with a grand *Flipping Of The Bird* gesture. Sam took the chopper up and veered off on a southeast course heading toward Orlando's *Herndon Airport* and eventual reunion with her team.

** ** **

Chapter Sixteen
Coming Together

Sam saw the welcoming lights of the Herndon Municipal Airport's tower. Perfectly situated in the center of Orlando, it was a popular hub for small aircraft and could accommodate up to medium-sized corporate jets. Less than a mile from Jason's Lake Eola Office, it was especially convenient. Sam reached down for the mic switch to announce her arrival. Oops! The space usually occupied by the radio was empty. *Well, that's pretty inconsiderate,* she thought. *They must have removed it just to piss me off* (of course she realized there was no way her Russian friends could have anticipated her stealing their damn helicopter - it's just...*well, she was in such a good mood*).

Her thoughts quickly returned to reality when she noticed the two Sheriff vehicles sitting on both sides of the helicopter pad. Sam gently set the helicopter down, shut off the motor, and slowly climbed out, raising both hands high in the air.

** ** **

Jaydan returned the cellphone to his pocket. Both Jason and Laura eyed him with quizzical expressions, tinged with annoyance. Laura prompted, "...And?"

"So," Jaydan said, "that was Director McBride. Sam landed a helicopter at Herndon Airport not fifteen minutes ago. Said helicopter is leased by Wildcat Courier Service. She is okay. Diane is *not* with her, but she, too, is okay. We are to retrieve Sam, bring her to the safe house and debrief her, after which I am to call Director McBride."

Jason looked at Emily, who was quietly standing next to Laura. "If you would be so kind," he sarcastically requested, "to fetch my partner and bring her back, I would be forever in your debt."

"No problem, Jason," replied the FBI Agent. "I'll need to take your car. Mine is temporarily out of service; stuck as it is under a rather large oak tree."

Jason dug his key fob out of his pocket and handed it to the agent. "Here ya go, Emily. Thanks...and sorry about the sarcasm, I'm just a little out of sorts."

"Sure, no worries," said Emily with a smile as she went out the door.

** ** **

Diane sat on the sofa, her recently sprained ankle propped up on the coffee table. She examined the wrap that - what was his name, oh yeah - Pavlov had applied after icing the ankle for her. Seemed like he knew what he was doing. And he had given her a pill for the pain. Which she never expected. She had to admit to astonishment for his...actually the entire teams' treatment of her. The injury occurred during an escape attempt after all. Not to mention Pavlov was the guy Sam took down on the porch. Despite their *almost kind* treatment, she was pretty worried. No more masks...and Asimov readily identified himself and Pavlov. *What* did that say about her future?

She looked back at the TV as news anchor Nancy Riggs announced the breaking news that *"earlier this morning a mysterious helicopter had landed at Herndon Airport and its sole occupant was taken into custody. According to the anonymous source, the person hasn't been seen since and the helicopter is now secured in a hangar, out of public view."* Nancy went on to say that a reporter was on the way to the scene and would soon be *"bringing the viewing audience up to date with all the details."* Diane smiled. *Sam. Good Girl...you made it.*

She heard the cabin door open, and Asimov immediately walked over to where she was sitting.

"Good morning, Diane," he said with a phony smile. "As you Americans like to say, 'the party is all done!'"

"I think," corrected Diane, "you mean: *the party is over.*"

"Whatever...," said the red-faced Russian. "We are leaving."

The cabin door opened again. Pavlov the medic and *Smelly Guy* came over to join Asimov. She steeled herself against the inevitable gagging fit when, unexpectedly, *Smelly Guy* continued walking over to the kitchen bar, at least fifteen feet away. Though she still got a whiff of his unique stench, he was far enough removed to ensure her olfactory comfort. *There is a God,* thought Diane, *and She's looking out for me.*

Aismov told her to stand up, then while the medic blindfolded her, he said they were going to a vehicle just outside the cabin. The medic handed her a pair of crutches. Asimov told her to step forward and that he would give directions she should carefully follow. In short order, she felt the sun and a pleasant light breeze. After a few more steps, Diane was told to stop. The Medic helped her into the car, then closed the door. As the car pulled onto the gravel road, a quick sniff confirmed *Smelly Guy* was *not* aboard. *Thank you, God.*

** ** **

It was just past 9:00 AM as Owen Whittaker closed the car door and headed for the Turnpike Plaza Restaurant's entrance. He noticed Dimitrov's car parked near the door. *Punctual bugger,* he thought, recalling their last rendezvous. As he came through the door, he saw the Russian in the same booth, with...yes, the same *Ms. Efficiency* waitress hovering over him. Dimitrov glimpsed the FBI Agent and waved him over.

Whittaker took the seat opposite Dimitrov saying: "*Doboye utro, comrade Sergei*" (Good morning my friend Sergei) in an effort to continue their more cordial relationship.

"Da (yes) Comrade. Doboye utro," replied a smiling Dimitrov. "I see you came through the hurricane intact. I took the liberty of ordering you a coffee which, I believe, will be arriving within the minute."

"Da," answered Whittaker, "and thanks for the coffee order." Right on cue and within the predicted minute - *Ms. Efficiency* arrived with Whittaker's coffee. She quickly took their orders, wheeled around and left them to their conversation.

"So," continued Whittaker, "I'm sure you are aware of last night's - *correction* - this morning's escape. I'm sure the *Samantha* women is reuniting with her partner as we speak. I trust our main 'bargaining chip' is well and has been moved to a more secure location."

"Correct my friend. She is in a secure location. In Kissimmee, actually. Secure and *convenient.* The woman sustained a sprained ankle in their escape attempt. *Most fortunate* for us. Otherwise, we would - how do you say - *be up shit's creek."*

"Yes," agreed Whittaker, "and if I may add *without a paddle.* A review of your security procedures may be in order...but that's for another time," observed the agent. "For now, we need to finally bring this *Project Expose'* to a successful conclusion."

"Da," replied the Russian just as *Ms. Efficiency* arrived with their breakfast orders.

** ** **

Sam saw Emily come in the hangar door. She again thanked Sheriff Brown for his help, especially for so quickly facilitating her release. Excusing herself, Sam turned, quickly walking toward her approaching friend, almost breaking into a run. They met at the halfway point, embracing in a prolonged hug of relief. Sam began weeping uncontrollably. Emily continued to embrace her friend until she was able to regain her composure.

"Sorry," said an embarrassed Sam. "I don't know where that came from. I'm usually the most stoic one in the group."

"No need to apologize," responded Emily. "I've been where you are too many times to count. We're like pressure cookers - gotta let off steam once in a while or we're just gonna blow! And we need you in one piece - so please...," handing her friend a handkerchief. Sam laughed as she wiped her eyes.

"C'mon," continued Emily, "let's get outta here...the Team's anxious to see you!" They turned and headed for the exit.

On the way to the safe house, Emily gave Sam the short version of events since her kidnapping: John Stockwell's revelation about Whittaker's involvement; the attempted assassination of Jason and Laura by Kaslov and his subsequent capture; new team member Jaydan Sanders; the arrival of his uncle, Baylin Sanders; the revised strategy for *Project Expose'*; and the nearly tragic falling tree incident at the safe house.

"Holy Crap!" Exclaimed Sam." You guys have really been busy. I see somehow y'all have been able to muddle through without *Moi*." The women laughed.

"So," asked Emily, "*What happened to you?*"

"Long story," replied Sam. "Wait 'til we get to the safe house...save me telling it twice. I can tell you this much. I made a friend. A *good* friend. Diane Stockwell, who is one tough cookie...and I'm going back for her."

"We're *All* going back for her," corrected Emily.

"Sorry...of course," said Sam. "I didn't mean to imply anything, it's just...well, the two of us have been though a lot. And you know," continued Sam, looking straight at Emily; "now that I think about it, I made another friend. A *good* friend!"

Smiling, Emily replied, "Thanks, Sam. My feeling exactly." The autopilot turned the car onto Randall Drive and announced, "arriving at destination." As they approached the house, Emily's car was barely visible underneath the branches of the fallen tree.

"Holy crap!" Exclaimed Sam. "That is one big tree!"

"Yeah," agreed Emily, "tell me about it. By the way, your partner saved *yours truly* from that very same tree."

** ** **

Dimitrov located their waitress two tables down and was able to catch her eye. She immediately headed over and asked, "Is there anything else I can get you gentlemen?"

"A couple more coffees would be great," said Whittaker with Dimitrov adding, "and I'll have a couple of cinnamon buns with my coffee."

"Certainly," acknowledged the waitress. "I'll be right back." She picked up their empty breakfast plates and scurried off. Whittaker was about to begin speaking when the Russian held up a finger. Before Whittaker could question the finger pause, *Ms. Efficiency* arrived with their coffee and bun order. The Agent could only smile, slowly shaking his head.

After she left, Whittaker remarked, "She's looking for that big tip." They both laughed. "Gotta say, she's certainly earned it...I wish my people were this efficient."

"Da," replied the Russian, the pair enjoying another laugh.

"Sergei, I've come up with a plan for the exchange I want to run by you." The Russian nodded for him to continue. "My idea is we do it in the courtyard of the Florida Mall. Right out in the open. In plain sight with lots of people around. Tell them we have people hidden among the crowd. Once our people verify it's good and not bugged, we release the woman and get the hell out of the country."

Dimitrov took all this in, and after several more minutes of contemplation, looked up at Whittaker finally saying, "Da! I like it...a good plan my friend!"

The rogue agent continued: "One thing...I know we've had our differences...I hope we can put them behind us. I want to go to Moscow - to live, and hopefully work for the SVR...to work for you. There is nothing left for me here. I have no family. What I do have is a vast amount of knowledge about the inner workings of the Bureau and its people. Consider what an asset I could be for Russian intelligence! I'm not looking for a big payday. Just a nice place to live and a comfortable income. For me, the joy of life is in the work. What do you say?"

Once again, the Russian sat silently, pondering what he had just heard. *A few days ago, I was ready to kill this guy, thought Dimitrov. Now I find myself admiring his skills. He has gone out of his way to mend our relationship. If he is truly willing to shift loyalties to Russia, this would be a coup for the SVR and a very big feather in my cap. Of course, he could be lying. But to what end? He has already been thoroughly vetted. I cannot see any way the SVR can lose.*

Dimitrov looked Whittaker hard in the eye. "I think we can work something out. Of course, I must get final approval from the Kremlin, but I don't think that will be a problem, especially if we are successful in our current venture. Welcome to the SVR, Comrade Owen!"

The two men stood, reaching across the table to shake hands.

** ** **

Jason announced, "They're here," opening the front door. Emily brushed past so Jason could have a moment with his partner. The two silently embraced, relieved and happy to be reunited.

Jason released Sam. "I really missed you, *partner*. It's really been tough without you here. Oh...we got your truck back safe and sound, its waiting for you at home."

Stepping back, she dabbed at her eyes before replying, "Missed you, too. The good news, I made a new friend. I'll tell you all about it later." She followed Jason into the house where she was greeted with a round of applause.

"Quit that," she said, blushing. "I didn't do anything special."

"The hell you say," interrupted Jason. "You got away from a professional espionage team without a scratch. In the middle of a hurricane, I might add."

"Not to mention in pretty spectacular fashion," added Laura. "I didn't know you could fly a helicopter, much less land one. You go girl! James Bond's got nothing on you," setting off a round of laughter.

Jason put a hand on Jaydan's shoulder and looked over at Sam. "Sam let me introduce Agent Jaydan Sanders. Agent Sanders, this is my partner, Samantha Talley."

The two shook hands and exchanged the customary "pleased to meet you" and stepped back.

Sam said, "And who is he..." looking directly at Kaslov who was standing between Laura and Emily.

"That," announced Jason, "is Vladimir Kaslov." Kaslov took a step forward and extended his hand.

In the blink of an eye, Sam raised her left arm and reared back. With her fist tightly clenched, she brought it forward with lightning speed, directly impacting the Russian's rather large nose. Letting out a yelp, he dropped to the floor, where he sat, rocking back and forth, covering his face with both hands.

"You were going to shoot my friends you son of a bitch!" Sam yelled at him while she shook her now very sore left hand. "You're lucky I didn't kill you."

"Take it easy, partner," Jason implored. "You coulda killed him with that punch."

"No way," replied Sam, rubbing her bruised knuckles, "I hit him with my *left* hand."

"Remind me not to get on your bad side," said Emily, with Laura chiming in, "Ditto."

Emily and Laura helped the Russian to his feet and walked him to the bathroom down the hall where they would do what they could for what was surely a broken nose. Sam asked where another bathroom might be with Jason directing her to the master bedroom.

As Sam left to tend to her sore paw, Jaydan turned to Jason inquiring, "Is she always like that?"

A *fair question* thought Jason. "She does have a bit of a temper," understated the detective, "but you have to consider *context*. What just happened was the result of her intense loyalty. Sorta like the mama bear looking out for her cubs...okay, poor analogy...but you get the idea. You couldn't have a worse enemy...or a better friend."

"Well," said Jaydan, "I don't know her yet, but I can tell you I already like her. She's a good person. While that's based purely on intuition, I can tell you my people are very intuitive."

"What," inquired Jason, "exactly do you mean by *'my people'*? Someone else I know described their intuitive capabilities in the very same way."

Before Jaydan could reply, Laura and Emily came down the hall to inform the men that Kaslov did indeed have a broken nose. Emily allowed that they had affected repairs as best they could but at some point he would require professional treatment.

Jaydan said he understood, but *that* would have to wait until the resolution of the current *Project Expose'* dilemma. Sam emerged from the master bedroom and joined the other four in the living room. They noticed her wrapped hand.

"Ice," Sam informed her colleagues. "For the swelling - it's gonna be fine."

Everyone settled in: Jason and Laura took the loveseat with Emily, Sam, and Jaydan sitting on the large sectional sofa. "So," requested

Jason, looking at Sam, "can you bring us up to date on your 'adventure'?"

"Sure," replied Sam, "so, after I came to in the helicopter..." Sam provided chapter and verse narration for all that had happened from that point until her arrival at Herndon Airport: the arrival at the cabin; meeting Diane; evaluating their captors; the unusually cordial environment given their status; planning the escape; using the storm for cover; Diane's sprained ankle; concluding with her escape in the helicopter.

The team took it all in, spellbound by her matter-of-fact narration of events.

"Where do we go from here?" Asked Sam, Diane very much on her mind.

Jason said, "For one thing, we'll have to find out what the Russians will want us to do. Beyond that, we need to get together with Tara and fine tune our own plan. I suggest we meet at the office...and soon." All the team members nodded in agreement.

Jason's phone vibrated, announcing an incoming call. He reached into his pocket, retrieving his phone. He held up a finger and announced, "It's Tara."

** ** **

Chapter Seventeen
Just Another Day At The Office

"Hello Tara," answered Jason. "How are you?... Good, how about John...and Tucker?...Yes, we are all okay. And if you didn't already know, we have Sam back safe and sound. I'm glad you called...the Team is meeting at my Office in about thirty minutes, I would like you to come...we need your expertise. Yes...Sam has a lot to tell you. Great...see ya at the Office, Bye."

Jason put his phone away then glanced up at Jaydan. "See if you can learn anything new from our Russian friend. I'll give you a call as soon as we're finished at the office. OK people, let's go!" The four of them went out the front door, glancing wistfully at Emily's still entombed car before piling into Jason's Lexus.

** ** **

Because it was a Saturday - actually a Saturday after a hurricane - the parking garage was virtually deserted save for a very old Porsche parked at the end of the first row. Jason parked mere feet away from the elevator...he couldn't remember ever having that option before. They got out, walked the short distance to the elevator where Jason slid his I.D. card through the scan slot. After everyone was in, he pressed the requisite button, sending the elevator up to the 6th floor; the door opening to the *McVay & Associates* office suite across the hall.

The security camera positioned above the entrance identified Jason and unlocked the door, which obligingly slid open to allow the group's entry. Jason said, "Shall we," indicating the conference room between his and Sam's offices. They entered the small, but well-appointed room and selected their seats; Jason at the head, Sam taking her usual place at the opposite end, Laura on Jason's left, and Emily on the right.

Jason's phone vibrated. It was Tara, just arrived in the parking garage. He gave her the code to access the elevator and told the others she was on the way up. Three minutes later, Jason looked at the security screen to see her leave the elevator and approach the office door, which he opened remotely.

"Come in, Tara," he invited, "we're in here." Tara walked over to the partially opened door, entering with a cheerful "Hello, everybody. Good to see you all again!" Everyone acknowledged with a smile and/or nod as she took a seat between Laura and Sam.

"So," began Jason, "Before we start working on getting Diane back, I'm gonna let Sam bring Tara up to date on her 'little adventure.'" Sam detailed everything that had happened to her beginning with the kidnapping and ending with her landing the helicopter at Herndon Airport.

Emily asked Sam for her assessment of the Russian team and what weaknesses she may have noticed. Before Sam could answer, Jason held up his hand to indicate he had an incoming call. It was Jaydan.

"Hey, Jaydan," he said. "What's up? We've only just started the meeting...WHAT!!! Say again...." Jason stood up with a look of disbelief spreading across his face. The women anxiously glanced back and forth, in-between eyeing Jason, all wearing the same alarmed expression as they listened to Jason's end of the conversation.

"*You've got to be kidding me!* And you verified all this..., what do you mean: *will call you back with the details?...* no, I *Don't* under-stand...yes, yes, I know she's your boss. No, I don't blame you...call me back right after you talk to her. OK, Bye." Jason pocketed his phone and shook his head before addressing the team, now in a state of high anxiety. "Well, this is just unbelievable! Director McBride called Jaydan about five minutes after we left. She told him to put Kaslov on the phone. After she was done with him, she told Jaydan to give Kaslov five hundred dollars, a burner phone, and, ominously, a loaded pistol, then immediately release him. Jaydan said he was dumbfounded, but after verifying that it was indeed McBride, he complied with her order; reluctantly letting Kaslov go with the money, phone...and gun."

"That was," he glanced at his watch, "just over an hour ago. He's awaiting a promised phone call from McBride detailing exactly what the hell is going on; he's gonna call us as soon as he has something."

"So," asked Tara, "...any guesses?"

"Frankly, I haven't a clue," replied the perplexed detective.

** ** **

The taxi dropped off Kaslov at the end of a long driveway leading up to a dilapidated farmhouse. Wildcat Courier Service had been renting the place for some time, telling the landlord they needed the place for additional storage. Located on the outskirts of Kissimmee, the rural location was perfect for a safe house. The surrounding woods added another layer of security; its proximity to the Orlando metro area an especially convenient feature.

Kaslov walked up the gravel driveway, past two foreboding signs: a No Trespassing sign pointing out that trespassers would be "prosecuted to the full extent of the law" and a second, more ominous sign warning of "Off-leash Bad Dogs Patrolling the Property." He glanced around warily as he approached the front door. At the front door he used the coded knock: two quick raps, pause; one rap, pause; one rap. The door opened, revealing a short, stocky man with a crooked nose and scraggly beard. "Yes?" said the bewhiskered one.

"My name is Vladimir Kaslov. I am here to see Sergei Dimitrov," said Kaslov using the tone of voice of a superior addressing his subordinate.

"Certainly, comrade Kaslov," said the man, immediately recognizing the name. "Please follow me." He led Kaslov down a long hall, turning into a rather large living room. Upon entering the room, Kaslov glanced around at the seven men seated around a large table. He immediately spotted Dimitrov and Andre Asimov; several of the others looked familiar, he couldn't recall their names. His nostrils suddenly flared, picking up a most unpleasant scent - rather like the combination of vomit and a dead thing. This distraction faded when he noticed the well-dressed man sitting at the middle of the table. Definitely not one of the crew.

Dimitrov, seated at the head of the table, stood and immediately headed toward Kaslov. The two men embraced, exchanging the customary European cheek kiss.

"Vladimir, you're looking well," said the burly Russian. "I heard you were in the area...what brings you to our humble house?"

Kaslov explained he had been captured by McVay and was able to escape when the detective and his team left for a meeting at his office, leaving just one man guarding him.

"Sergei, I have new instructions regarding the final phase of the *Project Expose'* mission. Much of the information is for your ears only, so if we could..."

Dimitrov nodded, "Da, please follow me...," indicating Kaslov should follow him to the hallway. As the two Russians made their way out of the room, Whittaker rose from his seat and discreetly fell in step a few feet behind. Just as the pair rounded the corner into the hallway, Whittaker quickened his pace just in time to see Kaslov reach into his pocket and retrieve the gun Jaydan had given him earlier. He raised it, aiming at Dimitrov's back, just three feet in front of him. Reaching around, Whittaker drew his Glock from the holster at the small of his back, simultaneously yelling: "SERGEI – GET DOWN!!!"

The Russian instinctively ducked just as Kaslov got off two quick shots which missed their mark. Whittaker fired a volley of shots at Kaslov, all of which went wide - the Agent's arm having brushed against the door frame just as he fired. Kaslov returned fire, missing Whittaker but wounding one of the crew who had responded when he heard the gunshots. Kaslov crashed through a window, tumbling onto the front porch. He quickly got up and headed for the adjacent woods. Several of the crew with guns drawn headed for the front door.

"NO!" Commanded Dimitrov as he stood up. "Let him go. Get the girl! We have to get out of here!... NOW!"

Pavlov, recognizing an opportunity to raise his standing, interjected, "I know where McVay's office is... this would be an ideal time - our enemies are all gathered together...it's the weekend, the place will be deserted. Three of us should be sufficient. Just say the word!" He implored.

"Yes...yes!" Said the infuriated Russian. "Kill them all!"

Pavlov quickly selected two men and gave them tactical instructions along with the address of the Lake Eola office building. As they were leaving, he turned to see Asimov glaring at him before issuing rapid fire orders for the immediate evacuation of the place.

Dimitrov grabbed Whittaker in a bear hug. "You saved my life! For this, I will be eternally grateful, my friend."

Whittaker modestly replied, "You would have done the same for me," not actually believing it.

** ** **

Resuming the meeting, Sam continued, "To fully answer Emily's question about my assessment of the Russian crew at the cabin would take...probably the rest of the afternoon. I can tell you this, the way they treated us was exactly the opposite of what you'd expect."

"How so?" Inquired Tara.

"Well," replied Sam, "we were treated more like resort guests than kidnap victims. We could move about freely, watch TV, make meals...pretty much do whatever we wanted - as long as we didn't try to leave the cabin."

Just then, Jason saw his phone vibrating on the tabletop. He picked it up. "Hello, Jaydan." The women watched in silence for the next five plus minutes as Jason mostly listened during the call, punctuated with his occasional, "I see," or "really," and an abundance of "uh, huhs," and finally; "Thanks, Jaydan, I'll be in touch." Jason placed his phone back on the table, then looked at his colleagues.

"That was Jaydan. Obviously. Anyway, he's shed some light on the current situation with our Russian friend. Apparently, Kaslov has, from time to time, worked with the CIA as a double agent. Director McBride has enough incriminating evidence to ensure his instant demise should the Agency ever reveal it to his Russian handlers. His assassination attempt on me and Laura was at the direction of the Kremlin and had nothing to do with the SVR or Dimitrov's little group. McBride doesn't know the Kremlin's motive for wanting a private investigator killed, much less why the SVR were kept out of the loop; but their working on it."

"She ordered Kaslov to go to the Russian safe house in Kissimmee and take out Dimitrov. We are *Not* to attempt a rescue at this time."

"And why the hell not?" Interrupted Sam.

"My best guess is it has to do with the software modification scheme Baylin described during our last meeting at Dynamadics. The Agency has something new in mind to ensure the *Project Expose'* thumb drive for Diane exchange goes smoothly," offered Jason.

"Goes smoothly...goes smoothly?...nothing's gone very smoothly so far," retorted an increasingly irritated Sam. "Plus, isn't hostage rescue in the purview of the FBI?"

"You're correct Sam," verified Emily. "This case, however, would be an exception, not knowing the extent of the 'rogue agent' thing."

Laura - for Sam's benefit - was about to expand on the Dynamadics meeting when she noticed an odd expression spread across Jason's face. She thought, *Uh, oh...*

Jason felt what had now become that all too frequent sense of foreboding. The familiar chill descended over him. Time froze as the *movie in his mind* began playing. He noticed Laura was getting ready to speak when he barely heard his office door slide open. The partially open door of the conference room was violently pushed all the way open. Suddenly, three men appeared at the door, leveling their assault rifles at the assembled group. Tara was shot in the back of her head before she could turn around, slumping down in her chair. Sam stood and quickly turned around to no avail. Before she could bring her gun to bear, she was hit multiple times in the head and torso, the impact slamming her body into the side wall. Laura had immediately stood, drawing her Beretta, but sustained multiple gunshots to the head and body, knocking her into the room's closed back door. Jason looked on in horror just before everything turned black. He was spared witnessing the subsequent shooting of Emily, who had been riddled with gunshots.

Real time resumed. Jason picked up his cellphone, put it to his ear and after about twenty seconds put it down. "Everyone listen to me and do *Exactly What I Tell You!* In just over a minute, three of the Russian crew are going to emerge from the elevator with assault rifles. Laura and I will take up positions at the corner about two office suites down from the elevator. Sam: you, Emily, and Tara head down the opposite side - there's a recessed entrance to the law office suite next to our suite where you can take cover. When the elevator door opens and they've all got out, I'll yell for their surrender. If they choose to engage, open fire!"

Everyone did as instructed; the entire group in position with just a minute to spare. Exactly two minutes after Jason's warning preview, the elevator door opened; three men, weapons at the ready, spilling out.

Jason yelled, "YOU'RE SURROUNDED! DROP YOUR WEAPONS AND RAISE YOUR ARMS NOW!!!"

One man let go of his rifle and dropped to the floor. The other two pointed their weapons in the direction of Jason's voice, firing a volley of shots. Simultaneously, the team opened fire from their positions at either end of the hall; the two who chose confrontation over surrender instantly falling to the floor where they laid in crumpled heaps next to their more prudent companion.

Jason and Laura ran over to the fallen Russians while Sam, Emily, and Tara maintained cover for them.

Sam commanded the uninjured Russian, "Slowly stand with your hands interlocked behind your head and walk backwards until you're told to stop." The man did precisely as instructed.

Laura said. "This one's dead," followed by Jason making the same proclamation about the other one.

Sam ordered, "OK, that's far enough. Stop. Cuffs anyone?" She asked. Emily stepped over and handed her cuffs to Sam who holstered her weapon. Emily likewise put her gun away as Tara kept the perp covered. Sam cuffed the guy and walked him to the office. Laura was on the phone to Sheriff Brown.

As Sam sat their captive down, she said, "I know you...you're the guy I jumped back at the cabin! You're...you're...*Pavlov!*" The Russian, barely fluent in English, looked up at her with a sullen expression and replied simply, *"Da."*

** ** **

"I have just the place to take her," said Dimitrov, turning toward Whittaker. As they watched Diane being placed in the back seat of his SUV, he continued, "it is the residence of a team member currently in Russia...a two-bedroom apartment that is minutes from the Florida Mall."

"Sounds perfect Sergei," replied Whittaker, "we only need to hold her one more day."

A crew member emerged from the front door and strode over to where Dimitrov and Whittaker were standing. He told Dimitrov in Russian that the house was now "clean" and they could leave with confidence there was no evidence of foul play remaining. Dimitrov nodded, instructing the man to join his comrade and take the SUV to the location he recently described to Whittaker. The Russian nodded, turned and walked to the vehicle containing their hostage.

Dimitrov told Whittaker the gist of the conversation he had just had. Whittaker informed him that he had understood most of what was said.

"Very good Owen!" He enthused. "We will have you speaking fluent Russian in no time."

"Da... yes indeed," replied Whittaker. "Would you care to ride with me to the apartment?"

"Da comrade Owen," he confirmed. "We have much to discuss." He waved at the man standing by at the SUV, signaling him to leave for the apartment.

** ** **

Chapter Eighteen
Tying Up A Few Loose Ends

Two staff members of the Medical Examiner's Response Team lifted the body bag containing the second of the two deceased perps onto the gurney and headed to the elevator, fortuitously just large enough for the equipment. Sheriff's Department CSI personnel were just finishing their work.

Sheriff Brown walked over to Jason and Laura, who were completing a joint interview with a Sheriff's Agent.

"How are you Sheriff Brown?" Inquired Jason, extending his hand.

"I'm good, thanks for asking, Jason," he replied. Glancing in Laura's direction he continued, "I see you and the little lady have been busy." With a smile, he amended his statement; "I didn't mean 'little' in the literal sense (acknowledging her near 6' height) - no offense."

Laura laughed as she reached over and gently touched him on the shoulder. "None taken, Sheriff. The CIA is very much in your debt...needless to say, we'd be in quite a fix without your help."

"My pleasure Agent Sparks. Kaitlyn and I go back a long way...I owe her a lot...my life actually. But that's a story for another day. That said, at the rate we're going, she's gonna have to seriously consider putting me on the payroll," the remark setting off a round of laughter. "I think we've got pretty much all we need...I've got to go speak to the media now, I'm sure we'll be crossing paths in the near future," provoking more laughter.

"Thanks again Sheriff...or should I say *Agent* Brown?" joked Jason; the Sheriff raising an arm in mock surrender as he walked away.

Jason walked over to Sam - currently sitting with their captive - while Laura headed in the direction of Emily and Tara; the pair currently engaged in an animated conversation.

"Everything good with the Orange County Sheriff Office?" Inquired Sam as Jason approached.

"Yeah," answered her partner, "Sheriff Brown has turned out to be one of our biggest assets. Not to mention a really good guy. Listen, I need you to get this clown over to Jaydan at the safe house. Tell him to find out what he can and get back to me."

"Sure thing. My pleasure, boss." She looked at the glum Pavlov, gesturing for him to get up. "Let's go," she said, grabbing the handcuffed man and escorting him to the elevator.

"Thanks Sam," he said to her back..., "and don't call me *Boss*!"

** ** **

Diane felt the vehicle slow, coming to a stop as Dimitrov announced, "We're here. Final stop before freedom or...," his voice trailing off ominously.

Back at the Kissimmee safe house, she had been placed in the middle row of the SUV, a non-English speaking Russian seated next to her (Diane's captors were still unaware of her Russian fluency). Dimitrov had handed her a pair of "blacked out" wrap-around sunglasses - effectively the same as wearing a blindfold - and told her to keep them on until instructed otherwise. She had absolutely no idea where they were. Dimitrov instructed her to hold his hand and he would guide her to their destination. As Diane stepped out of the SUV, she overheard a woman passing by tell her companion that "this part of the Orange Blossom Trail is close to the Florida Mall, almost walking distance...," before fading from her hearing range. *Good to know,* she thought, just as she felt a tug on her elbow while a door was being opened. An elevator ride later, followed by a short walk brought Diane to her newest "residence." A door opened and she was walked a few paces when Dimitrov suddenly stopped and let go of her hand.

Her captor announced, "You can remove your sunglasses now."

She took off the sunglasses to find herself standing next to a beige fabric sofa done in a rather quaint butterfly print. Glancing around the room, she noted a breakfast bar at the end of a small "galley style" kitchen. A four-person dining table a few feet from the bar transited into the living room. There was a hallway to her right which she assumed led to the bedrooms. She could hear the sounds of heavy vehicular traffic, a further confirmation of their location. Diane believed the apartment to be on the fifth floor, having deduced this from the number of chimes she heard during the elevator ride.

"Have a seat, Diane," said Dimitrov, indicating the sofa as he sat in a chair on the opposite side. Without a word, she did as instructed. Diane watched two of the crew leave while a third man headed down the hall and out of her view. She had never seen this guy before. Based on his dress and demeanor she thought he must be a professional, perhaps a lawyer. Curious.

"So," continued Dimitrov, "I am happy to tell you that your ordeal will soon be over and, I trust, will have a safe and satisfying conclusion for all the involved parties. You have been treated well...yes? At first, I was surprised to learn of your ill-advised escape attempt; but in light of your then-companion's profession, realized a certain inevitably to it."

"In response to your question," replied Diane, "I *have* been treated very well, for which I'm grateful. I am, however, curious; having been treated more like a guest than a hostage - completely counterintuitive to what one would expect in this situation."

With a smile, Dimitrov explained, "I cannot speak for my compatriots, but I believe disrespect and nasty treatment achieve nothing...especially in your case. Because of the position you occupy in this situation - the target's wife - you become *an incentive.* A means to an end. We are not animals after all. Once we have the required software in hand, you will be free to resume your normal life...a tad richer I might add."

** ** **

Sam parked Jason's Lexus in the street, deciding it was the better option, what with Emily's tree covered car still occupying most of the driveway. She tooted the horn to alert Jaydan of her arrival. A moment later, the young agent emerged from the front door, heading toward the car at a brisk pace. Sam buzzed the window down just as he arrived.

"This is our new 'Guest'," she indicated, thumbing toward the back seat. "His name is Pavlov. He doesn't speak much English."

"No problem," replied Jaydan, "I speak lots of Russian." He leaned in the window and looked directly at Pavlov, telling the Russian in his native tongue, exactly what was expected of him; their captive urgently bobbing his head up and down to indicate his understanding.

Turning toward Sam, he said, "I just told him I was coming around to remove the handcuffs and that he was to get out of the car, then walk with us - as if he was a friend - right up to the front door. I assured him you wouldn't hesitate to shoot him should he try anything...he was quick to indicate he would comply...apparently you two have a history?"

"That would be a big 10-4," confirmed Sam with a wry smile.

Sam shut the door as Jaydan disappeared down the hall with the Russian. A few minutes later, he returned to find Sam sitting at the dining table.

"Coffee?" He offered.

"Yeah, Thanks," she answered. As Jaydan went over to the Keurig, she continued, "What a hell of a day...scratch that...what a hell of a week!"

"No doubt!" Readily agreed the agent. "Lots of *firsts* for me...not the least of which was releasing a notorious foreign spy...ordered by the CIA Director herself!"

"'Firsts' for me too...of course I'm not a CIA Agent, but still...*never been kidnapped* before, so there's that. Not to mention a drunken redneck grabbing me by the..."

"Yeah," interrupted Jaydan, "heard about that too...remind me not to get on your bad side."

Sam responded, "Just don't grab me by the..."

"Right again," interrupted Jaydan. "Not to worry, this *gentleman* always asks first...my momma didn't raise any fools!"

They both erupted in laughter, Sam landing an affectionate slap on Jaydan's back. Jaydan got up, went over to the coffee machine, and returned in short order with their brews.

Once seated, Jason asked, "How well do you know Emily?"

"I only recently met her," replied Sam, "but I feel like I know her pretty well. Why do you ask?"

"Gotta say," said Jaydan, "I think she's great. Really pretty, too. Got a crush on her. Do you think she likes me?"

"I don't know," replied Sam mischievously, "do you want me to ask?"

"*Would you?*" Implored Jaydan hopefully.

"What is this...*high school?*" Responded Sam, grinning impishly.

Blushing, Jaydan said. "Oh, never mind...it's not a big deal."

Lightly laying her hand on his arm, Sam said, "I'm *just teasing* Silly...of course I will...and I promise to be tactful. I can't imagine her not, you're a really handsome guy...but you already know that."

Still blushing, Jaydan said, "I don't know about all that...but *thanks Sam.*"

"No problem, Jaydan, that's what friends do." He stood up, excusing himself to begin interrogating their Russian captive. She watched him disappear down the hall thinking what a perfect couple Jaydan and Emily would be. *Imagine...Samantha Talley, Matchmaker.*

Sam finished her coffee, pushed her chair back and headed to the front door. She opened the door, pausing to tell Jason she was leaving. She leaned her head toward the hall and somewhat loudly announced, "I'm gonna bring Jason's car back...see ya later buddy."

From behind the closed door down the hall she heard his muffled acknowledgment, "Okay Sam, see ya later."

** ** **

Dimitrov bid goodbye to Diane after confirming the ground rules during her stay in the apartment. Whittaker emerged from the hallway and the two men, attired in T-Shirts, shorts, and sandals exited through the door - headed, presumed Diane, for the complex's pool.

Confirming Diane's assumption, upon reaching the ground floor, the two men walked out the rear door entrance to the well-appointed pool area. There were perhaps a dozen people scattered about on chaise loungers or seated at the tiki bar enjoying the sun as they sipped their various drink concoctions. After ordering Mai-tais at the bar, the pair walked around to the shady side and selected a table in a remote corner, affording the two men a largely unobstructed view of the entire pool area.

"So," began Whittaker, a smile spreading across his face, "feels like vacation...almost."

"Almost," agreed the Russian, "until we recall this morning's little escapade."

"Yes ...quite the downer," replied Whittaker.

"Downer?" Inquired his confused companion.

"Sorry," explained Whittaker, "an old American expression meaning a depressing or disagreeable situation."

"Da...yes, a correct description of what happened...how you say... *really sucked*!"

"So how well do you know that guy?" Asked the agent. "Why do you think he wanted to kill you? I mean you're both on the same team...right?"

"Vladimir Kaslov is a Kremlin operative. Works out of the President's office, has no direct link to the SVR. His assignments would tend toward the political, not espionage."

"Why would he try to kill you? Do you two have a *history*? Was this an assignment ordered by the political leadership or was he acting on his own?" Whittaker sat back wearing a perplexed expression.

"I have had little to do with him," answered Dimitrov. "We exchanged information about an operation a couple of years ago...I can't recall anything else. Certainly, no disagreements. We are not rivals...we are on completely different career paths. As far as I know, the Kremlin has no issues with me. Frankly, I'm baffled. For the time being, we have to let it go; it is imperative we get that thumb drive...we have too much invested to fail now!"

"I agree Sergei, but we must stay aware of the continuing threat Kaslov poses. As you said, failure is not an option - all the more reason we keep this guy on our radar!"

"Da," concurred Dimitrov. "Now it is time make the final preparations for the exchange and get instructions to Stockwell."

** ** **

Jason glanced up from the Incident Report he had just completed to see Sam walking into his office.

"Hey, partner. Got our 'guest' all settled in?" inquired the detective.

"Safe and sound," replied Sam. "I left him in Jaydan's capable hands; matter of fact he was just beginning a 'conversation' as I was leaving."

"Excellent," said Jason, "He may have some information about Diane's current whereabouts. I'm sure Jaydan will find out whatever he knows in short order."

"About that," said Sam hesitantly, "I..um..placed a tracker on her watch before the escape attempt, so if she's wearing her watch, we can...um find her location."

'WHAT!" Exclaimed Jason. "You're telling me we've had the ability to find her, and *you didn't say anything?!*"

"Wait," pleaded a flummoxed Sam, "it's not like that, I...I didn't say anything at first because of what Director McBride said about 'hands off searching for her'. I knew your first instinct would be for us to tear out the door - you know, 'Calvary coming to the rescue' stuff...then we'd really be in the deep end of the pool. She must have had a good reason for us to stay away."

"Maybe," said a calmer Jason, "But that's *my* decision to make. You were wrong to withhold such critical information. What happened to *trust*? I'm disappointed Sam."

"Jason, I'm truly sorry. Poor judgement on my part, I see that now. It won't happen again."

"Okay then," acknowledged Jason. "Now let's move on. Let me think about our next move. I want to see what more we can learn from our Russian friend at the safe house."

Laura, Tara and Emily came into Jason's office to discuss what to do next. It was decided that Jason and Laura would head over to the safe house after a brief stop at home. Sam asked Emily if she would like to go home with her, where her truck was waiting, since Emily's car was still buried under the Oak. Tara offered to drop them off before going back to Dynamadics to wait with John Stockwell for "the call."

Everyone gathered their belongings and headed toward the door bound for their various destinations.

** ** **

197

Chapter Nineteen
Romance & Revelations

Jason fastened his seatbelt while he instructed the autopilot to "take us home." He looked over at Laura and asked in a mildly agitated tone, *"Can you believe Sam? She's had the ability to pinpoint Diane's location all along...and never said a word!"*

"Yeah, you're right Jason...but cut the girl a little slack, we've - all of us - been under a hell of a lot of pressure this past week. She's been shot at, kidnapped, escaped her captors in the middle of a hurricane - stealing their helicopter no less! Not to mention the shoot-out we just went through at the Office. I mean, C'mon...it was just a rookie mistake."

Acknowledging Laura's insight, he sheepishly admitted, "I over-reacted, no doubt. You're right, she's one helluva detective, plus one helluva *person*...I'm really, really lucky to have her." The autopilot parked the car in Jason's designated space when his ringtone sounded. It was CIA Director McBride. They remained in the vehicle as he took the call.

"Hello, Director, yes, she's sitting next to me...we just got home. Sure...I see...yes, go right ahead. Uh huh; uh huh." (Long pause as Jason listens to McBride) "I understand Director. I'll convey that to Laura. We won't do anything before checking in with the Agency. Tara will be with Stockwell for the call this afternoon. Yes...you as well. Goodbye."

After a couple minutes silence, Laura pointedly glanced at Jason and inquired, "So...? Was that all 'top secret' stuff, or what? I mean, *I am* the CIA agent here...right?"

Startled out of his reverie, Jason offered, "No, no... I'm sorry Laura, no slight intended...I was just caught up thinking about what she said."

"*Well...?*"

"Right," he began, "she said the entire situation has taken a new turn. Vladimir Kaslov is a double agent. Actually, that's not entirely accurate. He is, first and foremost, a Russian agent and his first loyalty is to Mother Russia. Apparently, McBride is holding something - she didn't say what - over his head. They have an arrangement. He will perform certain tasks for us but will not reveal any intelligence that would be detrimental to his country. We just saw an example of that - his attempted assassination of Dimitrov."

"What about us? The Agency wouldn't have told him to kill us...right?"

"No, of course not," affirmed the detective. "He was acting on instructions from the Kremlin. *You* were his target; I was just collateral."

"I was? But *why?*" Asked a perplexed Laura.

"McBride said she didn't know but wasn't sparing any effort to find out. As soon as she knows, you'll know. In the meantime, we need to be especially alert."

"*Especially alert?* The 'threat level' is higher than what already exists? *Really?*"

"Point taken," conceded Jason. "However, as they say, you can never be too careful."

"True," she replied, "but remember, *I've got you...and a Two Minute Warning!*"

** ** **

Tara watched the two women walk up the driveway and pause by Sam's truck as she gave her beloved ride a quick once-over before heading to the front door with Emily right behind her. Sam opened the door and they quickly disappeared inside. Tara waited a couple of minutes just to be on the safe side before instructing the autopilot to "Take me to Dynamadics."

As the car turned toward the highway and her destination, she found herself mentally reviewing the day's events; indeed, everything that had transpired since her close call at Dynamadics almost a week ago. She felt a shiver when recalling her near-death experience. *If it hadn't been for Jason McBride, well... Quite the team,* she thought, *all we've been through this past week. Shot at, car-bombed, kidnapped...jeez we could be a TV series...still got to get Diane back safe and sound* was her final thought as she drifted off to an unintentional - but well-deserved nap.

** ** **

"How about a beer?" offered Sam as she walked over to the fridge.

"Sure," answered Emily as she set her purse on the sofa, "sounds great. I could use a cold brew right about now. Frankly, I'm exhaust-ed, mentally and physically." She continued on to the bar, pulling out a stool for herself.

"Ditto," responded her host, returning from the fridge with two Heinekens and two frosty mugs in hand. Pouring their beverages, she observed, "You know Emily, when you get right down to it, it's the little things in life that make the big things matter. For instance: here, sharing a cold brew with a good friend is what makes the 'big thing' - my home - really matter. Gives it *life.* Without little things like this, it's no more than a 'four-walls with a roof' shelter."

"Look at you!" Exclaimed Emily. *"Sam the Philosopher.* Seriously, though, an astute observation...I couldn't agree more."

Reaching over, Sam gently laid her hand on Emily's forearm. "What...you think I'm all muscle and fight?" They both laughed, tak-ing healthy swigs of their beers before clinking their mugs in a mutual toast.

"If you ever want to join up with the FBI, let me know. We could sure use you; actually, we could use ten of you. You're a helluva an investigator, and with more than your fair share of brainpower!"

"Thanks, Emily, but I think I've found my calling with Jason. As an ex-Marine, I know all about how the government works...I like the freedom of the private sector."

"*Ex Marine?* I thought 'once a Marine always a Marine'," pointed out Emily.

"*Simper Fi',*" said Sam, "you are correct. Just sayin'."

"I get it," replied Emily. "Each of us has to follow his *or her,* own path: Tara with corporate; You and Jason as private investigators; me and D'arby with the FBI; Laura and Jaydan in the CIA... each of us on a dedicated path."

Seizing the moment, Sam said, "Let me ask you something...what do you think about Jaydan?"

"Jaydan?" Parroted Emily. "Do you mean professionally or personally?"

"Both."

"Well," continued Emily, "I obviously don't know him that well, but *professionally* he strikes me as being exceptional at what he does. *Personally,* well...gotta say...I think he's a very attractive man." After a short pause, "Actually he's downright handsome. Why do you ask?"

"Well," said Sam, "I think he's got a crush on you."

"*You're kidding,*" replied an incredulous Emily. "I'm certainly not in his league."

"Don't sell yourself short, I think you're very pretty, I'd say *beautiful.* I'd love to see you when you're all dressed up."

Blushing, Emily replied, "I don't see myself that way, but since you brought it up, I *do find myself attracted to the man.* Even had a fantasy or two, if I'm being honest."

"Great!" exclaimed Sam. "Girl, I see romance in your future!"

** ** **

"Real convenient living on the other side of the lake," observed Laura as they got out of the Lexus and headed toward the elevator. "What is it, about a half mile from the office?"

"Seven-tenths actually," answered Jason. "We could have just as easily walked. The top reason I rented this apartment. What is it they say...'location, location, location'?" They entered the elevator, and he punched the fourth-floor button. As they approached his apartment, the door opened, activated by the security system's facial recognition.

"Welcome home Jason...Ms. Laura," pronounced the invisible System Manager in his English Butler accent, "I trust the two of you had a delightful day."

"You don't know the half of it, Alfred," replied Jason sarcastically.

"Don't take it out on poor Alfred," teased Laura with mock indignation, "you programmed him after all. You're going to hurt his feelings."

"She's right you know," remarked the disembodied Alfred, "you programmed me this way."

"See," said a grinning Laura, "I told you so."

"Be quiet, the both of you," said Jason, breaking into a smile. "He's just a collection of algorithms, and you, you're...I don't know *what* you are!"

"I know one thing for sure," said Laura in a more subdued tone as she wrapped her arms around Jason in a tight embrace; "I love you with all my heart Jason McVay." He leaned down, whispering "Ditto," before kissing her passionately. They sat close together on the sofa, Jason encircling his mate with his arm as she laid her head on his shoulder. In his mind, Jason heard Laura say, *I will always love you Jason, we will be together in a most wonderful way.*

What do you mean, "a most wonderful way?" responded Jason in his mind. *"You scare me with this telepathy thing...how are you doing this?"*

Don't worry my Love, you will know everything very soon. Trust me. I love you.

Laura slowly sat upright. She glanced at Jason saying, "I'm pretty hungry. How about you?"

Jason looked at Laura with a now receding blank expression and replied, "Uh, yeah, right. I could eat something. What did you have in mind?"

"I've got a real craving for pizza. Since I have a quick errand to run, thought I could pick up a pie on the way back...what do you think?"

"Sure...errand? What kind of errand?" Quizzed Jason.

"Something I promised Jaydan," replied Laura. "Nothing to do with you...Agency stuff unrelated to our investigation. I'll explain later."

"All right, then," said a momentarily placated Jason as Laura headed for the door.

** ** **

John Stockwell continued pacing the length of his office, alternately looking out the window at the near empty parking lot and glancing at the clock on his desk - the one with the image of the spaceplane *Explorer* Diane had gifted him on his last birthday; *three o'clock...three-twenty...three-forty...almost four. It won't be long now,* he thought. As he paced by the window, he saw Tara's car pull into her reserved space. *Great!* he thought, watching her step out of her car and begin the short trek to the front entrance where she disappeared from view.

The entrance door slid open upon identifying her via facial recognition. One of the Security Officers rounded the corner near the elevators. Nodding in her direction, he acknowledged her arrival. "Good afternoon, Director Wayne, is there anything I can do for you?"

"Good afternoon, Officer Perez. I'm going to my office for a moment and then will be in conference with Mr. Stockwell at his office. If anyone besides senior staff arrives, let me know before admitting them."

"Very good, Director," he replied, confirming with another nod. He watched as she entered the elevator before turning to head for the front foyer.

Stockwell was now seated at his desk, drumming his fingers on the mahogany surface as he awaited Tara's arrival. After what seemed to him an inordinate amount of time, he heard a knock on his door. Glancing at his desk clock, he noted it was now three fifty-five, only five minutes since he had last checked.

"Please... come in," he said. The tension drained from his body as he watched her enter. She had that effect on him. "Please have a seat," he invited, indicating the two identical chairs in front of his desk.

"Anyone in particular?" She inquired, a twinkle in her eye.

"Dealer's choice," he said with a smile.

She selected the one on the right, commenting with mock seriousness, "Well, I'm glad we got that out of the way," as they enjoyed a light laugh, further reducing the tension of the moment. She was about to give him a brief summation of the day's earlier events when his cellphone's ringtone announced *The Call*...it was precisely four o'clock. He looked furtively in her direction. She nodded back; he tapped *accept,* simultaneously placing the phone in *speaker* mode.

"Hello John," greeted an even-toned Whittaker. "We have finally arrived at the moment of reckoning. *If* you do as directed...follow these instructions *precisely*...you will experience a satisfying and profitable outcome. Your wife back safe and sound together with more money than you will ever need. And, as promised, your prior academic record will be permanently 'corrected'. If, on the other hand, these instructions are not followed precisely...and *I mean to the letter*...the outcome will be most unpleasant. Do we understand one another?"

Stockwell looked across at Wayne as he soberly stated, "Yes."

"Good," responded Whittaker. "Write down these instructions exactly as I read them to you. Stop me if you need clarification. When I'm done, I'll have you read them back. Ready?"

"Ready," said Stockwell, pen poised above paper.

** ** **

Jaydan was watching the Red Sox head for the dugout after tying the game at three apiece in the bottom of the eighth when he heard his phone chime. Glancing at the screen he saw it was Laura Sparks calling.

"Hello Agent Sparks, what can I do for you?"

"Hello Jaydan," she answered, "please...it's *Laura,* and it's more of a matter of what I can do for you. I'm pulling up to the house as we speak...are you hungry?"

"Always," was his enthusiastic reply.

"Great, I just left Pizza Palace and I have a still warm meat-lover's pizza ready to be served. Interested?" She heard him click off just as the front door opened to reveal a grinning Jaydan.

Laura opened the passenger door, slid out, and proceeded to the door, pizza box in hand. He held the door open while Laura headed to the kitchen where she laid the pizza on the kitchen table. After a slight detour to the living room to shut off the TV, Jaydan came into the kitchen, heading straight to the fridge.

"Want a beer?" He offered.

"Sure, the autopilot's driving," she joked.

Smiling, he returned with two cans. "Would you like a glass?" he asked.

"No, the can is fine...sit down and have some pizza."

"Thanks, Laura," he said, opening the box and taking a slice. He nudged the box back in her direction.

"No, thanks, it's all for you, I'm gonna pick up another pie on the way home for me and Jason."

"Well, I sure appreciate the pizza. Really thoughtful," said Jaydan, "you didn't have to do that."

"My pleasure, Jaydan," replied Laura, "but if I'm being honest, I have an ulterior motive."

"Oh," said Jaydan, taking another bite, "and what might that be?"

"First, how *private* is our conversation...I'm thinking about our 'guest'."

"He can't hear anything outside the room. It's been soundproofed by our people, so no worries."

"Good," acknowledged Laura. "You were right when you said we had met before. I worked with your Uncle Baylin as a fellow member of the CIA's Serendipity Team - before either of us knew the true identity of the other. At the time, you were working as a "special messenger," hand delivering highly classified communiques to specially involved people. I was one of those individuals. That was sixteen years ago."

"Yes, now I remember," recalled Jaydan. "You said something about my family resemblance with Baylin."

"Exactly!" confirmed Laura. "And that we would meet again in the future. That future is now."

"So, what happens next?" Inquired the young Agent.

"Still to be determined," replied Laura with a twinkle in her eye. "For the moment, finish your Pizza."

"Thanks, Laura. I appreciate your honesty. We have more in common than I realized."

"True," she responded. "Always important to know who's who, right?" She pushed her chair out, saying, "I've gotta get back to Pizza Palace and pick up Jason's pie. He's probably famished by now."

Jaydan stood. "Right, okay, I'll see ya later. Thanks... and for dinner, too." He sat back down, thinking, *I knew I'd seen her before...*

** ** **

Chapter Twenty
The End Game

Jason had just finished his last bite of the last remaining slice of pizza when his ringtone sounded. It was Jaydan. The call lasted a little over five minutes with most of the conversation coming from the caller's end. As soon as he disconnected, Jason glanced at Laura, who, once again, was patiently awaiting a detailed summation.

"That was Jaydan," he said.

"Uh, huh. And..." prompted his mate.

"...And, he finished a session with Pavlov," reported Jason. "Who was most cooperative. Started with Sam and Diane's escape attempt from the cabin. He was embarrassed to say the escape began when he was overpowered by Sam. He said Diane was recaptured after spraining her ankle, which *he* treated, being a trained medical tech. I didn't know - Sam never mentioned that part."

"He provided chapter and verse about Kaslov's assassination attempt on Dimitrov. Further, the guy provided a good description of his teammates and his assessment of their personalities. He has no idea where they took Diane since he had left early with the assault team we confronted at the office. Jaydan sent a report of the interrogation to McBride."

"Well, that intelligence is going to be a big plus going forward," observed Laura. "Speaking of 'going forward' ...I wonder where things stand with John Stockwell?"

"You're right," responded the detective, glancing at his watch. "It's 4:45...he should have heard something by now."

As if in acknowledgment, his ringtone announced an incoming call. It was Tara Wayne.

** ** **

Jaydan pocketed his phone, pushed his chair away from the computer desk, and headed for the living room, plopping down on the sofa. Satisfied that he had completed all the required briefings, he considered resuming the Red Sox game then thought better of it. He sat in silence for a few minutes, musing about recent events.

He thought, *it was a "helluva week" as Sam had so succinctly put it. Talk about living on the edge...they certainly had more than enough excitement this past week! Meanwhile, I've been stuck here doin' grunt work. Still, can't complain, they're a great team. And then there's Emily.*

** ** **

"I'm gonna go give my truck a more thorough inspection...make sure the Russian crew didn't leave any more surprises for me," announced Sam, pushing her stool away from the bar.

"Good idea," affirmed Emily. "Want some help?"

"Nah, I know the drill...but thanks...sit and finish your beer. I'll only be a couple of minutes."

"Okay," acknowledged Emily. "So... you see romance in my future, huh?"

Sam, halfway through the front door, paused, turned her head, and said, "I have no doubt," before disappearing from view.

Emily sat staring at her half-gone mug of Heineken. *Romance in my future. With Jaydan Sanders. ...Nah. Maybe...Nah.*

** ** **

Vladimir Kaslov clicked off on the burner phone. More instructions from Kaitlyn McBride. He sat staring out the window of his third-floor room in the downtown Orlando Hyatt Hotel, courtesy of the CIA. On Lake Eola, the opposite side from Jason McVay's Office. The irony didn't escape him. What had Kaitlyn said when he pointed out the proximity...*ah yes, 'Keep your friends close, but keep your enemies closer.'* She was still pressuring him to reveal why the Kremlin had targeted Laura Sparks for elimination. He continued to resist...that piece of information being the only bargaining chip he had left.

Kaslov reflected on her call: "You have unfinished business," she had said. "Sergei Dimitrov MUST be terminated." He was to complete that assignment during tomorrow's exchange of the *Project Expose'* thumb drive for Diane Stockwell...details to follow. *That bitch is going to get me killed,* ran through his mind.

** ** **

Jason glanced at Laura as he pocketed his iPhone. "That was Tara. John just got off the phone with Whittaker. Time to head over to Dynamadics. Call Sam... I'll grab the 'Go bag.'" Laura nodded in acknowledgement as she headed for her phone on the coffee table.

** ** **

Emily was sitting at the bar immersed in a most pleasant daydream when Sam came in through the front door engaged in a phone conversation. "Yes...right. We're on the way. See ya in about twenty," then slid the phone into her jean's pocket.

Emily said, "Dynamadics?" Which Sam quickly affirmed. "I haven't got my Go Bag with me," noted Emily.

"No problem," replied Sam, "I just finished getting the truck ready...we're loaded for bear...let's go!"

Emily snatched her purse from the sofa as she followed Sam out the door.

** ** **

"Well Tara," said Stockwell as he looked over the instruction list, he had just completed, "I guess this is it."

"Almost," she replied, "the Team's on the way over now to discuss tomorrow's 'exchange'...make sure we have all our ducks in a row. John, you've certainly done your part to make this work. Tomorrow at this time you'll be reunited with Diane."

"That's my expectation," he said optimistically, equal parts hope and fear in his expression.

** ** **

Diane was sitting quietly on the sofa when Dimitrov rounded the corner from the hallway and approached her. He was holding a box with a *Sofisticate* label prominently displayed on top. She was quite familiar with *Sofisticate,* an upscale lady's clothing store located in the Florida Mall.

Smiling, he laid the package on the coffee table in front of her. "Something for you Mrs. Stockwell."

She looked up at him suspiciously, yet obviously curious. With some trepidation she asked, "Should I open it now?"

"Please."

Diane opened the box, slowly lifting out a pale-yellow chiffon dress, the $689 price tag still attached. "It's beautiful," was her instinctive feminine response. "What's the occasion?" she said, half-jokingly.

"Yes," replied Dimitrov. "*The occasion.* We have come to the proverbial end of the road. Tomorrow is...how you American's say, 'the moment of truth'. You will be happily reunited with your husband, and we will finally be in possession of the *Project Expose'* thumb drive. Or not. Which would be most unfortunate for all parties concerned. But optimist that I am, I fully anticipate a positive outcome."

"So, I assume the dress is part of your plan?" speculated Diane.

"You are correct, madame," confirmed Dimitrov. The dress will serve to make you readily identifiable - for both sides - should things suddenly go south. Incidentally, I believe the dress will fit...I took the liberty of checking your size with Mr. Stockwell. Oh, and I'm happy to inform you, after the transaction is complete, it is yours to keep with my compliments. Consider it a small token of appreciation for your cooperation and patience during this ordeal."

At this, Dimitrov bowed slightly; with a smile turned and left.

** ** **

Jason and Laura noted the nearly empty Dynamadics' parking lot as the car pulled in the main entrance. Laura said, "Look, there's Tara's car," pointing out the parked vehicle.

"Release control," Jason instructed the autopilot, manually driving the car over to park adjacent to Tara. They stepped out of the Lexus in time to see Sam's truck turn into the parking lot. Both Jason and Laura waved them over; Sam noticing immediately and a moment later pulling in beside them. She and Emily exited the vehicle, "Long time, no see," joked Sam.

"It's been a long day," observed Laura.

"And it's not over yet," added Emily.

The foursome made their way to the front entrance.

"They're here," announced Stockwell, watching the group disappear as they approached the main entrance. He returned to his desk and sat. Less than a minute later his desk phone rang. Tara immediately reached for it.

"Hello, Officer Perez. Yes. Please send them up to Mr. Stockwell's office. Thank you."

Three minutes later, they arrived at Stockwell's office, where he and Tara were standing outside the office door. Everyone exchanged greetings, then followed Tara back to the elevator, headed to the fourth-floor conference room.

Upon entering the room, Tara took the head chair, John Stockwell to her right and Jason on her left. Laura and Sam sat adjacent to Jason while Emily took a seat next to Stockwell.

After everyone was seated, Tara stood to speak. "This will be our final meeting, barring unforeseen circumstances, so we need to be sure we've got all bases covered." Taking her seat she said, "John will detail the instructions he got from Whittaker, then the group can slice and dice all of that before we put our plan together." Glancing at Stockwell, she continued, "John, if you would..."

Stockwell remained seated as he began, "Everything is pretty straightforward...I do want to point out that Whittaker was quite emphatic about following his instructions - as he put it - 'to the letter', and I have no doubt of his resolve in this regard. I have made a copy of his instructions for each of you. This is what he said, verbatim:"

"The Exchange will occur tomorrow at precisely 11:00 AM at the Center Courtyard of the Florida Mall. Diane Stockwell will be seated at the northeast corner table with her back to the Food Court."

"She will be dressed in a pale-yellow chiffon dress. Seated to her left will be Sergei Dimitrov. Another of our associates will be seated on her right."

"There is a bank of personal lockers located on the wall directly across from Diane's table. The Thumb Drive is to be placed in Locker number thirteen. Secure it and take the key to Dimitrov. There is to be no conversation. After delivering the key to him, immediately turn and depart via the West Hall. For reference, the Apple Store is the first facility."

"The Associate on Diane's right will go to the locker, retrieve the Thumb Drive, and exit via the East Hall. Within five minutes he will verify the Thumb Drive is authentic. Once verified, Diane will be allowed to leave via the West Section while Dimitrov will simultaneously exit via the East Section. At that point, our business is finished."

"Any deviation from this arrangement will result in Mrs. Stockwell's demise."

"Pretty smart, if you ask me," observed Sam. "They set the meet up in a public place with numerous exit points, plus a crowd to get lost in."

"I agree," said Jason. "Boxing them in is going to be difficult, if not impossible. Any miscalculation on our part could be fatal for Diane."

John Stockwell looked over at Jason, a look of terror spreading across his face.

"John...John, we're *not going to let that happen!*" interjected Tara. "I have the greatest confidence in this team. You're looking at many years of combined experience, not to mention the full resources of the United States government. We're going to get Diane back safe and sound, I promise!"

Stockwell now relaxed somewhat. "I know...I believe that. It's just..."

"John," interrupted Emily, "I've been with the Bureau for over ten years. Five of those years were spent on the primary Hostage Rescue Team. Our team *never* lost a hostage. We've got this."

Stockwell nodded as he sat back in his chair, seemingly more at ease after listening to the FBI Agent's reassuring words.

Tara was about to speak when Jason's ringtone announced a call. He glanced at the screen, holding up a finger, silently requesting a pause. "Hello, Director. The Team is having a meeting as we speak. Yes, I have them right here."

Everyone listened as Jason read the exchange instructions to McBride. After a few moments of silence, he laid his phone on the table. "Director McBride wishes to address the Team."

The phone now in speaker mode, McBride began; "First I want to commend everyone on the outstanding work you all have done. What I am about to tell you is classified at the Code Blue level, which Agents Sparks and Cast can explain to you later. Suffice it to say that the outcome of this operation is of extreme importance to the security of our nation."

McBride continued, "The instructions you have received are to be followed exactly. In fact, your Team *is to ensure that the Russians successfully escape. There is to be no attempt to follow them or otherwise impede their departure.* Is that understood?"

In unison, the table responded with a "Yes, Director."

"Again, my thanks to each and every one. Agent Sparks, if I may have a word..."

Jason took the phone off speaker mode and handed it to Laura.

"Yes, Director," she began. After a nearly five-minute conversation, most of which was one-sided, Laura said, "Thank you, Director McBride," then clicked off, handing Jason his phone.

"Well, I guess we won't have to worry about a confrontation now," said a perplexed Jason.

"Rest assured there is rhyme and reason to all this, in spite of appearances," Laura said reassuringly.

"All right, then," said Tara. "I guess we can adjourn until tomorrow. Jason?"

"Yes. Let's meet at the office...say 9:00 AM. You too, John," amended Jason, glancing in Stockwell's direction.

** ** **

Chapter Twenty-One
Tomorrow

Whittaker put the burner phone on the table and looked across at Dimitrov.

"Well, that's done," he said. "Tomorrow will be the end of it."

"Or the end of us," replied Dimitrov, ominously.

"What!? Rather uncharacteristic of you, Sergei. Where is your optimism? Your confidence? We - you and I - have put in the hard work. Our plan *will* be successful, trust me."

"*Da*," sighed the Russian. "It's just...I don't know... *a feeling*, I can't put it into words."

"It's going to be fine," Whittaker said reassuringly. "Right here at this place."

"Yes. It begins and ends at this very table," observed Dimitrov as he surveyed the mall's courtyard from his seat, positioned in the corner adjacent to the East Hall...their exit point. He had a direct view of the bank of storage lockers on the opposite side of the courtyard. Looking up, he saw construction preparations underway on the second level. The six retail units there were now closed, to soon be replaced with a small auditorium for community events. That area was roped off to mall foot traffic, providing the Russians a further security advantage.

"The whole process should take less than ten minutes," noted Whittaker. "The multiple hand-offs of the 'package' will prevent any effective tracking. Frankly, I don't think McVay's team would risk it...they're focused on getting Diane Stockwell back. I'm telling you Sergei, *we got this*! Two days from now you and I will be sipping champagne in the Kremlin with President Sarov."

"Da, Comrade Owen," replied Dimitrov. "I very much look forward to that moment," his still pensive expression at counterpoint to his cheerful tone.

They rose from their chairs simultaneously to head for the adjacent food court; Chinese takeout having been promised for tonight's dinner back at the apartment.

** ** **

Kaitlyn McBride sat at the desk in her study, gazing out at the Potomac River as it lazily wound its way by her Georgetown townhouse. Not the best viewing what with the mist hanging over the constant drizzle. On the other hand, the scene was in keeping with her currently somber mood.

She had just got off the phone with her counterpart at the FBI, Ken Upton. They had been colleagues since together forming the Serendipity Team...what, 16 years ago. A good and trusted friend. During his stewardship of the FBI, they had partnered together many times in a "hand in glove" manner not experienced before in the usually contentious relationship between the two agencies. Nonetheless, their differing missions and modis operendi would occasionally come into conflict. Like now. McBride had been poised to resolve one of her biggest headaches - one Sergei Dimitrov...until Ken Upton called. Now she has to do a - metaphorically speaking - "180". No other option. For the good of the Country. Sighing, she picked up her cellphone.

** ** **

Laura sat on the sofa mentally debating whether she would shower now or wait until morning when Jason popped his head out the bedroom door and announced, "I'm gonna grab a quick shower, Love."

That takes care of that, she thought. "Sure, Honey. I'll call the Team to let them know about breakfast tomorrow." On the drive home Jason told Laura he felt they should have a last strategy session over breakfast with Laura readily agreeing. They decided on *The Breakfast Place* restaurant, located just two blocks from the Mall. She reached for her phone just as the ringtone announced an incoming call. She saw it was Kaitlyn McBride calling from the encrypted number. *Uh, oh* quickly crossed her mind.

"Good evening, Director," greeted Laura.

"Good evening. Are you alone?" Asked McBride.

"I am. Jason's in the shower at the moment."

"Good," replied the Director. "I mean *good that you're* alone," amended McBride, ever the wit. "What I'm about to tell you is highly classified and for *your ears only*...understood?"

"Yes Director," affirmed Laura. She began listening with one ear cocked in the direction of the bathroom as her mate showered.

** ** **

Kaslov stood by the window of his hotel room, looking out at the small pond they'd dubbed *Lake Eola* but was actually seeing nothing; his mind focused exclusively on the instructions the McBride bitch had given him little more than an hour ago:

"As soon as the Mall opens, head to the second level above the central courtyard. Carefully enter the now empty third store down - The Bridal Path - using the keypad code 0709. A case containing a sniper rifle, silencer, and all the accessories you'll need is on the floor at the left rear of the store. Dimitrov will be seated at a table located at the northeast corner of the first-floor courtyard, adjacent to the food court. You will have a clear shot. Take your shot at precisely 11:00 AM. The timing is critical. Depart immediately; take nothing with you, the weapon is untraceable. Go back to the hotel where I will contact you."

Kaslov stepped away from the window and began pacing the length of the hotel room, McBride's instructions looping through his mind over and over again.

** ** **

"Want a Heineken?" Offered Sam as she opened the fridge door.

"No thanks," answered the FBI Agent. "Wait…yeah, what the hell. I think I will. We're done with the serious stuff, right?"

"For tonight. Tomorrow's a different story," ventured Sam. "The moment of truth, as they say. But I'm confident. This is one hell of a talented group of people!" She continued, handing Emily a frosted mug of ice-cold Heineken. Sam reached into the freezer and came out with another frosty mug; promptly pouring her bottle of Heineken into it. Sam raised her mug, "To Diane!"

"To the Team!" Added Emily.

"To Success!" They both exclaimed in near unison, clinking their mugs together.

Emily's ringtone sounded. It was Laura.

** ** **

Jaydan sat at the kitchen table, eyeing his freshly made cup of coffee while enjoying the rare silence. It had been little more than an hour since Agent Janet Walker had picked up his charge, Pavlov Kruska, bound for parts unknown. Then came the call from Jason. He was to join up with the Team at the *Breakfast Place* for a strategy session prior to the *Exchange* meeting. Which made him very happy. Maybe…just maybe, a little excitement for a change. At the very least, a welcome change of pace from his usual routine.

Sipping his coffee, his thoughts turned to Laura Sparks. Kindred spirit. Like his Uncle Baylin. The three of them the same. Well, not exactly. She was from a different place. Her people had welcomed Jaydan's people with open arms. Her place was now *their* place. He knew his and Laura's true identities had to remain secret. For now.

** ** **

Laura snuggled up to her lover, lying quietly on his side. After all the phone calls, they had settled in for a moment together. Not the most ideal time for romance. On the other hand, a welcome respite from the tension of the day...indeed the whole week. An evening of wine and lovemaking - the best possible stress reliever. She still felt that special after-glow; the warmth of his body next to hers. She loved him more every day.

Jason relished the comforting feel of Laura as she lay against his back. He loved her so much; it was becoming more difficult to deal with their inevitable partings. That had to end. It was time to make the final commitment. Still, he had a sense of dread... he knew that Laura was different; *how different* he truly had no idea.

** ** **

Tara sat on her sofa enjoying a glass of Chardonnay, a small pleasure in this moment of stress as light classical played softly in the background. She loved her new home; it was little more than a year since she had moved in. At five bedrooms, a bit large for a single woman...but what the hell, she had to spend her money on something. It occurred to her that she lived only a mile from Briar Patch Estates, where John and Diane Stockwell's home was located. *Where this whole thing started.* She thought, *the most significant event during her long career in the security field - with the exception of working with Baylin Sanders and the Serendipity Team sixteen years ago.* A few moments later, she fell asleep, the long day catching up with her.

** ** **

Diane lay quietly in the bed, listening to the traffic noise rising above the hum of the air conditioner. It had been a long week and, if she was being completely honest, an *exciting* week. Now about to end…she believed, in a good way. Diane drifted off to peaceful slumber.

** ** **

Chapter Twenty-Two
The Buck Stops Here

Laura looked around the table as the waitress cleared the last of the breakfast dishes. She stood saying, "If I could have everyone's attention for a moment. Before Jason gives you your assignments, I want to pass along more information concerning Director McBride. She has been working with FBI Director Upton on this particular situation since its beginning. Jason's Agency, along with Tara, had actually 'stumbled' into an ongoing CIA/FBI joint investigation, the result of the unforeseen kidnapping of Diane Stockwell."

"I can verify what Laura is telling you," chimed in Emily. "I, too have been in touch with Director Upton about this case, which goes deeper than the rest of you are currently aware. I'm sure you understand Laura and I have to adhere to the confidentiality of our respective agencies."

"Yes," resumed Laura, "You are all professionals, no disrespect intended. As a matter of fact, Director McBride is most impressed with your entire team, Jason. And that includes you, Tara. I can promise you all that once this mission is concluded, you will all be 'read in'. For now, I need to relay the parameters of today's action:

"First - and most important - THERE IS TO BE NO ATTEMPT TO PREVENT THE RUSSIAN TEAM FROM OBTAINING THE THUMB DRIVE. NO ATTEMPT WILL BE MADE TO HINDER THEIR SUCCESSFUL ESCAPE IN ANY WAY. This is imperative for the success of the mission. Everything will make a bit more sense if you think back to Baylin Sanders visit. Second, this whole operation *must be as low key as possible.* We damn sure don't need any publicity!"

Laura took her seat as Jason tapped the side of his water glass. "Now it's time for your individual assignments during *the exchange* process."

Jason began with Laura, who would be leaving almost immediately to conduct reconnaissance; Sam and Jaydan were to continually patrol the lower-level Courtyard perimeter while Emily would perform the same function on the less travelled upper level portion overlooking the Courtyard. Jason would place the package containing the thumb drive in locker #13 and deliver the key to the Russian across from Dimitrov, who would retrieve the thumb drive from the locker and exit via the East Hall. Once Dimitrov signaled the "Okay" with a pre-arranged simple nod, Tara would proceed to the Russian's table as Dimitrov exited to the East Hall; returning with Diane to Jason's table, where John would be awaiting his wife.

At that point, Jason would make quick phone contact with everyone individually before they proceeded to Dynamadics.

Jason glanced around the table. "Everyone good?" He queried. The Team nodded in unison.

Laura stood, saying, "If you'll excuse me...Good luck! I'll see you all at Dynamadics."

She pushed out her chair and headed for the door as their waitress arrived with more coffee and their check.

** ** **

During the short trip to the Florida Mall, Laura focused on her *other* assignment, recalling in detail what McBride told her. The original plan had called for Kaslov to take out Dimitrov as soon as the other Russian had left the premises with the Thumb Drive.

Kaslov had gone incommunicado after his last conversation with McBride. She explained it was part of his personal ritual before an assigned assassination. For luck or something. Bottom line, she wouldn't be able to reach him before the event. Laura's job was to stop him without seriously harming him, then ensure he could escape. Oh, and make sure he didn't know who was responsible. When she asked McBride *how* she was supposed to do that, her reply was, "That's up to you *Senior* Agent Sparks...use your ingenuity."

Sure, thought Laura, *easy for you to say. Well, I really didn't want to pull this particular rabbit out of the hat just yet, but desperate times call for desperate measures.*

As she approached the West Entrance, she glanced at her watch, noting it was 10:05, the Mall open barely five minutes. She came through the door, literally unseen by anyone and headed for the escalator at the Central Courtyard. Once on the second level, she made her way over to *The Bridal Path* store. Upon entering the access code, the door slid open.

Laura walked in, immediately touching the *Close* button on the interior keypad. She scanned the near empty store; the only items there were three plastic chairs - one in a rear corner and the other two placed near the front entrance. In the opposite rear corner was the case containing the sniper rifle.

She walked a few paces and stood next to the chair furthest from the door; there to await the arrival of her quarry. She touched the outside of her pants pocket and felt the reassuring bulge of the syringe.

** ** **

Whittaker stood on the sidewalk watching Dimitrov give Asimov his final instructions.

Asimov nodded occasionally as Dimitrov spoke. The Russian stepped back from the SUV and watched Asimov and his crew of six exit the parking lot on their way to the Florida Mall.

He walked the short distance to the sidewalk where Whittaker awaited. "Well Owen," he said, "the final chapter has begun. I hope at the end of the day the two of us are enjoying a well-deserved dinner and drinks, though I must confess some measure of trepidation."

Whittaker clapped his hand on the Russian's broad shoulder. "Comrade Sergei, you worry too much. This is going to go so smoothly...I promise."

"Da...I hope so. We have left nothing to chance. As you say, smooth as...*the glass?*"

They both laughed as they headed toward the rear elevator.

Diane sat on the sofa, awaiting the return of Dimitrov and his companion, who Dimitrov addressed as *Owen.* For whatever reason, he had never seen fit to introduce them. The two men came in the door and stood in front of Diane.

"I must say," Mrs. Stockwell, *yellow* becomes you. The dress is beautiful, as is its wearer. I must confess to envying your husband. If all goes well - as I fully expect - the two of you will be reunited short-ly. I regret this past week's ordeal. On the other hand, you can think of it as an adventure...imagine the tale you can tell your chil-dren...and later, grandchildren! And don't forget to check your bank account later, I'm sure you'll be pleased with your compensation."

"I must thank you for treating me so well under the circumstances," said Diane with sincere appreciation. "I don't understand...but thank you."

"You're welcome," replied Dimitrov. "As I said before, we are not animals after all. Now, it is time to go. All that is required of you is to just sit quietly. No blindfold sunglasses this time. You are going home." Diane stood and the trio headed to the door.

** ** **

Kaslov walked through the Mall's East Entrance and casually strolled down the hall toward the Center Courtyard. He was dressed like a maintenance man and carried a small toolbox. Upon reaching the Courtyard he stepped on the escalator to the Upper Level. On the ride up, he looked around, observing only a small number of people about. He stepped off the escalator and nonchalantly headed to the roped-off north side, where his destination, the now closed *The*

Bridal Path store awaited him. He unfastened the rope, stepped across, then refastened it. At the store entrance, he looked around before entering the *0709* entry code into the keypad, the door sliding open in response. Once inside, he pressed the *Close* button; the door quickly sliding shut. He set the empty toolbox down and looked at his watch. 10:15. He had less than an hour.

Something didn't feel right. He glanced around the empty store. To his right, a couple of chairs were placed along the front, about four feet from the entrance. In the rear, another chair was in a corner. In the opposite corner he saw the case containing his sniper rifle. Still, he couldn't shake the feeling that he wasn't alone. Suddenly, the hairs on the back of his neck stood up. His heart was racing. Then, he felt a *presence* behind him just before a sudden sharp sting in his arm. Before he could touch his arm, everything went black.

**** ** ****

Laura watched Kaslov approach the store, enter the access code, and come into the store. As he looked around the store, she pulled the syringe from her pocket, uncapped the needle, and walked up behind Kaslov. She jabbed the needle into his right arm, simultaneously pushing the plunger all the way down. In less than two seconds, he dropped to the floor, where he would lay unconscious for the better part of an hour. Laura walked back to the door, let herself out, and walked over to the glass wall overlooking the Courtyard.

**** ** ****

At 10:25, Diane Stockwell, along with Dimitrov, entered the Center Courtyard and headed directly to the table located at the southeast corner where Asimov was already seated. She took the center seat with Asimov on her right and Dimitrov sliding into the seat on her left.

Glancing at Asimov, Dimitrov queried, "So...?"

"So," responded the other man, "everything is as it should be. The crew are in position; strategically located around the Mall and out-side in the parking lot. Everything appears normal. We haven't detected any government agents, though the arrival of McVay's Team is imminent I'm sure…we know all of them by sight."

"Very good," acknowledged his boss. "Whittaker has taken up a position on the Upper Level to monitor the situation.

"Ah," announced Asimov, "there they are now!"

Diane and Dimitrov followed Asimov's glance in the direction of the West Hall to see Jason McVay, Tara Wayne, and John Stockwell come into the Courtyard and head to the designated table at the middle of the west side. At the same time, Dimitrov noticed Jaydan and Sam Talley begin casually strolling around the Courtyard perimeter. Sam playfully waved in Asimov's direction, the Russian nodding in acknowledgement.

Leaning toward Dimitrov, Asimov asked, "Who is that with the Talley woman?"

"That," curtly replied Dimitrov, "is CIA Agent Jaydan Sanders, an interrogation specialist. Pavlov is currently in his custody."

On the Upper Level, Whittaker noticed Agent Cast about halfway up on the Escalator. Not wanting to be seen by Emily, he melded into the increasing mall traffic, working his way around to the "down" escalator. He realized she was already aware of his "rogue" status, but he wasn't eager to have a verbal confrontation, especially in the current circumstances. As he approached the escalator, Laura Sparks suddenly materialized directly in front of him, seemingly out of thin air.

"Hello, Agent Whittaker," Laura said demurely, "fancy meeting you here."

Whittaker, both startled and taken aback by her comment replied, "I…uh…I didn't see you, Agent Sparks…I..uh, I have to go now."

Fixing him with an icy stare, Laura coldly said, *"I'm sure,"* before suddenly vanishing.

The now totally befuddled Whittaker looked all around him before getting on the escalator. He continued nervously looking around all the way down.

At Jason's table, Tara suddenly pointed at the down escalator. "Isn't that Agent Whittaker?" She asked Jason.

"It is," he quickly answered. "I wonder what the hell he's doing here. You wouldn't think he'd be showing up, even though he's a big part of the plot. Piece of shit, if you ask me."

Nervously tapping his fingers on the table, Stockwell looked over at Diane, then glanced at his watch. "It's 10:45," he announced.

Jason looked at his own watch confirming, "Your right, John. Almost time."

** ** **

At 10:55, Jason, who had spent the last ten minutes fixed on Sergei Dimitrov, saw him pick up his cellphone. After a couple of minutes, he put the phone down and looked over at Jason, nodding his head. Apparently he had received the *all-clear* from his crew.

The detective got up and headed straight for the bank of personal convenience lockers on the north side of the Courtyard. As prearranged, at the lockers' payment panel, he slid his debit card through the slot and selected locker 13. He walked over to the locker, pulled the key from its slot, the locker door springing open. He reached into his pocket and retrieved the small package containing the precious Thumb Drive, sliding the package in and closing the locker.

Jason walked directly over to Dimitrov's table. Without a word, he handed the locker key to Asimov, turned, and walked back to his table. Once Jason was seated, Asimov rose, pushed his chair out and quickly walked over to locker 13. He opened the locker, pulled out the package and after a cursory inspection, put it in his pocket. The Russian turned and walked through the Courtyard, disappearing down the East Hall.

Halfway down the East Hall, he smoothly handed off the package to an associate heading back to the Courtyard. At the Courtyard, this person turned and proceeded down the North Hall, where he repeated the earlier handoff maneuver with yet another associate. When this person reached the courtyard, he headed down the South Hall.

Meanwhile, the second associate continued down the North Hall and out the door where he walked down the sidewalk, cutting into the parking lot five rows down. He was in possession of the Thumb Drive, *having convincingly faked the earlier handoff.* He quickly disappeared into a nondescript white van parked four spaces down the row. Inside the van, he handed the Thumb Drive to the computer expert inside, one of the top computer engineers in the SVR; who immediately set about his work.

** ** **

Trying to stay calm, Diane glanced back and forth between Dimitrov, who was sitting stoically and Jason who looked her way with what he hoped was a reassuring expression. It seemed like an eternity since Asimov had left with the Thumb Drive to have its authenticity verified.

Tara looked at her watch. 11:15. Felt a lot later than that.

Dimitrov picked his phone up. He listened intently for about a minute, then stood up, pocketing his phone. With a wide smile he nodded, first at Jason, then, taking Diane's hand, at her. He released her hand, turned, then quickly disappeared down the East Hall. Tara immediately got up, almost breaking into a run. When she reached Diane, who was already standing, the two quickly hugged before returning to Jason's table, where John was waiting. Diane and John embraced and kissed, both with tears of joy...and relief. No one spoke for several minutes. Finally, John whispered into his wife's ear, "It's over. *I love you so much!*" Still unable to speak, she responded with a series of kisses.

Laura suddenly appeared at Jason's side. "Shall we...?" she said, indicating the West Hall.

"Right!" Acknowledged Jason. "Let's all meet up at Dynamadics."

The entire Team walked down the West Hall, leaving John and Diane to enjoy some private moments together.

** ** **

Chapter Twenty -Three
A Not So Dull Day After All

Jason, Laura, Sam, and Emily began the short trek down the West Hall while Tara stayed behind in the Courtyard. Diane and John would be riding back to Dynamadics with her, and she was allowing them a little more reunion time before heading out.

While all the Team were happy for the uneventful conclusion; Sam, in particular, was annoyed that the Russians were essentially given a "free Pass". Voicing her frustration she exclaimed, "I mean, what the hell, *they kidnapped us,* but get off scott-free! Damn."

"You're right of course," acknowledged Jason. "But no one got hurt. Plus, as kidnappings go, you guys were treated like VIPs."

"...and I still haven't figured *that* out," replied Sam.

"Don't look a gift horse in the mouth," Jason retorted.

"For my part," observed Emily, "I'm more than satisfied everything went so smoothly. In my experience, more often than not, that's just not the case." Stealing a glance at Laura she continued, "Besides, after we debrief at Dynamadics, I think you'll see things quite differently."

Laura said simply, "Agreed. As you pointed out Emily, dull...but safe." *As long as you don't include my encounter with Kaslov,* ran through her mind...*when I put him beddy-byes. Or my little run-in with the Whittaker Traitor. Now THAT was rewarding.*

Reaching the door, Jason politely let the women exit in front of him. They walked the short distance to Jason's car where Sam's truck was conveniently parked in the adjacent slot.

As everyone got into their respective vehicles, Sam shouted, "Just another quiet day at the ranch," drawing smiles from the team. She pulled out with Jason right behind her. Just as Sam was beginning to turn onto the perimeter road, she slammed on the brakes, forcing Jason to do the same. An old, beat-up car had swerved in front of Sam's truck, with screeching brakes announcing a panic stop.

Sam exclaimed, "WHAT THE HELL! ..." just as a teenage girl tumbled roughly out onto the pavement. The driver's side opened and a skinny guy with a scraggly beard leapt out and ran around to the girl on the other side. He grabbed her, dragging her by the hair to the still open passenger side door; all the while the girl kicking and screaming. Sam and Emily simultaneously leapt out of her truck. The perp saw them coming; letting go of the girl, he ran around to the driver's side, jumping in just ahead of Sam's outstretched arms. He pulled the door shut as he punched the accelerator, tires screaming under the sudden force. Emily grabbed the girl and dove toward Sam's truck, barely avoiding the two of them being run over.

Laura punched her window's *down* button, yelling, "YOU OKAY, EMILY?"

Emily, still holding onto the girl, nodded in affirmation. Laura looked over at Jason, who put the Lexus in gear; deftly pulling around Sam's truck, ending up on the bumper of the perp, who was pushing the dilapidated car for all it was worth. He turned from the perimeter road onto the Orange Blossom Trail, the inertial force slamming the passenger side door shut. Jason backed off slightly, putting a few car lengths between his much faster Lexus and the shit-bomb in front of him.

"Careful, Jason," cautioned Laura, "this looks like a really busy road... Sunday not withstanding!"

"I know this area well," he replied. "I think I can keep him in sight until we can get help!"

Laura touched her phone's 911 button. Once connected via the car's hands-free audio system she quickly explained the situation and began calling out streets as they stayed back far enough so as not to unduly panic the perp into doing something even more dangerous.

Suddenly, she felt an intuitive dread. She looked at Jason, who appeared to be in a trance.

...Oh shit, immediately entered her mind.

The now all-too-frequent chill descended upon Jason. The *movie in his mind* began playing: The perp must have concluded he wouldn't be able to lose the more powerful and nimble Lexus, because his next move was born of desperation. Suddenly, the perp's car swerved into the opposing traffic lanes as he began heading the *wrong way.* Jason stayed right behind him, believing that if he could get close enough, he could spin the perp out, hopefully avoiding a tragedy.

Before he could reach the car's rear bumper, the perp hit the brakes and turned down a little-used access road. Jason duplicated the maneuver and began closing on the perp's bumper. Suddenly out of nowhere, a tanker truck laden with a full load of propane appeared in front of the perp's car, its horn blaring and tires screeching as the trucker hit the brakes. Before Jason could react, his car slid into perp's car just as that vehicle met the huge tractor-trailer head on. A blinding white flash was quickly followed by a black void. Then real time resumed.

Laura watched Jason intently as the perp, with Jason still on his tail, changed direction, heading the wrong way into oncoming traffic. The perp suddenly turned right onto an empty road.

Jason hit the brakes, turning in the opposite direction. The Lexus' autopilot instantly took control of the vehicle - just as it was designed to do when perceiving a vehicle control issue - safely guiding the car across two lanes of traffic before stopping on the shoulder. Suddenly the car was lifted almost a foot off the ground by the concussive blast from a huge explosion somewhere on the other side of the road. The car settled back; Jason and Laura turning to see a rapidly rising black plume from the fading fireball of the explosion.

Traffic on both sides of the road came to an abrupt halt as the sound of emergency vehicles approaching from all directions grew increasingly louder. Jason and Laura got out, walked to the front of the Lexus, and silently watched the horrific scene about a half mile down from where the street intersected with the Orange Blossom Trail. An unmarked Orange County Sheriff Department SUV came to a stop behind Jason's car. Sheriff Brown stepped out and walked toward the couple. With a wry smile, he extended his hand to Jason, then Laura.

"We meet again, Detective McVay. Please tell me this has nothing to do with Kaitlyn McBride and her agency?" he said with just a touch of sarcasm.

"No...not this time," volunteered Laura. "It appears to be your run-of-the-mill, ordinary abduction gone awry. If you have your investigators speak with Sam Talley, she can give you all the details. She has the intended victim with her. That girl is one little warrior."

"Thanks," replied Brown, obviously relieved it wouldn't be necessary for him to do any *fixing* this time. "You two appear to be all right."

"We are," confirmed Jason. "It was just a case of 'right time, right place' for us. Lucky girl, that young lady. I'm really happy we were there to help her. One thing, Sheriff Brown..."

"I know," anticipated Brown, "You would be grateful if I kept your names out of it."

"Right," confirmed Jason with a sheepish smile. "Thanks. If ever I can do anything for you...and I do mean *anything*...don't hesitate to ask."

"My pleasure, Detective McVay...and thanks for the offer. I'll have one of my agents take your statements, then you can get out of here." Once again, he shook hands with the pair before turning toward a couple of Sheriff Investigators.

Laura reached for her phone. "Hello Sam…"

** ** **

Sam answered her phone the instant Laura's face popped up on the screen. *"What the hell happened?!"* she asked with barely contained excitement.

Laura relayed the details of the car chase - avoiding Jason's *two-minute warning* part - including the perp's car colliding with the tanker truck resulting in the huge fireball easily visible from Sam's vantage point.

"Oh," Laura continued, "Heads up…a Sheriff's Investigator is heading over for your witness statement. How's the girl doing? From what we saw, she put up quite a fight."

"Yeah, she did," affirmed Sam. "She's fine except for some bumps and bruises from the spill on the pavement. Said she managed to kick him in the face before he grabbed her hair. Anyway, her Mom is on the way over to us. They were shopping in different stores when the girl got taken."

"Gotta go, that Investigator you were talking about just pulled up. Plus, it's crazy over here, they're evacuating the mall now. We'll see y'all at Dynamadics as soon as we can get out of here."

"Okay," replied Laura, "see ya at Dynamadics." She ended the call then told Siri to "Call Tara." A moment later Tara answered. "Hi Tara. Are you and the Stockwells all right?"

Tara allowed that they were Okay and just now learning more details about the explosion that had rocked the entire Mall as they made their way out with everyone else. She said they would probably be arriving late due to the circumstances, said goodbye, and clicked off.

As soon as Tara ended the call Laura thought: *just one more call,* before instructing Siri to "Call Kaitlyn McBride."

** ** **

Vladimir Kaslov was laying on his bed staring at the ceiling as he tried to make sense of today's earlier events when his train of thought was broken by the vibration of the bed and the window suddenly rattling. He got up and walked over to the window; arriving just in time to see a rapidly fading red glow off to the south. In the direction of the Florida Mall, where he had just come from. He walked back to the TV, picked up the remote, and turned it on.

"...breaking news. There are calls pouring into the 911 Center about a massive explosion at or near the Florida Mall. We have the Channel 9 Chopper heading there now along with a ground team," said the excited announcer. *"We will be coming back with more details after these words from our partners at Kirby Ford."* As the screen filled with a row of shiny new pickup trucks, he hit the *mute* button and sat down on the bed. After the commercials were over, he reactivated the sound to be informed that *"there has been some sort of explosion near the Mall. The Mall itself is apparently unaffected, although it is being evacuated as a precaution."* As the scene changed between various reporters, he was able to surmise that the explosion was most likely the result of an accident; the only significant consequences being loss of life and the serious disruption of traffic in south Orlando.

Kaslov walked back to the hotel room window, gazing at Lake Eola and its famous fountain jetting plumes of water hundreds of feet in the air. He played over what little he could remember about the morning's events, his mind still foggy. He recalled entering *The Bridal Path* store to set up for his "shoot" at 11:00 sharp. That was at 10:15. Next thing he remembered was sitting up in the empty store with a splitting headache. That was at 11:25. He got up, immediately leaving the store, *along with the sniper rifle still ensconced in its case,* behind. Kaslov left the now busy Mall and returned to his hotel room to await a call from McBride. Hopefully, she could shed some light on what exactly had happened.

** ** **

Sam dropped her phone in her pocket and walked around to the passenger side of her truck where the two Emily's - turned out the girl's name was Emily -were chattering away.

"How you two doin'?" Inquired Sam, with a warm smile.

"Great!" Exclaimed Emily the Younger. "I didn't know Emily is *an FBI Agent!*"

"So," asked Sam, "How old are you Emily?"

"I'll be fourteen next month…on the 12th, actually."

"*My birthday is on the twelfth, too,*" said Emily the Elder, "but six months from now."

"You guys seem to have a lot in common," observed Sam.

The two Emily's looked at one another, simultaneously exclaiming, "Yeah!"

Emily announced, "That's my Mom!" Pointing at an attractive forty-something woman walking rapidly toward the three of them.

** ** **

Chapter Twenty-Four
Didn't See That Coming

Whittaker tossed his suitcase in the back of the SUV, walked around to the already open front passenger door and climbed in, closing the door behind him. As he fastened his seat belt, he glanced over at a stoic Dimitrov, grinning ear-to ear as he fastened his seatbelt.

"Let's go," he said simply.

They had both packed light for the trip to Mother Russia. Four of the crew remained at the apartment. They would resume their "cover" - Wildcat Courier Service - while awaiting the next assignment. Asimov was being reassigned to the Washington cell, a significant promotion for him. In less than an hour, the pair would be taking off on a private jet leaving the Herndon Airport bound for Moscow. As they pulled onto Northbound Orange Blossom trail, they heard a huge explosion relatively close by. Dimitrov saw a bright orange glow in the rear-view mirror.

"What the hell was that?!" Exclaimed Dimitrov.

"Looks like something happened near the Mall," speculated Whittaker. "Whatever...just keep driving, we've got a plane to catch!"

"Da," answered his companion. "We can find out on the news later on."

"Mission accomplished!" exclaimed Whittaker, patting the small package on his lap. "I can hardly wait to get to Moscow with this thing...the final piece of the puzzle. Russia will be able to level the playing field with this cloaking technology. And you…what a coup…I predict a bright future for you Sergei, the soon to be Director of the SVR!"

"Thank you, my friend. In no small part due to your expert assistance. You will be occupying a very big place at the table - this I can guarantee. Together, we will take the SVR to new heights!"

As they neared their turn onto the Crosstown Expressway, they saw a convoy of emergency vehicles speeding south toward the site of the explosion.

** ** **

Vladimir Kaslov sat on the bed awaiting the arrival of the *associate* who had been tasked with helping him get to Dimitrov before he could make his escape. During his just concluded phone conversation with McBride, he learned he had been a victim of a gas leak that affected several of the stores on the second level, including the unit he was in. The problem had been quickly detected and fixed, but not before it had rendered him unconscious. So, he was in no way being held responsible for not completing his assigned mission. In fact, she was sending a trained operative to assist him in completing his original assignment. That provided him a measure of relief, yet he felt something was off.

He heard a knock at the door; two raps followed by one rap followed by two raps - exactly the code McBride had provided. He got up, walked over to the door and opened it. Facing him was a tall, fit looking white guy. "Vladimir Kaslov?" Asked the man, in a thick Russian accent.

"Da," replied Kaslov, pleased to meet a fellow countryman. That was the last thing he ever saw.

** ** **

As soon as the door opened, Pavlov had the man verify his identity. Satisfied it was Kaslov, he raised the silenced Beretta and in rapid succession fired two shots; the first to the head and the second to the heart in the traditional "double tap" style favored by assassins. A tradition with which Kaslov was most familiar. Pavlov looked around as he quickly unscrewed the silencer, pocketing it along with the pistol, then pulled the door shut. He walked across the hall to the elevator he had left locked open, entered and punched in *Lobby. The irony*, he thought. *As a medic he had been trained to save lives NOT take them.* Unfortunately, this distasteful assignment was the price of his freedom.

** ** **

In the sumptuous back seat of Tara's Lincoln, John and Diane Stockwell continued looking at one another in silence. Tara, in a moment of romantic whimsy, had told the couple to take her car to the Dynamadics debrief meeting and that she would catch a ride with Sam and Emily. The couple readily accepted, expressing gratitude for her thoughtfulness. The autopilot announced they would reach their destination in twenty minutes. That was five minutes ago.

John was first to speak. "Diane, *I am so sorry.* Without a doubt, the most bone-headed thing I've ever done in my life. I've treated you terribly, brought shame on us, but through this whole ordeal I've come to realize that you are the most important thing in my life. I love you more than I can put into words...if you'll give me another chance..."

Diane gently touched two fingers to his lips, silencing him for a moment. "While I was stuck in that cabin, I had a lot of time to think...to reflect...I came to believe that in my heart, I do love you, that we were meant to be together. I know, I know...it looked like you betrayed our country...I didn't believe that then - I *don't* believe that now - Tara told me the whole story. You can hold your head high John. You *have redeemed yourself.* I love you and will stand with you through whatever lies ahead." She leaned over and gently kissed him, then brushed his wet cheek. Ahead they could see the exit ramp for the road to Dynamadics.

** ** **

The hot morning had given way to a hotter afternoon. There had been a dearth of the usual afternoon thunderstorms that dropped temperatures ten, sometimes fifteen degrees cooler; usually taking the edge off the relentless Florida summer heat. Jason stood just outside his car, looking up at a cloud-free sky as Laura emerged from the passenger side.

"Damn it's hot," she observed, "where's the rain when you really need it?"

"Like it doesn't get hot in D.C.," retorted Jason. "Looks like we're the first ones here."

Walking around to join Jason she replied, "No telling when everyone will finally get here, traffic around the mall is a big mess. It's gonna take a while to clear that scene."

Anxious to get back into an air-conditioned environment, they quickened their pace to the main entrance, where a security associate was awaiting them.

"Good afternoon Mr. McVay...Ms. Sparks," he greeted, buzzing the door open for them.

"Good afternoon," they replied in unison; the welcoming blast of cold air displacing the *egg-frying* temperature outside. They checked their weapons and walked through the scanner before taking a seat on a comfortable couch near the empty Reception Desk.

Jason was about to speak when Laura said, "Oh, look. Sam and Emily are here."

He replied, "I'm kinda surprised...I thought they'd probably be last, what with having to make statements. Not to mention, they were actually at the perimeter of the mall when everything literally exploded." They watched Sam park her truck next to Jason's car.

"Tara's with them," observed Laura. "I'll bet she lent her car to the Stockwells."

"I think you're right," Jason readily agreed.

The trio made their way to the entrance and were promptly checked in. Tara took the Security Officer off to the side while Sam and Emily went straight over to Jason and Laura. The group had a rather animated conversation about the car chase; the resulting horrific crash, and meeting with Sheriff Brown who, once again, expedited matters for them. Sam and Emily were beginning to tell about their time with *Emily the Younger* when Tara joined them.

"I suggest we head up to the Conference Room. John and Diane are on the way and will be joining us shortly." Everyone nodded in agreement and the group headed for the elevator.

On the fourth floor, the Team followed Tara down the hall to the Executive Office Suite, leading them through the Reception Area to the Conference Room door, which she held open for them. They were pleasantly surprised to see an assortment of sandwiches, side salads, fresh fruit, a selection of deserts, and the obligatory pods of various coffees.

With a broad smile, Tara turned toward her comrades: "Anyone hungry?"

"Does a cat have a climbing gear?" Quipped Sam.

Everyone - apparently hungrier than they realized - lined up to get some of the tantalizing food displayed in front of them.

Tara walked over to the door to answer the light knock and welcomed John and Diane Stockwell. The rest of the team acknowledged their arrival as the pair joined them at the end of the line.

After about twenty minutes of enjoying their repast accompanied by light conversation, Tara took her place at the head of the table; silently signaling it was time to begin the meeting. Taking her cue, the team began heading to their usual places, John and Diane sitting at the end adjacent to Emily. After everyone was settled in, Tara stood to speak.

Looking directly at the Stockwells she said, "Welcome back, Diane! We are all thrilled and relieved to have you back safe and sound! Made possible in large part by the efforts of your husband, John."

The entire group applauded the couple.

Tara continued, "You all need to give yourselves a round of applause for a job well done. John and Diane stood to join Tara in applauding the Team as they remained silently seated in a moment of awkward modesty.

Taking the hint, Tara moved on. "I know there are questions about how this thing ended. Laura and Emily have some information to share." As she took her seat, Tara said, "Whichever one of you wants to speak first..."

Laura stood up. "In my role as a CIA Agent, I have information that can now be shared with the Team. However, Director McBride has requested a videoconference and will incorporate my remarks in her presentation. If you'll turn your attention to the monitor..."

Everyone turned toward the large flatscreen monitor mounted on the front wall behind Tara. CIA Director Kaitlyn McBride came into view.

"Good to finally see you all. First, my congratulations on a job well done. Jason, I'll bet you never thought you'd be partnered up with the CIA." (smiling, he nodded). If you ever want a career with the Agency, call me. That goes for all of you - except Emily. Director Upton would *never* let you go." (Emily blushed at the backhanded compliment).

"What I'm about to tell you is classified at the highest level...it doesn't leave this room. If you'll recall, Agent Sanders inserted hidden coding in the *Project Expose'* software loaded in the thumb drive that is now in their possession. I know their computer engineers will do a thorough analysis of that thumb drive. I also know there is no way they will discover the malware inserted by Baylin."

"Coupled with the hardware they had previously stolen, they will now believe that they have the same cloaking capabilities for their aircraft that we enjoy...true to an extent. No other country will be able to detect their warplanes...*except us.* Our military will be able to track their aircraft - and spacecraft - with precision...thanks to Baylin's *Trojan Horse* coding."

"And that, people, is why it was essential that they be allowed to escape with the *Project Expose'* software. You folks have unwittingly been a significant part of a joint CIA/FBI mission we have dubbed *Operation Trojan Horse.* This mission has been ongoing for over two years; we have just successfully concluded the first stage. To more fully explain the extent of this operation, I have authorized the CIA's local Project Coordinator to read you in." On screen, McBride sat quietly, hands folded on her desk. Just then came a knock on the Conference Room door. Tara said, "Please come in." The door opened, revealing Agent Jaydan Sanders. Walking in right behind him was...*Asimov.*

"What the hell...," uttered a startled Sam; murmurs erupted all around the table. The two men continued into the room with Jaydan taking the last seat on Jason's side. Asimov stood at the end of the table directly opposite Tara.

He looked around the table. Everyone (except Laura and Emily) with perplexed expressions. On the monitor, McBride, a bemused smile breaking, was quite enjoying the moment.

"Good afternoon, everyone. Yes...*it's Asimov.* My full name is Andre Asimov. *Agent* Andre Asimov. I have been with the CIA since graduating college sixteen years ago. Both my parents were Russian immigrants, now U.S. citizens. My Dad retired from the Army with the rank of Colonel. My Mom taught high school in New York City for twenty years."

"We are a proud American family. I am a proud American patriot. For the last eight years, I have been in deep cover as a Russian operative, most of that time assigned to the Orlando cell, headed by the soon-to-be new SVR Director, Sergei Dimitrov. My primary assignment has been to monitor his activities."

"He had been targeted for elimination, but that designation has been changed. We now believe it is in our government's best interest if he is Director of the SVR. You will understand why later on in the Debrief session. Any questions?"

"I have one," said Sam. "Was my kidnapping planned? Oh, and I notice you speak perfect English. Not the broken English Diane and I were treated to."

"In answer to the first part…no, your abduction was definitely not planned and was done over my objections. Some of my crew didn't have two I.Q. Points to rub together. They served as 'muscle' and caused me more grief than I want to think about…your kidnapping is a case in point. As to your second observation, my 'broken English' is a part of my cover…I'm pleased you bought into it. Anyone else?"

Jason said, "Obviously a great job, Agent Asimov. Are you going to continue with your undercover work here in Orlando?"

"Please…call me *Andre*. And no, I have been *promoted*…assigned to the Washington cell; considered a plum assignment. Actually, this is great news for the Agency, an unexpected bonus if you will. Any other questions?"

The rest of the Team demurred and as Asimov took his seat, Jaydan reached over, clapping him on the back in a sign of respect.

From the monitor, McBride once again addressed the Team. "Okay everyone, in just a moment, I'm going to defer to FBI Special Agent Cast, who has been working with our Agent Sparks since the beginning of the operation."

"On behalf of the United States, I thank you for your extraordinary work. I look forward to meeting you all in person in the near future."

As the screen darkened, Emily stood up. "I, like Laura, am standing before you representing my agency. Like Laura, I had prepared remarks about *Project Trojan Horse* that I have now been authorized to share with you." Suddenly smiling, she continued, "But the FBI

Director has requested to speak to the Team as well. So...I now defer to Director Upton."

Upton came into view on the monitor screen. Like his CIA counterpart, he was sitting behind his desk, a large FBI Agency emblem displayed on the wall behind him.

"Good afternoon, everyone," he began, "I see Mr. McVay, Ms. Talley, Agents Sparks, Sanders, and Asimov; of course Agent Cast; along with Mr. and Mrs. Stockwell. Especially good to see you safe and sound, Diane - may I call you Diane? - (she quickly assented with a nod). I assure you your abduction was *not* a planned part of this operation. Lastly, I want to acknowledge Ms. Tara Wayne and express the Agency's sincere gratitude for all the help afforded by Dynamadics Corporation. Please express my thanks to Tucker as well."

"All of you have done outstanding work under the most dangerous circumstances; with even a hurricane thrown in for good measure. You already know most of the details of Operation *Trojan Horse* from Director McBride and Agent Asimov's remarks. Does anyone have a question at this point?"

"I do Director," said Emily. "Actually," she continued, "more of a personal observation. I get that Dimitrov had to escape to Russia in order for the next phase of the operation to begin. But...did we really need to allow the traitor Whittaker to get away as well? As a veteran Agent, I can't tell you how much he disgusts me...he is the anthesis of all we stand for!"

"About that," replied Upton, "I was going to cover that situation in some detail in a few minutes, but since you brought it up..."

"Okay, people...fasten your seatbelts. Things are not always as they appear. Agent Whittaker Is *NOT* a traitor. To the contrary, he is one of the bravest people I have ever known."

Around the table, one could hear the proverbial pin drop. The group was collectively dumbfounded. Jaws went slack. Eyes glazed over. Everyone hung on every word Upton spoke.

"Owen Whittaker has been a part of Operation Trojan Horse from its inception. In fact, the operation evolved from one of his suggestions. He was very much involved in planning the operation and is now, without a doubt, its key player."

"The point is to get a deep-cover operative - Agent Whittaker - embedded in the SVR as close to upper management as possible. We are well on our way to achieving that goal. Dimitrov, politically well-connected and a Kremlin favorite, was a major contender to replace the retiring SVR Director. Unfortunately, he has been a major thorn in our side and up until a day ago was at the top of Director McBride's list for termination, the result of miscommunication between our Agencies. Luckily, we corrected this at the last minute; in the bargain terminating another major problem, one Vladimir Kaslov."

"Agent Whittaker has managed to skillfully ingratiate himself; Dimitrov completely trusts him and now considers our Agent to be his best friend. You can readily see the intelligence advantage we will enjoy! I have to pinch myself...I almost feel like I've died and gone to FBI heaven! What a coup! And all of this due in no small part to the intelligence, bravery, and yes - *Patriotism* - of our own Special Agent Owen Whittaker."

"Until this point, only Director McBride and myself have been aware of Agent Whittaker's status. Since he is now leaving the country to begin the most dangerous part of his mission, we agreed that you all deserved to know the truth, especially you, Agent Cast. This man is a hero, *not a traitor.* Unfortunately, we have to allow this perception to continue in order for him to be safe and effective."

"Thank you for sharing that with us, Director Upton," said Emily. "I feel very good about what he is doing for us. Now, knowing the truth, I respect and admire him...a true role model for the rest of us. I hope that one day I can thank him personally."

"I believe Agent Cast speaks for all of us," added Jason. "He is a true American hero," the rest of the team signaling their agreement.

Director Upton concluded by again thanking everyone and hinting that they may be seeing him in person in the near future. Shortly after Director Upton signed off, Tara formally adjourned the meet-

ing, and the next hour was spent talking over the stunning revela-
tions about Asimov and Whittaker. Everybody headed to individual
destinations; Jason and Laura to their apartment; The Stockwells to
their home; Tara and Sam inviting Asimov to join them for drinks at
O'Doul's Pub; Jaydan and Emily off to have dinner.

** ** **

Chapter Twenty-Five
Through The Looking Glass

They all left Dynamadics at the same time. In deference to the 97-degree temperature, there were no farewell conversations beyond a brief "goodbye, see you later." The heat - in a word - was stifling. Jason and Laura were headed straight home; Jaydan was taking Emily home before returning later in the afternoon to pick her up for a dinner date. Sam, Tara, and Andre Asimov were destined for O'Doul's Pub, while Diane and John were headed home in Tara's Lincoln; she having insisted they continue using her car for the time being.

** ** **

Owen Whittaker looked out the portal as the small jet gained the necessary momentum for lift-off, then rapidly ascend before making a turn east toward the Atlantic Ocean and their ultimate destination, Moscow. As he felt the plane leave the ground, he tightened up; a reaction to the cumulative stress of the past week coupled with the entirely new situation waiting on the horizon.

All things considered; he was pleased with how things had turned out. If he succeeded in cementing his relationship with Dimitrov, the Agency will have achieved an unprecedented intelligence coup. He had given up much to get to this point. Not the least of which was his reputation. A necessary personal sacrifice to achieve the larger goal. His train of thought was interrupted by the sudden appearance of a very attractive flight attendant, who leaned over to speak to Dimitrov in Russian.

"Da…DA!" He responded, laughing heartily. She stood and returned to the rear of the cabin.

"So…," inquired Whittaker, "what was that all about?"

"Well," said Dimitrov, a mischievous glint in his eye, "First, she's bringing us cocktails. Second, she says you are a *very good-looking man*. She is wondering what you are doing after we land." With that he burst out laughing again. Blushing, Whittaker was at a loss for words.

"So, my friend, I can make the necessary arrangements if you wish."

"No, No!" quickly retorted Whittaker. "*Not* that I'm not flattered. She is beautiful. I'm just not quite ready to indulge…"

"It's Okay, Owen…I understand," interrupted Dimitrov. "I will handle this - in a tactful way. Don't worry my friend."

The attendant arrived with their drinks; Dimitrov speaking to her briefly in Russian. As she handed Whittaker his drink, she smiled and said in perfect English, "If you change your mind at any point, Sergei always knows where to find me."

After she left, Whittaker said, "She speaks English…and apparently already knows you."

"Da, this is true," his remark once again punctuated with boisterous laughter.

** ** **

The apartment door had no sooner shut behind them when they heard: "Welcome home, Jason. Welcome home Laura. I trust the two of you have had a pleasant, if not *downright adventurous,* day?" said the unseen Alfred in his usual whimsical English Butler voice.

"*Adventurous*? What would you know about adventurous?" challenged Jason.

"Only what you allow me to know…Sir," answered the virtual butler.

"Wait a minute," interjected Laura, "Was that *sarcasm*?"

"Ask *him*," responded Alfred, "*he programmed me!*"

"Guilty as charged," admitted Jason. "Just trying to make him more interesting."

"*Interesting*?" Stated the virtual Butler. "Excuse me for trying to make your lives a little more entertaining," said the butler in a *faux* put-upon tone.

The couple broke out in laughter, Jason adding, "Keep up the good work, Alfred."

"Yes Sir," replied Alfred, ending their repartee.

"What a day," observed Laura.

"What a week," added Jason. "I'm gonna need another week just to catch my breath."

"Amen," concurred Laura. "So where do we go from here, Mr. McVay?"

"I've given that a little thought," began Jason. "We love each other. Of that, I'm sure. Before I formally ask for your hand, I think we have some things to work out. You love your job with the CIA. I can't ask you to give that up. I know you have to stay in Virginia - be near Langley - for the foreseeable future. Likewise, I'm not ready to give up my practice...at least for a few more years."

"Jason...," she interrupted.

"No, wait," said Jason, cutting her off. "Let me finish. Here's my suggestion: we have *two* residences, one in Savannah Heights and one here in Orlando. Not *yours* or *mine,* but *Ours!* We've managed a long-distance relationship for almost twelve years. Why can't we have a long-distance marriage? We can work out the financial arrangements to make it work."

"I agree 100%," replied Laura, "and financial arrangements won't be a problem. The long-distance relationship issue - I've got a solution for that, too. Everything will come together."

** ** **

Jaydan clicked off the call. He was beside himself with glee. He couldn't believe his good fortune. He had called Jason to ask if he might have any suggestions where he could take Emily for their first date. Without missing a beat, he had said, "Absolutely my friend. Tonight, you and Emily will dine at the *Starlight Terrace.* You may have heard of the place…it's at the newest Disney Hotel, *The Centennial.* Tell me what time you want to dine…eight is good? Very well, eight it is. When you get there, tell the maitre'd your name and he will take it from there. Oh, and your dinners are compliments of the McVay Agency. All you need pay is the gratuity."

When Jaydan insisted on paying, Jason said that was non-negotiable: he felt it was the least he could do for the couple. Besides, he had explained, "It will help me out with my taxes." *Right,* thought Jayden. So, he graciously accepted, believing Jason might feel insulted if he declined.

Jaydan sat in silence for a few minutes to calm himself. He picked up his phone and called Emily.

"Hi, Emily…I wanted to call you about our dinner date…yes, everything is fine…I just wanted you to know we're going to a fine dining establishment…what…no, I don't want to say where, I want to surprise you. Anyway, I needed to let you know how to dress…. Well, you're welcome. I'll pick you up - say seven? Great, see you then."

** ** **

They pushed through the old-timey western-style swing doors at O'Doul's Pub and stepped off to the side. Sam turned toward Tara and Asimov. "Table or bar?"

Tara replied, "Bar's fine with me," glancing at Asimov who nodded in agreement.

"Bar it is," affirmed Sam. The trio strode over and selected three empty stools on the mostly vacant side facing the entrance. As soon as they were seated, the bartender came over to get their drink orders. He made a point of trying not to make eye contact with Sam.

"Well, Hello Al," greeted Sam. "Remember me?"

"Yes indeed, Ms. Talley," he replied. "Your usual?"

"Please," she responded.

Turning toward Tara and Asimov, he asked, "and what would you folks like?"

Tara ordered a rum and coke, while Asimov ordered vodka on the rocks. As Al left to fetch their drinks, Asimov said, "What's up with the bartender…he seems almost *afraid* of you Sam."

Tara glanced at Sam and chuckled.

Sam looked back at Tara. "*What…??*"

Al returned with their drinks, including Sam's signature Heineken.

Sam looked pointedly at Al. "Mug," said Sam, "a *frosty* mug please."

"Right. Sorry. I forgot. Be right back," he said as he scurried off to the opposite side of the bar.

"So," said Tara, a wicked gleam in her eye. "Do you want to tell it…or should I?"

"Okay, Okay," replied a somewhat perturbed Sam. "I'll tell it." She proceeded to relate the Nogudum incident, beginning with the breast-grabbing and ending with the devastating right hook that left the asshole laid out cold on the barroom floor. Asimov laughed so hard he almost fell off his stool, drawing Tara, then Sam into his infectious laughing fit. Al, who came back with Sam's frosty mug, beat a hasty retreat, correctly surmising what the laughter was all about.

** ** **

It was 6:55 PM. He was five minutes early. Jaydan rang the doorbell one time and waited. Through the door he heard, "C'mon in Jaydan, the door's unlocked."

He entered, gently closing the door behind him. Looking around, he noted a sofa, loveseat, and recliner - all upholstered in fine beige leather. Off to the left side was a small dining table with a galley-style kitchen lying just beyond. The place was immaculate, certainly a reflection of Emily's fastidious nature.

From somewhere down the hall he heard, "Make yourself at home, I'll be right there."

He chose the loveseat since it was facing in the general direction of her voice. Sitting down, he was immediately impressed with the chair's luxurious feel and comfort.

A few moments later, he heard footsteps as Emily emerged from the hall. He quickly stood, looking her over head to toe. He was mesmerized by her sudden transformation from the consummate professional FBI Agent to this...this beautiful creature before him. She was wearing a gorgeous light pink formal gown that fit her perfectly, subtly accenting her already exceptional feminine attributes. And just enough make-up to highlight her facial features. He thought, *she is radiant... just so beautiful.*

"Well, look at you all dressed up," she said smiling. "Jaydan...Jaydan, are you there?"

Regaining his composure, the smitten man answered, "Sorry. Your dress is perfect. You look beautiful! I can't believe you're the same person...wait, that didn't come out right. I mean I've just never seen you all dressed up before."

With a slight giggle, Emily sought to put him at ease, "It's Okay Jaydan, I know what you meant. Really. And thank you, I'm very flattered, coming from such a handsome man. And I'm really happy you like the dress."

"Oh, and I really like your apartment, it's cozy and warm. I have reservations at a place I think you're really going to like…shall we go?"

Emily picked up a small purse from the coffee table and looked over at Jaydan. With a warm smile she replied, "By all means, Mr. Sanders," extending her hand for him to take.

** ** **

Sam, Tara, and Asimov had spent the last couple of hours regaling one another with *war stories* from their careers. Asimov was in the midst of one such anecdote when Sam said, "Excuse me Andre, I have to take this call," as she got up and walked toward the door. She suddenly turned back and obviously alarmed, said to Tara, "It's the hospital…My Aunt Maddy's in the Emergency Room!!"

** ** **

James, the Maitre'd, glanced up just as Jaydan and Emily arrived at his station. "Good Evening Sir…Madame. And who do I have the pleasure of assisting?"

"Good evening, I'm Jaydan Sanders and this is Emily Cast. Mr. McVay said you would take care of us."

"Ah yes, Mr. Sanders, we've been expecting you." He picked up a pair of menus. "If you'll follow me…," he led the way to the far corner of the terrace where Jason's usual table awaited. On the table was a vase with a single red rose. Next to the vase was a bottle of vintage champagne. James held out Emily's chair and seated her. Jason took his seat and looked over at Emily. James handed them their menus, allowing that "the Wine Steward will be with you momentarily. Enjoy your evening."

Jason thanked him; James smiled and bowed slightly before returning to his station.

Emily reached over and touched Jason's hand. "The *Starlight Terrace*. I can't believe it. I know people who have waited weeks to get a reservation. You sure know how to impress a girl!" she exclaimed. "This is *wonderful!*"

"Actually, this is all Jason's doing," confessed Jaydan. "Though, if I could have got a table for us tonight, I surely would have." He went on to explain about Jason's lifetime reservation that included a personal table, then told her about Jason's insistence on treating them to a unique dining experience.

"He's a really great guy," opined Emily, "but he didn't have to do all this."

"I know," agreed Jaydan, "but that's what makes it so special."

They spent the next two hours enjoying their five course gourmet dinners; he chose a beef selection while Emily opted for seafood. By the time desert arrived, each knew the basic life story of the other. Anyone watching the couple would immediately surmise that they were smitten with one another. They spent the next hour and a half dancing and drinking; doing just enough of the former to keep the effects of the latter under control.

"The girl in me doesn't want this magical night to end," said Emily reluctantly, "but the woman that I am knows her limits. It's time for Prince Charming to take his Cinderella home."

"As you wish, my lady," replied a weary but happy Jaydan.

Jaydan left a generous gratuity. They took the elevator down to the ground level where their car was awaiting them. The autopilot got them to Emily's apartment in just under 25 minutes. Jaydan got out and walked around to the other side to let Emily out. They walked up to the front door, pausing for a moment. Then they kissed. Long and passionately. They parted slightly, looking deeply into the other's eyes. Emily broke the silence. "Would you like to come in?" she asked softly.

** ** **

Jason put his phone down. Seeing the distressed look on his face, Laura quickly asked, "What's wrong, Jason?"

"It's Maddy. They've taken her to the Emergency Room."

** ** **

Chapter Twenty-Six
New Beginnings

The Security Officer quickly cleared the two, buzzing open the entrance door to the I.C.U. Waiting Room. They were looking for Sam when Laura, pointing toward the Nurse's Station said, "Look, there's Tara." At about the same time, Tara noticed them, immediately heading in their direction. They met about halfway.

"So," Jason urgently inquired, "What's going on?"

"All I know," responded Tara, "is she was brought in unconscious. Her neighbor, who happened to be sitting on her porch, saw Maddy walk to her car, but before she could open the door she suddenly collapsed in a heap. The neighbor ran over; couldn't revive her and called 911."

"Where's Sam?" Asked Laura.

"She's in with her Aunt...the doctor went in to talk to her about ten minutes ago."

Just then Sam came through the I.C.U. door into the Waiting Room. She saw her friends and quickly walked over. She had a very worried look on her face as she hugged Jason and Laura in turn. They could see that Sam was struggling mightily to keep her emotions under control. Finally, she spoke. "The doctor said she experienced a massive stroke. She's comatose. He said...," at this point - Sam, no longer able to keep her anxiety at bay - began stuttering..." he sa-sa-said that he di-di-didn't believe she-she would wa-wa-wake up fro-fro-from the coma."

Sam started sobbing. Tara embraced her, trying her best to comfort the distraught woman. She gently guided her to a chair and helped her sit down, seating herself in the adjacent chair.

As Tara continued trying to comfort Sam, Jason and Laura looked at one another. Laura subtly nodded toward the Waiting Room door, silently indicating she wanted Jason to follow her out. She held a finger up in front of Tara to indicate they were leaving for a moment. Tara acknowledged with a nod.

Once outside, Laura said to Jason, "I may be able to help her."

Jason, with an expression of incredulity, responded, "Really?...How?"

"You know about my ESP. Part of that involves an ability to heal. How it works? I don't really know...I just know it works. Certainly, worth a try."

"Yes, of course. You're right. How can I help?"

Laura told Jason when they go back inside he needed to tell Sam what she had just told him. "If she believes I can help her Aunt," Laura continued, "then she should ask the nurse if I can have a few minutes alone with her - Sam can say it's a family religious rite or something - and I'll go in and try...I'm really confident I can help."

After they went back inside, Jason took Sam aside to explain Laura's proposal. As Laura looked on, she saw Sam brighten, nodding as Jason spoke. Jason returned, taking a seat next to Laura. They both watched Sam walk over to the Nurse's station and engage the duty nurse in conversation. A few minutes later, the nurse beckoned Laura to come over. Sam returned to her seat next to Jason and Tara. They watched Laura nod at the nurse, then disappear into the I.C.U. About five minutes later, Laura reappeared from the I.C.U., quickly walking over to take her seat next to Jason. He glanced at Laura, who briefly smiled while taking his hand and squeezing ever so slightly.

The four of them had been sitting in somber silence for several minutes when a loud commotion could be heard coming from the I.C.U. A few more minutes passed before a nurse emerged and headed straight for Sam, asking her to come with her; the pair then disappearing through the door. Tara, appearing extremely stressed, turned toward Jason to ask, "Oh, no...do you think Maddy..."

Laura quickly cut her off. "Wait...just hang on, we shouldn't jump to any conclusions yet."

A moment later, Sam burst through the I.C.U. door. Sporting a wide grin, she ran to her friends who were already on their feet. She excitedly told them that Maddy had suddenly awakened, sitting straight up, hollering for the nurse. The nurse immediately contacted the doctor who couldn't believe his eyes. They did a rapid-assessment scan and found the damaged part of her brain now appeared normal. All her vital signs had also returned to normal. They would do a more detailed scan later, but the Doctor was confident she was cured.

He said he had never seen a patient recover from this type of brain damage. He pronounced the event "a miracle."

The four of them joyously chattered away about the "miracle." Laura was momentarily overwhelmed by the experience, her eyes watering even as she smiled. The nurse told them they could go in to visit as soon as a few confirming tests were completed.

** ** **

The next two weeks proved to be a time of new directions for some and a period of settling in for others.

Tara decided to take some vacation time to "wind down" from all of the excitement of the past week. She was headed to New Hampshire to spend time with her niece and her family at their summer home on Lake Winnipesaukee. She looked forward to the respite from the Florida summer heat. Jesse, the aforementioned niece, had been raised by Tara from the age of twelve, when she lost her parents - her Mom was Tara's sister - in an aircraft crash. Jesse's husband of ten years was one of the current Senators from New Hampshire. Tara was looking forward to being with her great niece and nephew; she hadn't seen them since Christmas.

Likewise, the Stockwells opted to take a vacation as well. On Tuesday morning, they received a phone call from FBI Director Upton informing John that his name and reputation were now restored; the false college information had been expunged from the system. Moreover, Tucker Henry assured him that his position with Dynamadics was secure.

And the $250,000 they found deposited in their bank account was theirs to keep. Director Upton explained that it was Russian government money and as far as he was concerned, fair compensation for Diane's abduction and week spent in captivity.

John and Diane had resolved their marriage issues: he promised to be much more attentive; they would be "equal partners." Diane revealed her Mensa membership to him. When he said he now felt "intellectually humbled;" she responded, "It doesn't work that way…remember, "equal partners." They both decided John would continue at Dynamadics as Vice-president of Research & Development. She told John that the other big plus from the experience was her new friendship with Samantha Talley. For him, it was an affirmation of *who he was* and what the really important things are.

** ** **

Jason looked up to see Jaydan walking toward his table with a waitress right behind. As he took a seat opposite Jason, the waitress asked, "Coffee?" To which they both replied in the affirmative. She smiled, setting their menus on the table, then turned to leave.

As Jason picked up his menu, Jaydan said, "I wanted to thank you in person for the wonderful dinner Emily and I had at the *Starlight Terrace.* And to let you know that we are beginning a pretty serious relationship. I know it's kinda fast. We both feel the same way…I don't know how to explain it…"

"I get it," interrupted Jason. "I know *exactly* how you feel. The same thing happened between me and Laura twelve years ago."

Jaydan nodded slowly. "Good to know. So…has marriage ever come up? How would that work for you guys…She's a top tier Agent assigned to the Director's Office in D.C., and you've got a successful practice here in Orlando?"

"Yeah," replied Jason vaguely, "we're seriously considering marriage now…we kind of have a plan in the works…"

The waitress arrived with their coffees. "Ready to order?" she asked.

They both picked up their menus to peruse the selections. After a moment, Jason ordered his usual French Toast Special, Jaydan saying he'd have the same. The waitress picked up their menus and left to put in their orders.

"The long-distance thing is tough," continued Jason, "it will certainly test the strength of your relationship, but you can make it work if you really try."

"Well," said Jaydan, "fortunately, that's not going to be an issue for us. Director Upton has given Emily her choice of assignment. She has chosen FBI Headquarters in Washington," he continued with a big smile, "so, looks like we'll be moving in together in the D.C. area."

"Good for you guys!" Exclaimed Jason, thinking, *we should be so lucky.*

** ** **

Sam was sitting on the sofa musing about Emily and Jaydan when she heard a vehicle pull into her driveway. She got up and looked out the window to see Tara's Lincoln. She thought, *I wonder what she's doing here?* when, to her surprise, Emily got out. She opened the door, greeting her with a bright smile. "Hey girlfriend! Come on in."

Emily dropped her purse on the coffee table as she followed Sam over to the breakfast bar.

"Coffee?" asked Sam. "I was about to fix myself a cup. Wait…are you hungry? I can make us some breakfast."

"Yes to the coffee, no to breakfast, but thanks for the offer," said Emily with a warm smile. "Just wanted to share some really good news."

"Well, great!" Enthused Sam as she headed for the coffee cup rack. "Oh, what's up with Tara's Lincoln? I thought the Stockwells were using it. She should start a rental car agency."

"Long story short," explained Emily, "I called Tara to tell her I was leaving in a few days..."

"Wait...what?" interrupted Sam. "Your *leaving*...leaving for *where*?"

"That's part of what I have to tell you," Emily continued. "As you know, my car is under the fallen oak at the Safe House; it's totaled. Anyway, Tara is going on vacation and won't be needing her car...so she offered it to me to use for transportation until I leave."

While Sam made their coffees, Emily went on to tell her - in great detail - about the evening at the Starlight Terrace and - in somewhat less detail - Jaydan spending the night at her place.

"I think...no, I *know* I'm in love with him, Sam," said Emily. "He feels the same. I know...*we just met*...I'm not normally an impulsive woman. It just feels right. Director Upton offered me my choice of assignment and a two-step grade promotion; the equivalent of Laura's *Senior* Agent rank. Anyway, I chose the Washington Headquarters...as you know, Jaydan's assigned to CIA Headquarters at Langley."

Sam, filled with joy for her friend, hugged Emily tightly. "I'm really, really happy for you. I'm gonna miss you. If you need a warm place to visit when the weather gets cold up there...well, you're always welcome to stay here."

"Thanks, Sam. Likewise, I want you to come up for a visit after we're settled in."

The pair spent the next couple hours talking about the past week's "adventure" and future plans. Sam told Emily that Asimov allowed he was behind the exceptional treatment she and Diane experienced during their abduction by manipulating Dimitrov's soft side for women.

As Emily was getting ready to leave, there was a knock at the door. It was a Post Office delivery person. She handed Sam a registered letter, asking for her recipient's signature. Sam immediately opened the envelope as Emily kept a discreet distance. Sam read the several pages, then put them on the bar saying, "OH MY GOD!!!"

Emily, with an alarmed look asked, "What is it...is everything all right?"

"Yes, yes...everything is GREAT! I can't believe it! MY HOUSE IS PAID FOR!"

"Paid for...what do you mean?" Asked Emily.

Sam went on to explain the letter was from her mortgage holder. It said that her mortgage had been paid in full by an anonymous source and that she now owned her house free and clear. It went on to state that she would receive the property title within a few days by registered mail.

Neither Sam nor Emily could think of anyone who had the financial resources, much less a motive, to pay off her mortgage.

Emily said, "Well, I wouldn't look a gift horse in the mouth," Sam quickly nodding in agreement. The women said their goodbyes, promising to stay in touch and nurture their friendship.

** ** **

"Okay," said Jason, setting his coffee on the bar, "I have to tell you what's bothering me. It's the telepathy and the mind-melding thing you do. And now what you did for Maddy - which was wonderful...you gave her back her life...still, it kind of frightens me. And we've never talked about your past...your parents, relatives..."

Laura was staring down at her empty coffee mug. After a moment she looked up, meeting his gaze. "You're right. It's time you learn about my past. I was born (she paused for a beat}, I was born in Alexandria, Virginia. My Dad was a corporate lawyer and my Mom was a college professor - she taught theoretical physics…"

"Wait," interrupted Jason, "you said *'was'* about both of them…"

"I was getting to that," she replied. "They were both killed in a car accident in 2012. I had just finished my freshman year at Syracuse University. Being 18, I didn't need guardianship. I decided to leave school for a while and on a whim enlisted in the Marines for two years, doing a tour in Afghanistan. After my enlistment was over, I returned to Syracuse and finished my degree. The best thing about that was I met your sister and…well, you already know that story. So, after graduation, I joined the FBI and, ironically, got paired with Sandy as a joint FBI/CIA Special Ops team. I later left the FBI for the CIA, where I've been teamed with Sandy ever since."

"I'm sorry about your parents," he said. "I can't imagine how hard that must have been."

She reminded Jason, "Look, you're unique, too. Your future-casting gift is amazing; how many times has that special ability saved your…our lives?"

"*Not* the same thing," he retorted. "Not even in the same ballpark."

They sat quietly, both pondering the future…*their future.*

Jason broke the silence. "I don't know what to think, Laura. What kind of future could we have? What about children? What would they be like?"

"*What would they be like?*" Repeated Laura, somewhat incredulously. "They'd be normal children, that's *what they'd be like*! What - you think they'd be these little green creatures with antenna sticking out of their heads?!" she said, obviously hurt by his question.

"No, no…of course not," he replied. "I'm just…I don't know…really, really confused. I don't know what to think."

Placing her hand over his, he heard in his mind, "*I Love You. With Every Fiber Of My Being.* If that's not good enough... then, well...*I* don't know what to think."

** ** **

Epilogue

*F*ive Months Later...

Laura walked over, wine glass in hand, to join Jason, seated at one end of the oversized sofa. He was still digesting what she had just so casually said: "Oh by the way, we won't be having any financial issues. I - we - have a net worth north of a billion dollars. My Dad was an astute investor."

She set her glass on the coffee table, then snuggled up to her husband. "Only a week 'til Christmas," she said, rapidly changing the subject. Wrapping an arm around her, he replied, "You're right...and only a month 'til our 'half-a-versary'. Pretty soon, we'll be 'old-married folks,'" he joked.

"I hardly think a marriage of a mere five months qualifies you for 'old-married folks' status." Opined Alfred, their virtual butler.

Remembering a similar conversation during the past summer, Laura couldn't resist the urge to engage Jason's creation in yet another round of banter.

"And who invited you into this conversation Alfred?" demanded Laura, in what she hoped was a sufficiently indignant tone.

"Just an observation Madame," replied the disembodied butler, "no need to get our feathers ruffled."

"Here's an *observation* for you, Alfred;" said an amused Laura, "that was a very un-butler-like remark."

"Sorry," replied Alfred. "If you're offended, I suggest you talk to *him.*"

"Him?" Parroted Laura.

"Jason," clarified the butler, "the one who programmed me."

Jason suddenly burst out laughing with Laura quickly joining in. Alfred - his feelings...er, algorithms hurt, indignantly said, *"Well,* if you people don't appreciate my views...I'll just, I don't know...return to the ethereal wilderness from whence I came." He shut himself down, sparking another round of laughter from the bemused couple.

Laura glanced at her watch, then stood up. "Time we get ready for our Celebration at Tucker's place. I'll shower first...then, by the time you're done, I'll be finished with the makeup and hair."

He looked up lovingly at his new wife, saying simply, "Sure, honey." Jason watched her until she vanished from sight into their bedroom. His thoughts drifted back to that day five months ago; the day she had erased all doubt from his mind. After he had told her, *I don't know what to think,* she touched his hand; in his mind he heard: *I love you with every fiber of my being, if that's not enough...*not only had he heard her thoughts - he *felt* the sincerity in her heart. Then that joyous moment when he said, "Laura, I love you with all my heart. Will you be my wife?"

** ** **

"You two really blindsided us with that *Justice of the Peace* number," said Jaydan, playfully poking Jason in the ribs.

"Speaking of blindsides," remarked Laura, "what about all this?" Gesturing with a wave of her hand around the huge great room of Tucker Henry's mansion.

"I can only say that one good blindside deserves another," remarked the host, who happened to be standing next to the two couples. "All kidding aside Tucker," said Jason, "we appreciate your generous hospitality. Having our wedding celebration in your beautiful home will surely be a *forever* memory for us."

"My distinct pleasure Jason…and Laura," replied Tucker with a polite bow toward Laura. "Jane (his wife) and I will be having a small holiday gathering next Wednesday between the Christmas and New Year's holidays and are hoping you can attend."

"Thanks for the invitation, Tucker," said Jason. "We look forward to coming." Just then, Tucker's wife waved at him from the opposite side of the room.

"Excuse me," their host said smiling, "the wife needs me for something or other," nodding politely before walking across the room in her direction.

Tucker Henry and Tara had arranged this celebration five months earlier after learning of Jason and Laura's discreet marriage at Laura's Georgetown residence in D.C. Laura's boss, CIA Director Kaitlyn McBride had collaborated with Tucker, resulting in this intimate gathering of friends and family to celebrate their marriage. In attendance were the Henrys; Kaitlyn McBride; Jason's sister, Sandy; Laura's cousin, Stafford Var; Jaydan Sanders; his fiancé, Emily Cast; John and Diane Stockwell; Jason's partner, Samantha Talley; and her Aunt (Jason's Secretary) Maddy Winslow. Also present were a small number of Tucker and his wife's relatives who were enjoying the holiday season in Orlando at the Henry residence.

Since the conclusion of the *Project Expose'* caper, everyone had settled into their routines: Jason offered Sam a partnership in the firm - which she eagerly accepted - now named *The McVay, Talley, & Associate Investigative Services Agency* (Maddy being the "& Associate") …this arrangement making for a very tight knit group.

McBride assigned Jaydan as the coordinator of the top-secret External Threat Unit, based in D.C., not far from his new fiancée, Emily; now a special projects Agent reporting directly to FBI Director Ken Upton. The couple were currently renting a home in Savannah Heights, Va. Laura McVay continued in her Special Assignments role with her longtime partner - now sister-in-law - Sandy McVay.

John Stockwell was back directing research and development at Dynamadics while Diane had become quite active at the local community college teaching computer programming. She and Sam had become close friends and saw each other frequently.

While Emily was grateful for her promotion and happy to be with Jaydan, she was becoming increasingly bored with her administrative duties. Likewise, Laura - while enjoying her new life with Jason - found herself, along with her partner Sandy, growing more restless by the day. That would all change in the not-too-distant future.

** ** **

Six months later...

Jason looked out the window of his wife's Georgetown apartment. It was a beautiful late May Day in D.C. Soon the humidity would be rising making it feel more like their other home in Orlando. Thinking of which, he must remember to check in with Maddy later. Ever since the New year everything had been running smoothly, Sam was pretty much able to handle the day-to-day stuff; her administrative skills had greatly improved. Truth be told, everyone was getting bored. Your run-of-the mill investigative cases: divorces, embezzle-ments, missing persons - paid the bills but really didn't excite. Not like the *Project Expose'* caper. Likewise, Laura and Sandy were suf-fering the blahs of boredom.

Then his phone's ringtone announced a call from Laura.

"What's up, honey?" He answered.

"Guess who I just talked to?" She teased.

"I give up...Who?"

"Emily Cast," she replied, "And things are 'a-poppin.'"

"How so," implored Jason.

"Well, Emily got an encrypted message from Owen Whittaker - remember him, our very deep-cover agent in Moscow - highest priority. It said a *very serious situation* existed at the top of the

Russian government. It appears that the top leadership is being replaced by - get this - *clones,* one by one. He says he has hard evidence. Furthermore, only he and Sergei Dimitrov are cognizant of what's going on."

"McBride is activating the External Threat Team. This is some really serious stuff, Jason. You need to come down to Langley ASAP."

"On my way!" He replied as he headed for the bedroom and a quick change of clothes.

Be Careful What You Wish For...

THE END

If you enjoyed this book, please take a few moments to write a review and refer it to anyone you think will enjoy it.